BLOOD ATONEMENT

Barbara Townsend

Praise for *Blood Atonement*:

A powerful and haunting novel. Barbara Townsend has an uncanny ability to evoke the lives of Mormon women in 1846 shortly after the proclamation of plural marriage. We root for the women as they struggle for their rights in a world turned upside down. Read *Blood Atonement* for the history, the compassion and the understanding that Townsend brings to her characters, and for the spellbinding story. Just read it!

~ Margaret Coel, *Killing Custer*

I thoroughly enjoyed *Blood Atonement*, the new historical thriller written by Barbara Townsend.

After reading and loving *Under the Banner of Heaven* by Jon Krakauer ten years ago, and seeing a great documentary about Mountain Meadows, I became interested in the darker details of Mormon pioneer history. Barbara Townsend's book touches on that history—it conveys a real sense of historic detail and accuracy, yet at the same time it manages to be a real page-turner.

This book is a great window into a fascinating chapter in the American Pioneer experience—and is a satisfying crime novel to boot. If you know anything about the Mormon's migration west—or if you know nothing about it at all, you will enjoy this book.

~ Robert Ben Garant, Screenwriter

Enter a world where women share a husband—only a curtain separates intimate moments as jealously, pain, and despair build each day in their male dominated world. Discover a tenderness between sisters rent apart as evil individuals twist a religious course to fit their malicious intentions. Don't miss this absorbing mystery of a pioneer journey of Latter-day Saints, its blessings and curses in the infancy of its church.

~ Patricia Frolander, Wyoming Poet Laureate, 2011 - 2013

Blood Atonement
Second edition, published May 2016
Second printing, February 2022
by Fine Nib Publishing, Wyoming, USA

Copyright © 2013, 2016, 2022 by Barbara Townsend

Originally trade published in August 2013
and entitled *Blood Atonement; A Pioneer Trail Mystery*

Cover design, Roger Carpenter

ISBN-10: 0-9972340-6-7
ISBN-13: 978-0-9972340-6-0

*To the Old West pioneers
who struggled and sacrificed
in the hope of a better life.*

Acknowledgments

I send a warm thank you to Ann Marie Lane, curator for the Toppan Rare Books Library in the University of Wyoming, for your guidance and without whom I would have no novel.

To Gail Holmes and Terry Latey of the Pioneer Research Library, Mormon Trail Center, at Historic Winter Quarters, Nebraska, for sharing your time and knowledge.

To the members of *Absolute Write*, the Internet writers' forum, for being so generous in providing information, encouragement, and the necessary kicks in the backside.

To the members of the *Writers Bloc*, the writers group in our tiny Wyoming mountain town: Philippina Halstead, Jo Trumble, Marjane Ambler, and Robert Townsend. Your friendship, encouragement, and laughter kept away cabin fever and made writing a joy in my life.

Foreword

Many teachings, philosophies, and tenets of the Church of Jesus Christ of Latter-day Saints have evolved since its inception. For example, the church now forbids its members from drinking coffee, tea, and alcohol, but in the early years such activities were acceptable.

The early decades of the Latter-day Saints were chaotic and the Mormons were often forced from their property. Both Mormons and Gentiles were guilty of criminal acts against the other. Tension, intolerance, and anger grew until the situation exploded into bloodshed.

The Afterword includes more information about the times, actual persons in the novel, and the Danites.

Additionally, interested readers will find a Suggested Readings list for information relevant to this era, the pioneer trail, and the Mormon faith from varying perspectives.

Prologue

October 1838
Carroll County, Missouri

Eliza turned from the window as her sister Esther groaned and writhed on the bed. The glow from the oil lamp's small flame barely lit Esther's sweat-soaked face and that of the older woman tending her. The sparse furniture's shadows on the log walls spasmed in time to the dancing blaze in the fireplace.

"Bite down on this belt," Mother whispered as she pressed the cracked leather onto Esther's lips. Esther opened her mouth just enough for the strap to slip between her teeth and clamped down. A sharp moan escaped through her clenched teeth. She arched her back as agony coursed through her body.

"I know, honey," Mother spoke gently. "I know." She lifted the bunched hem of Esther's nightgown and peered into the dimness. The crown of a dark head bulged from between white thighs. "I can see the babe's head. Push now."

Esther coiled as she made herself sit up. Her face creased in a grimace as she forced her muscles to push. Rivulets of sweat cascaded down her face from the strain. With a cry, she fell back onto the bed and spit out the belt. She gasped for air.

Eliza turned back to the window and pushed aside the curtain to peek outside.

"What are they doing?" Mother dabbed a damp cloth on Esther's forehead.

"They're arguing with Lucas," Eliza murmured.

The yelling outside the log cabin was clearer now. Jumbled hollers separated into words.

"Get out, Mormon!"

"Better run, Saints!"

"We'll burn ye out an' eat yer cow!"

Foul jokes about Mormons and polygamy circled the cabin as curses echoed off the log walls, followed by a clear and chilling "you got five minutes to clear out before the torches land on your house!"

Eliza gasped and jumped away from the window. She and her mother exchanged horrified looks.

A low voice rumbled, trying to reason with the mounted Gentile mob. "I beg of ye, my wife is birthing. Let her have the babe in peace. Then we'll go."

"Nah, sir, that'd be just one more Mormon we'd have ta get rid of."

"We don't need more of yer thievin' kind here," a higher-pitched voice shouted.

Wood popping in the fireplace and Esther's groans broke the thick silence.

"Four minutes."

Eliza fought a wave of panic and ran to grab a blanket for protection from the night's cold air. Her eyes searched the small cabin for anything they needed for Esther and for their escape, but her mind raced too fast to think.

Esther screamed, "No! My babe—"

"Three minutes."

Through the walls, Lucas' voice vibrated. "I have four women and two boys with me." Tension laced his voice. "We have harmed no one. We tried to be good neighbors. Mister Matthews, we threshed together. Mister Jones, I helped ye raise your barn. Allow my wife to give birth. Then we'll leave peaceably."

"How many wives you got, boy?" A round of chuckles echoed from the mob.

"Like you, I have but one wife."

Lucas is trying to connect with them, Eliza thought.

"Two minutes."

Eliza looked between Esther's legs. The baby's head hadn't moved. She ran to the window and pushed aside the curtain.

Esther cried openly in pain and fear.

Mother looked up, her face stricken. "Levi. Jack. Eleanor. Where are they?"

"Levi's at the neighbors. Eleanor took Jack to the barn when Esther's time came."

"Do what ye will to me. I give myself unto ye, freely." Lucas began to weep. He tossed his musket onto the ground and held out his arms. "Here I am for ye. I pray ye leave my family be."

Laughter exploded from the mob. Eliza didn't hear the joke for the roaring in her ears.

"One minute."

Eliza ran to Esther. "Mother, help me!" She heaved Esther to the bed's edge. Esther cried out. Her weight was full on her haunches to stop herself from sitting on her baby's head.

"Eliza, find Jack! Find Eleanor!"

"Mother, they can run out the barn's back door." Eliza's eyes flooded with tears as she panted in terror.

Weeping, Mother grabbed the quilt. With Esther's arm over her shoulders, Eliza gripped her sister's waist and together they staggered to the door. She flung it open.

Mounted horsemen ringed the house. Flares from their burning torches hurt her eyes. The mob fell silent as they studied the three women.

Lucas ran to Esther and hefted her in his arms. She groaned and clutched her abdomen.

"In the name of all that is holy, can ye not see? Will ye let my wife birth in the safety of her home?" Tears streamed down Lucas' face. "I beg of ye —"

"*Time!*"

Whoops erupted as the riders spurred their horses. Several flung their torches onto the house's shake roof. The dry wood exploded into flames.

Eliza and her mother ran into the darkness for the cottonwood grove to the west. Lucas ran behind them carrying his shrieking wife.

Mother turned back. "Jack! Eleanor!"

Eliza grabbed her mother's hand and pulled her along.

Screaming horses and the hollers and curses of the riders pushed her onward. The roar of the flames engulfing the house muffled the gunshots.

The sounds of brutality dimmed behind them as they neared the grove. Eliza's lungs burned from the frozen night air. She gripped her mother's hand and dragged the woman when she fell. Lucas' boots thumped behind her, his breaths ragged.

Behind them, Eliza caught sight of Jack and Eleanor leading the cow from the burning barn. They fought off the mobsters from grabbing the cow's harness.

A rifle butt smashed down on the boy's head. A horseman dragged off Eleanor.

Eliza, Mother, and Lucas ran deep into the grove. Hidden behind thick bushes, Eliza and her mother collapsed. Lucas tripped over the brambles and crumpled beside them, dumping Esther onto the ground. He knelt, bellowing in grief. Lungs heaved as Eliza and her mother knelt by Esther. They placed their hands on her face and stroked her hair. "Esther!"

She didn't respond.

Chapter 1

November 1846
Winter Quarters, Missouri Territory

The bridal party of three sat around the makeshift altar—a plank table. Sixteen-year-old Aveline Bowmore sat erect across from her groom-elect, Washington Avery. Beside him hunched Dorris Avery, his wife of nineteen years. Behind Avery stood Bishop Lang, the ward's bishop.

Aveline's heart thumped in her chest as Dorris' red-rimmed eyes stared at a dark corner of the log cabin.

"As a sign of your willingness to give this woman to your husband to be his lawful wife, place her right hand within the right hand of your husband." Lang held out his hand indicating for Dorris to proceed.

Stiffly, Dorris reached for Washington's hand. With her other hand, her icy fingers trembled as she lifted Aveline's hand off the table. Dorris joined Washington and Aveline's hands. With this act she had demonstrated her approval of this polygamous union.

Dorris' eyes welled with tears. A soft hiccup choked off a sob. To Aveline, Dorris' place in heaven was assured, yet the act seemed to fill the old woman's soul with despair.

Aveline's hand disappeared in her new husband's cupped palm. She didn't feel comfortable touching this man she had met only a month earlier.

Now being married to a married man spiked her anxiety. Her hand felt cold, stiff. *His hand is so warm.* She flinched as he squeezed hard, a signal that she belonged to him and for her to get used to his touch.

Lang intoned the final marriage blessing. The gathered witnesses echoed "Amen." The wedding ceremony in the Bowmores' log cabin concluded.

A plural wife now, Aveline was the second wife of the First Counselor of the Ninth Ward, Winter Quarters. A jolt of pride shot through her. *His first wife might be queen of the household, but she's old and worn. I'm young and fresh, now the preferred woman of his household.*

Dorris Avery said nothing to her new sister-wife, to Washington, or to Aveline's parents. She pulled her shawl tight over her head and shoulders and fled the cabin. The door slammed behind her.

Aveline's parents, Lyda and Royal Bowmore, silently shook the bishop's hand, their bodies jerky from tension. Older sister Frances pressed against the wall beside their parents, bent over the bed from the crush of bodies in the tiny cabin. The bishop nodded to Aveline, shook Washington's hand, and left.

Frances hugged Aveline, now a sister-wife like herself, in a long embrace. Frances had arrived alone just before the ceremony began, and Aveline had had no time to speak with her. "I'm so happy you were able to come! I haven't seen you since you married. I have so much to tell you!" Aveline cried.

Frances' wedding to Lucas Bates had been two weeks earlier. She wore the gold comb Lucas gave her as a wedding gift. Small pearls dangled from the arch of gold, dramatic against her dark, upswept hair.

Aveline studied her older sister. Frances' mouth turned up in a quick smile. *How thin she's gotten since she married.* Her left hand's fingers brushed her hairline, but they couldn't hide the bruised cheekbone that had faded to a light rust.

She recalled Frances' wedding to Lucas Bates. Eliza, the first wife, had not attended the ceremony. The sisters had exchanged horrified glances after realizing Eliza's defiance. A first wife must consent to polygamy or, if she refused to consent, her sin would cause her damnation.

Alarm swept over Aveline for Frances' circumstances.

Ma and Pa embraced her tightly. Each was overcome with emotion. *Their last child is leaving their home. They are alone.* Aveline blinked back tears.

Washington excused himself. "The Lord's work calls." To Aveline he said, "I will be home after dark."

He shook hands with Pa then he left the Bowmore house without another word.

Frances hugged Aveline, too tight. Her mouth close to Aveline's ear, she whispered, "Let me help you prepare tonight." Aveline nodded, unable to speak from shock at the sight of Frances' bruised face and apprehension at what might happen to herself in the Avery household.

Alone with her parents and sister, Aveline tried to calm her nerves. She busied herself by checking and rechecking her packed trunks. Afraid to go to her new home to live with distressed sister-wife Dorris, Aveline sat on her stump and chewed her fingernails.

So much has happened so quickly this past month. …

Chapter 2

October 1846

Beyond Winter Quarters, the nearly frozen Missouri River crawled on its journey south. A shroud of smoke from more than a hundred cooking fires settled over the town and obscured the prairie beyond. Aveline stood on the slope above the town and watched the Camp of Israel begin its day.

The morning sounds, diffused in the calm air like a ripple after a tossed pebble in a still pond, reached Aveline. Horses whinnied in their tack. Boots crunched on the frost as men walked toward the stockyard south of town to tend the Saints' lowing beasts. An infant wailed its discomfort.

Stretched before her, the entire world was brown, a dead brown, from beast-packed dirt streets to log cabins standing in rows like a battalion of wood soldiers, smoke drifting from their chimney mouths.

The uniform brown rows of cabins and straight roads were interrupted by scattered white canvas wagon tops. *Even with the coming winter, these wagons will be home for many Saints. Some will have to live through the winter in tents.* She shivered at the thought.

She remembered how quickly the Saints had erected this temporary settlement. Here, they would wait for spring. She imagined how the families would then pack their meager belongings and head west to Zion, to the land outside the United States where they'd be free to practice their faith without persecution.

Lyda Bowmore, Aveline's mother, a strikingly handsome woman with auburn hair, carried a package as she hurried down the dirt road. She looked up the knoll toward Aveline and waved before ducking into their new log home. Aveline headed down the slope.

A thick bacon slab and three brown eggs sat on a plate, ready to fry in the skillet. Smaller bacon slices and one egg lay segregated on another plate.

"Pa gets a treat today," Aveline said, eyeing the large slab and three eggs.

"Your father has worked very hard, not just building our cabin, but other cabins too. He's almost breaking his back getting Brother Tyler's cabin ready so their baby girl can get out of the weather. He didn't eat breakfast this morning." Ma stated adamantly, "When he does eat, he should eat well."

The sheet curtain moved aside and Frances stepped from behind the curtain that hid their shared bed. Her fingers fumbled as she buttoned her gingham dress.

"Well, look who's up! You'll sleep through the second coming of the Lord," Aveline teased her year-older sister.

Frances wrinkled her nose in response and lifted the coffee pot. A disappointed look crossed her face at the heft of the empty coffee pot.

"Oh, I'm sorry, m' lady, but the servants don't have your coffee ready yet." Aveline bent in a deep curtsy as she spoke.

Behind their mother's back, Frances stuck out her tongue at Aveline. "I'll fetch some water. If I go walking around at least I bring back something." Frances grabbed the water bucket's handle, leaned from the weight of the wood and left the cabin for the well.

Four occupants crowded the twelve-foot-square cabin. *If Bedford were here ...* Aveline tamped down the feeling of dread for her brother's safety in the Army's Mormon Battalion.

Two beds—more accurately, one very large bed—took up almost half the cabin. A square frame of horizontal logs etched into the log walls, and ropes strung from log to log provided support for the straw mattresses. An old sheet, hung by twine from the bottom of the tiny loft, split the beds into two sections to provide some measure of privacy. Trunks tucked under the bed provided opportunities for stubbing one's toe in the dim light. Rough shelves lined the wall above where their heads lay, providing food storage and protection from hungry mice and rats.

In the other half of the cabin, Ma's rocker and Pa's straight chair faced the fireplace in the center of the wall. Two tiny tables flanked the fireplace. One makeshift table held her grandmother's oil lamp for a desk, and the other served as their kitchen counter. The washbasin and washtub nested on the packed dirt floor under the counter beside the wood water bucket. Pots and pans hung from nails on the wall. Windowless, the few pieces of furniture were bathed in the sunlight streaming in through the open wood-slat door.

Aveline hauled out the coffee grinder and scooped out the leftover grounds she had roasted and ground yesterday. Movement beyond the open door caught her eye, and she looked up to watch her father, Royal Bowmore, stride toward them. In the chill air, his ruddy face beamed with a glow of pride. His sagging trousers and ripped overcoat did not diminish his quiet dignity.

Another man marched to her father's right. The stranger was tall, and as he strode, his long brown hair waved behind him in time with his flowing unbuttoned overcoat. Even from this distance, the shadow cast by his top hat's brim did not hide his piercing dark eyes. A third man, a hulk whose sheepskin coat was taut across his stomach, lumbered on Pa's other side. The man's bulk made Pa and the tall man look like the runts of a mixed litter.

"Ma, here comes Pa. Two gentlemen are with him."

Ma spun and watched the men approach. Her hand rubbed her forehead as she stared at the plates of uncooked food as if calculating how to stretch it for six mouths.

"Mornin', my dear," Pa sang to his wife. Ma blushed at his familiarity in front of strangers and looked at the ground, hands folded.

"This here is my wife, Sister Lyda. Dear, this is Brother Washington Avery. He's the First Counselor in our new ward." Pa held out his hand toward his wife. Avery touched the brim's edge of his top hat in salute and nodded as Ma bobbed a small curtsy, but she kept her hands folded in front.

Avery turned to Aveline. His brown eyes darkened.

"My youngest, Aveline," Pa said. "She's sixteen."

Avery nodded and stared at Aveline. She curtsied and folded her hands. He was so good looking she wanted to rest her chin on her cupped hands and gaze into his eyes. Instead, she focused at the ground and fought the urge to peek at him.

"Brother Lucas Bates. He's Brother Brigham Young's right-hand man," Pa continued.

Bates resembled the image Aveline had in her head of a superhuman backwoodsman in a fable Ma had read to her. He dipped a rough bow to Ma and nodded his head in Aveline's direction. As his head tilted downward, a small clod of dirt rolled off the ragged brim and landed on the ground. Aveline forced herself not to look at what else could have found a home on his hat.

"Where's Frances?"

"She went to fetch water. She should be back directly." Ma looked from Avery to Bates. "Brothers, if you could stay for breakfast, I can have it ready for you both in a few moments."

"Most kind of you, Sister, but Brother Brigham has ordered me on a mission to Mount Pisgah, and I must leave immediately. Saints are still evacuating Illinois and are arriving unprepared. Our people suffer greatly, and they require my assistance." While he spoke, Avery stared at Aveline until she looked away.

Whispered reports about the Saints' troubles arrived daily. Around the Saints' church headquarters in Nauvoo, Illinois, tension between the Saints and their Gentile neighbors had built up for years. Mistrust, thefts, religious prejudice—perpetrated by both sides—spiraled out of control. The Saints' leader, Joseph Smith, Junior, and his brother, Hyrum, were murdered. Aveline had listened, wide-eyed, to the stories told around the campfires of how Mormons fled their homes at musket point. Some were fortunate enough to escape with their belongings, food, and beasts. Some escaped with only the clothes on their backs.

As the Bowmores had traveled toward Illinois, Bishop Riter had warned them to divert for the Missouri Territory. They passed thousands of refugees in temporary settlements like Mount Pisgah, Iowa Territory. Each family member helped others to find food, pitch tents, build fires, or dig graves. At Winter Quarters, Aveline watched the daily stream of mourners trudging to the cemetery.

"We wish you well, Brother, in alleviating their suffering." Ma bent to shift the skillet away from the fire.

Avery turned to Pa. "Only one wife, Brother?"

Pa froze at the blunt question. His face pinched from tension. Ma straightened slowly, her face a stony mask. With a glance to his wife, Pa squared his shoulders and faced Avery. "I have one wife, Brother Avery."

Avery's face grew stern. "Doubtless, you know of our prophet's blessed principle of plural marriage, a required undertaking for the faithful in order to reach heaven's highest plane. Brother Bates and I intend to enter into salvation. As obedient Saints, fulfilling God's word is our highest duty." Behind Avery, Bates nodded. Avery turned to Aveline. "Do you agree, Miss Bowmore?"

Aveline's breath caught in her throat, not prepared for strangers' eyes watching her or their ears listening for her response. Only one answer was correct, yet her constricted throat would not let her speak.

The weighty silence was broken when Frances staggered through the door under the weight of the full wooden bucket. Grateful for the distraction, Aveline hustled toward Frances to grip half the bucket handle. They lugged the bucket between them to the kitchen table.

Frances panted from the exertion. Her skirt was wet on one side where the water had sloshed out of the bucket. She pulled the clinging material off her leg, curtsied toward the men, and gave a small smile.

"Brothers, my eldest daughter, Frances. Daughter, Brother Avery is our ward's first counselor," Pa said. "And Brother Lucas Bates."

Bates affixed his gaze on Frances with such ferocity, Frances' smile vanished. She glanced at her mother before dropping her gaze to the ground.

"When I return from my mission, we'll talk again, Brother Bowmore. I find you've already made a fine addition to our ward with your charity and tithe work." Washington tipped his hat to Aveline's father, ducked under the low doorway, and walked away without a word to the women. Bates gave Ma another awkward bow and shuffled off after Avery, having never said a word.

Pa watched the two men hurry away before he turned to his wife. He slouched as tension left his body. "They stopped by while I was on Brother Tyler's roof. Avery asked about me and the family. I told him about you, the two girls, and Bedford serving in the Mormon Battalion."

Aveline glanced at her mother. Any mention of her first-born, Bedford, sent her into fits of panic for his safety. He and other soldiers marched toward the California Republic in the service of the United States after the government had declared war against Mexico.

One day in July, her tall, lanky brother had sported a crooked grin while he tormented his sisters with pranks. The next day, he had been one of the first to step forward when Brigham Young called for volunteers to enlist in the Army's "Mormon Battalion". Like most of the five hundred volunteers, much of the pay he received he gave to his family.

As the new soldiers marched away from the Camp of Israel, Pa, Ma, Frances, and Aveline stood with their arms locked around each other.

They watched the departing men until they could no longer see Private Bowmore and the dirt cloud the column had kicked up. Since the battalion had departed, the Bowmores had not heard from him.

Pa's eyes narrowed as he turned to Aveline. "I was not happy our first counselor put such a question to you." His mouth set in a tight line.

Aveline's face grew hot.

"Your breakfast will be ready soon, Royal," Ma said, too quickly. "Girls, get your father's coffee going."

Frances giggled. "Though I missed most of your meeting, a blind man would see Aveline had bewitched Brother Avery." She nudged Aveline's arm. "He probably thinks you're at the right marrying age."

Ma and Pa exchanged dismayed glances.

~*~

Ma leaned back on the chair in front of the hearth and watched the bacon sizzle. Frances ladled water from the bucket into the coffee pot. Aveline set out the cups. "When we leave to head west, Poppy Wallace says we can make the journey in about three months."

"Oh, you and that Poppy." Ma waved her hand in dismissal. "Even back in Pennsylvania, you three and Em and Carissa were always chattering up a storm."

The cabin door creaked open, and her father stooped to enter the low opening. "Good morning, my dears! It's a Lord's Day; serene, the air is fresh, and the beasts are fed."

Ma lifted her cheek to accept Pa's kiss and gave him a small smile. The smell of cold air laced with manure and hay swirled around him. He sat heavily on his grandmother's straight-back chair, lovingly hauled from back east.

Aveline smiled at her father calling the day a Lord's Day, a phrase he described years ago as a day that "feels like a celebration gifted by the Lord".

Ma removed her husband's boots, one at a time. She set each foot on a stump close to the fire to warm.

Frances handed her father the plate laden with sizzling bacon and fried eggs. From behind him, Aveline tucked a napkin into his shirt's neck and kissed the top of his head.

Pa looked around the cabin and at the women in his life, then down to the full plate. Even in the flickering of the fire's low flames, Aveline could see the love glow from his face. "If I was a bettin' man, even Brother Brigham can't be as happy as I am right now."

Ma stroked her husband's wayward honey blonde hair that matched Aveline's. "If I was a betting woman, that's a bet I would not take." She sat beside Pa in the rocking chair he had built for her as a wedding gift almost two decades before.

From the iron skillet, Aveline placed bacon slices and the eggs, one each, on the remaining plates. She handed the first plate to her mother, the second to Frances. The daughters sat on their cottonwood stumps and leaned against the wall. Except for the firewood popping, silence settled in the Bowmore cabin.

"Pa, before chores are done today, I'd like to go with Poppy to Whitney's store. She has some wine she'd like to trade for some cloth," Frances said.

"That's *Bishop* Whitney's store, young lady. Show respect," Ma snapped. She glared from under her eyebrows. Fierceness blazed in her gaze.

"Bishop Whitney's store. She needs my help to carry the jugs." Frances blushed.

"I'm going with them to see if I can trade my handkerchiefs. I'm so nervous to see what he thinks of my work," Aveline said, clenching her hands into fists of anxiousness. "Then I'm going to head over to the Abernethy cabin on Smith Street. Sister Mary Richards has been there a couple days now, helping out. I want to give her a rest from the children."

"Has Sister Abernethy heard from her husband yet?" Ma asked.

"Nothing so far, but I would imagine he can't write often from France. With such a time lag between letters, she's very lonely."

Frances finished putting away the utensils from the meal. "I just cannot imagine why Brother Abernethy was sent to France. He has four children living and his wife is sick. Couldn't they have sent another?"

"Do not criticize our leaders, Frances." Pa's voice was stern, deep. "They are privy to revelations we cannot understand. It is God's will and our duty to obey as best we can. You must try harder to show respect and reverence."

Frances blushed and lowered her head, "Yes, Father. I'll try to do better."

~*~

That afternoon, Aveline raced into the cabin. "Look what I got for my handkerchiefs, Ma, Pa!" Aveline sang out as she whipped off her shawl. Frances and Poppy Wallace pushed in behind her.

Frances held out a bolt of deep blue cloth, a bottle of ink, and a journal. "Aveline is a success," Frances exclaimed.

"Bishop Whitney saw the handkerchiefs, and he proclaimed the pieces were a treasure he'd never seen the likes of," Poppy said. "Others in the store saw them and wanted to trade for one right then."

The chirps of Poppy's naturally high voice peeped louder in her enthusiasm. She looked and sounded like a nestling: small, vulnerable, and covered with curly hair that looked like down.

Aveline's shoulders lifted in a quick shrug. She felt proud that a bishop praised her work then worried that her pride was sinful. Every night she had spent hunkered near the tallow candle, stitched linen into a perfect square and tried to perfect the tatted edging. "I shall make more. It will help us buy what we need for the journey west."

"I'm proud of you, Daughter." Pa's voice cracked.

"Poppy, will you stay for tea?" Ma waved a hand for Poppy to sit in her chair.

Poppy looked wistfully at the kettle and the cup of tea in Ma's hand. She seemed to wrestle with her answer. "Thank you, no, Sister Lyda. Anson decided we shall follow the prophet Joseph Smith's Word of Wisdom. Anson commanded, 'We will not partake of hot drinks anymore'." She watched, not with condemnation, but with longing as Frances took a sip of tea. "Tobacco and liquor I've never touched, but the coffee and tea ..."

"The Word's not mandatory," Frances said. "It's only Smith's recommendation."

"Frances!" Sharpness threaded Ma's voice. "Never include 'only' when you describe the prophet's words. He is our prophet, the seer, and the revelator. May he rest in peace. Even if we choose not to follow his recommendations, his words must be treated with respect, and revered."

At her mother's rebuke, Frances shrank against the wall.

"Oh, we know that, Frances." Poppy's words were heavy with disappointment. "But Anson believes if we deny ourselves the hot drinks and whiskey, we would be blessed and more worthy in heaven. Although, I daresay, I can smell tobacco on his coat when he returns from the stockyard." Irritation laced her voice.

"Well, I was so excited I had to come tell you." Aveline wanted to change the subject. The tension in the cabin had risen because of her mother's biting chastisement toward Frances. "Now we need to head to Brother Abernethy's to help Sister Richards." She reached for her shawl.

Pa cleared his throat loudly. Aveline's hand froze on her shawl where it hung from the nail. "Girls, you both need to stay home today. There's a matter of import we must discuss."

Poppy understood. "I'll leave for the Abernethys' cabin. Godspeed." She pushed the door closed behind her.

Pa shifted in his chair and held his wife's gaze. "Brother Avery, our first counselor, has returned from his mission and is coming by soon. He spoke to me this morning whilst I was feeding the oxen. He stopped here right after you stepped out to go next door and the girls left for Bishop Whitney's store." Pa cleared his voice again. "He has a proposal of marriage."

A shocked silence gripped the women. Ma, then Frances, turned to Aveline, their eyes wide. Pa saw their glances and took a deep breath. "The proposal is not from Brother Avery, but from Lucas Bates … for Frances."

Ma shoved herself from her rocking chair and stood in front of the fire, her back to her husband. Frances' face paled as she lowered her head to stare at the dirt floor. She swallowed hard. "Pa, what do I do?"

Her father pulled on his boots and stood. He stroked his daughter's hair. With a soft voice he said, "Frances, Brother Avery said you have been called by the Lord to be the wife of Brother Lucas Bates. You will accept your duty and fulfill it. Brother Avery assures me that Brother Bates is a kind man, and he'll take care of you. Brother Bates is close to Brother Brigham. He's a man our leader trusts."

Ma spun around and opened her mouth to speak. Struggling, she stammered, "He's married."

"Yes." Pa kissed Frances' forehead. "Brother Avery said you have been chosen by revelation to become a plural wife. As such, you will be exalted in heaven. He said Sister Eliza Bates will be of great assistance to you."

"When will he propose to Frances?" Ma whispered.

"Soon."

Frances squeezed between the wall and the table that served as the cabin's kitchen. She yanked her skirt hem to release the cloth from the snag jutting from the log wall, and kicked the tub under the table. Her hands shook as she insisted on washing the dishes although that was Aveline's chore for the day. "I need to keep busy," she whispered.

~*~

Pa had left to work on building cabins for incoming Saints. Since he had gone, the three women hadn't spoken. As the dishes dried on a towel on the table, the silence pressed against them. Frances suddenly sobbed and cried, "Ma!"

Ma held her daughter while both wept. When the tears stopped flowing, Aveline said, "Don't be sad, Frances. Brother Bates may be kind and Sister Bates. You may marry into a wonderful family, like the Paddocks."

"All three of them grew up together," Frances cried. "Carissa was raised by Em's parents. They were practically sisters already."

"Brother Bates is high in the church. You shouldn't want for anything." Ma wiped the tears from Frances' face. "You must protect your chance at salvation. You cannot refuse a divine revelation. A woman's greatest responsibility is fulfilling her duty of marriage." She hugged Frances in a tight embrace then sat in her rocking chair and forced it back and forth. Frances and Aveline sat on their stumps. Frances rocked as she picked at her fingernails.

The cabin door squeaked open, and the three women jumped to their feet. Pa stooped to enter, followed by Washington Avery and Lucas Bates. With the tension and with six adults, the cabin was crowded, the air close. With a shaky voice and trembling hands, Pa formally presented Brother Lucas to Frances.

She bobbed a curtsy, folded her hands in front, and stared at the floor. Her neck veins throbbed, exposing her racing heartbeat. Keeping her head low, she tried not to stare at the man she would marry.

Lucas wore homespun trousers and a cotton shirt. The hand stitching wasn't straight; the buttons unevenly spaced. His long, loose hair draped over his shoulders and covered his barrel chest. His eyes were gentle, but when Frances noticed him studying her, she lowered her eyes. Her nose twitched at the scent of unwashed clothing and body.

In the awkward silence, Pa cleared his throat. "Brother Bates, you have something to ask of Frances?"

Lucas' deep voice rumbled from his chest. "Brother Avery informed me that the Lord sent him a revelation. The Lord commands us to marry. I shall exalt ye in the celestial kingdom, if ye will agree."

All eyes turned to Frances. A squeak dribbled from her mouth. She nodded her consent.

"Splendid," Lucas said. The fire's flickering light revealed a smile of crooked or missing teeth. From his coat pocket, he pulled out a small package. "For ye, Miss Bowmore, a gift." He held out the package, tiny in his large hands. The white silk wrap contrasted with sunburned calluses.

Frances hesitated, too nervous to touch her groom-elect. She plucked the package from his hands. Under everyone's watchful eyes, she peeled back the silk. "Oh, how beautiful!" With both hands, she held up a hair comb of ivory and gold. Small pearls dangled from the half circle of gold. The precious metal sparkled in the flickering light from the fireplace. Aveline and her parents exclaimed over the treasure.

"It shall look lovely in yer hair," Lucas said. "Ye shall honor me if ye would wear it tomorrow."

"Tomorrow?" Frances looked confused.

Washington Avery spoke up for the first time. "Tomorrow. Bishop Lang will arrive here at eleven. We'll hold the ceremony here." Avery turned to Pa. "If you consent, Brother Bowmore."

"Of course, of course," Pa stammered. "So quickly," he muttered. "Holding the ceremony in my home would be my honor."

"There is one more matter to be settled," Avery said.

"What is that, Counselor?" Pa asked.

Avery's chest puffed out in pride. "The Lord has granted me another revelation. He has revealed to me that I, too, shall marry another and my plural wife shall exalt me in heaven."

His eyes darkened as he turned toward Aveline. "That plural wife shall be Aveline."

Chapter 3

November 1846

Pa cleared his throat. Aveline jerked as the sound broke her reminiscing. She trembled as she realized that he was standing by her stacked trunks beside the door.

His voice cracked. "Aveline, it's time for you to go home."

~*~

Aveline knocked on the door of her new home. The Avery cabin stood on the corner of Ward Nine and faced south on Russell Street near the center of Winter Quarters. The cabin looked like the rest in Ward Nine: small and windowless; a thin stream of smoke curled from the rock chimney. The cabin was about twelve feet square, the same as the Bowmore cabin.

Pa and Frances stood behind her for moral support. Her small trunks, one dragged by her father, the other hauled on her father's back, were stacked behind them.

The wood hinges creaked as the door pushed open. Dorris Avery peeped through the crack. Her eyelids were puffy and, at the sight of Aveline, her eyes turned hard. Without a word, she turned, leaving the door ajar.

Aveline glanced at Frances, pulled the door open, and stepped into her new life. The fire in the hearth was little more than a tiny flame, straining to stay lit. Dorris trudged to the other side of the cabin and stepped behind a quilt that hung from the loft. The quilt separated two wrought iron bedsteads. With a jolt, Aveline realized she would bed a man only a few feet from his wife.

Frances' hand on Aveline's back propelled her forward. "This is your home too," Frances whispered in her ear.

Pa dragged in Aveline's two trunks. He took off his hat, gave a slight bow in Dorris' direction and asked, too loud in order to break the tension, "Sister, where would you prefer Aveline's trunks?"

Dorris nodded in the direction of the other bed. Pa set them, one on top of the other, beside a large chest, presumably Washington's. Pa pulled Aveline to him and held her. "May the Lord bless you and grant you a contented and fruitful life, Daughter." Tears welled in his eyes. He kissed her forehead and walked out the door.

Fighting tears herself, Aveline looked to her older sister for guidance. Frances flicked her eyes in the direction of the woman hiding on the other side of the quilt and whispered, "Remember, she is the first wife. Exaltation in heaven aside, she has agreed to give her husband to you. Be kind."

Aveline nodded her head.

"Perhaps you could offer her a cup of tea."

She nodded her head again. Her voice cracked while she asked the curtain: "Mother Avery, may I make you a cup of tea?" *Mother* was a term of respect used by younger wives toward the first wife.

The quilt whipped aside as Dorris sprang to her feet. "You will address me as *Sister* Avery." Fury boiled from under creased brows.

Unnerved by the sudden anger provoked by what Aveline thought was a benevolent question and a sign of respect, she stood frozen, not knowing what to do next. Dorris whipped the quilt back into place, disappearing behind it.

Frances pressed her fingers against her forehead and sighed, "Call her Sister Avery then."

Aveline asked in a quaking voice, "Sister Avery, may I make you a cup of tea?"

A sharp voice jabbed at Aveline's feelings from behind the curtain, "Will your sister always direct your actions or will you ever stand on your own feet?"

Shame flooded Aveline. With Frances' hovering, she must have appeared weak to her new sister-wife. Frances waved her hand dismissively. "Come, let's get you settled. This must be your bed." The foot of Aveline's bed reached to the doorway. Dorris' bed was in the far corner, away from the chilling draft that seeped through the cracks in and around the door. The quilt curtain hanging from the purlin that separated the two beds was old, thin, and had tears in a few places.

Frances opened one trunk and pulled out Aveline's quilt and her nightgown. She draped the quilt on the bed. At the sight of the nightgown, Aveline realized how close she was to having a man for the first time. She sat on the bed's edge to hide her jitters.

Frances studied Aveline and appeared to know how she was feeling. She sat beside Aveline. "Don't worry. Brother Avery knows what to do."

"Was, was it difficult for you?"

Frances' eyes flooded with tears. "Mister Bates was kind at first. He's a gentle man. Eliza—Sister Bates—has had great difficulty reconciling herself to plural marriage. I remind her we can expect happiness in heaven, but she cannot abide it."

In the dim light of the weak fire, Aveline discerned Frances' hollow cheeks and sunken eyes. "Are you happy in your life?"

The flames' light reflected the tracks spilling down Frances' cheeks. Stifling her sobs, Frances shook her head. "Sister Bates makes both our lives miserable. She reveals her grief through various ways—often, with a belt. Her sister, Eleanor, lives next door. She goads Eliza into believing I am the cause of her unhappiness."

"She beats you?" Aveline whispered, appalled. "Have you asked Brother Bates to stop it?"

Frances nodded. "For a strong man, Mister Bates is weak before his wife. After she had complained—screamed is more like it—for the hundredth time, he said I am to provide him children to build his kingdom. Beyond that, I am to make my own life. I don't know how long I can endure it."

Aveline reached for Frances and held her. "But you must, for your own salvation." She shivered in anger for her sister's misery and fear for herself with what lay ahead with the angry Dorris.

"Come, let's get you prepared for him." Frances wiped off her wet face with her hands.

After Aveline removed her dress, Frances helped her tug the nightgown over her sacred undergarment. The nightgown clung to the long underwear that symbolized a Mormon's devotion. Looking down at herself Aveline asked, "How do we manage wearing all these clothes?"

Frances giggled. "With the greatest of difficulty, but remember, he knows what to do."

Frances pulled on her coat, gave Aveline a hug and kissed her cheek. "Be strong, Sister."

Aveline pulled Frances back to her. "Be strong, Sister."

After Frances pushed the door closed behind her, Aveline crawled into bed under her quilt but into strange sheets. Shivering to warm the cold bedding, she stared at the fire, feeling as strong as the weakest flame.

The cabin's door creaked open then her husband latched the door closed behind him. Cold air whirled and settled on her quilt. Aveline peeked from under the covers and watched Washington's silhouette against the fire. He stepped behind the curtain. His voice rumbled, low, as he spoke to Dorris. She didn't hear if Dorris replied.

A moment later, Washington stepped around the curtain then undressed near her bed. Too embarrassed to watch, but too curious to shield her eyes, she noticed his handmade muslin undergarment and that he did not take it off before he slipped under the quilt beside Aveline. They laid flat on their backs, staring at the ceiling.

After several moments, Aveline wondered whether she should turn over and try to sleep when Washington reached below the quilt to pull up Aveline's nightgown. Too mortified to move, she lay still. As Washington tugged on the gown, he murmured, "You have to help."

She squirmed out of her nightgown. Washington helped her tug both legs out of her undergarment. With her legs exposed, he seemed satisfied that she was bare enough then slipped out one leg from his undergarment. He lay on top of Aveline. His long hair draped across her face. She struggled to breathe with his weight on her chest. She felt a hot prodding, a pressure between her legs, then a sharp, stabbing pain. Aveline bit her lips and tried not to cry out. Realizing Dorris was listening only a few feet away spiraled her embarrassment, and she winced in time to Washington's soft grunting.

Washington moaned and stopped thrusting. His raspy breath tickled her ear. As he pushed off her onto his elbow, her chest expanded with welcome air. She slipped her legs into the undergarment Washington held for her. The nightgown was tangled, and Aveline held up her arms while he tugged it over her head. He pushed his leg into his garment leg, kissed Aveline on the cheek, and rolled over.

Numb, Aveline stared at the flickering light on the cabin wall. The night's silence was broken by Dorris' soft sobs from the other side of the quilt. Aveline stared into the dimness until she fell asleep when, hours later, the flame went out.

Chapter 4

Pots banging on the hearth awoke Aveline. She blinked in the strange surroundings but couldn't get her bearings. *Ma?*

While preparing coffee and breakfast, Dorris took out her anger on the skillet, the teakettle, against the hearth, the table, across any surface she could reach. Washington was gone.

Aveline threw back the covers. She lurched from the ache in her chest and between her legs. *Am I to feel this way every time?* She shivered out of her nightgown and into her dress, hustling in the hope that her rising from bed would make Dorris stop beating the utensils. "I'm sorry for sleeping late, Sister Avery," Aveline called out while hurrying to pull on her boots and to lace them. "I'll be right there to help you."

No response came from Dorris, but the pots stopped banging. Aveline pulled up her quilt and fluffed the two feather pillows. She tucked the quilt under the ticking the best she could.

Aveline walked, hunched in achiness, the few steps to the hearth. With the fire flaring like Dorris' temper, the cabin was well lit and warm. She looked around the room. Clothes draped the two chairs. Dorris' sheets and bedspread were mounded on the mattress. Soiled plates smeared with food bits were jumbled into a battered washbasin. A chamber pot needed emptying.

Dorris sat on the clothes draped over her chair's seat and rocked. Her face was as hard as the stone hearth.

"What can I do for you this morning, Sister Avery?"

"You're helpless since your sister's not here?"

Aveline fought to be patient. "I'm not helpless. I don't know your habits. What do you wish for me to do first?"

"Leave. First, I wish for you to leave." Dorris' eyes never left the fire. The anger in her eyes was as hot as the fire's coals. "But that will not happen, will it?"

"Sister, I understand you're upset with my being here—"

"You understand nothing. You needed your sister to help you. How weak."

Be kind. Frances' words rang in her head, but Aveline chose to ignore them. "We are in this marriage, you and I, because of our belief in the revelation and sanctity of plural marriage. We want exaltation in heaven. Here on earth, we can make life much easier for both of us. We are married to the same man. Keep this in mind: I am also Sister Avery." Pride came through Aveline's voice. "*Sister*." The sneer in her voice lingered.

Dorris launched herself from the chair and, in a flash, slapped Aveline.

Aveline gasped and staggered back. Her hand flew to the stinging handprint on her face.

"You are *not* Sister Avery. You are Sister Bowmore. A plural wife never uses her husband's name. *Never!* That honor is reserved for me, the first wife. Didn't your sister instruct you on that?" Dorris' face contorted with rage. "If you have to be told what to do, here, fetch water." Dorris kicked the wood bucket by her feet. "Dump the chamber pot and that slop jar … every day. That is your duty. It's what you're suited for."

Dorris sat down on her rocker and ignored the tears flowing down her cheeks.

Aveline swallowed. Blinking back tears, she considered her new station in life. Married to a married man she barely knew, she must live in a soiled home filled with resentment from a furious sister-wife. Without a word, she draped her shawl over her head. She balanced the chamber pot on the slop jar and headed to the outhouse.

~*~

Through the following week, Aveline sought to blend into the walls to stay out of Dorris' way. Whether Washington was home or absent, Dorris never threw anything at Aveline, and she didn't lash out like she had that first morning. She calmed herself by acting as if she were alone. Aveline didn't mind so much about being ignored; at least the cabin was quiet.

The peace ended when Washington returned home. Dorris and Washington bickered constantly. His church duties kept him away for a day or two at a time. Dorris complained loud and often that he neglected her as his primary wife. Washington would reply that if she were in a more compatible mood, he might feel like attending her.

He complained of how he slaved to execute what the leadership bid of him in order to rise in the church, yet all he had been selected for was first counselor of one of the smallest wards in Winter Quarters. By now, he had expected to be at the next level: bishop.

When their tantrums escalated, Aveline retreated to her place behind the quilt. She sat on her bed or huddled near her trunks and hoped Washington would not follow her. A couple times she left the cabin to sit in the outhouse she shared with their next-door neighbors and the neighbors in the two cabins behind them. She felt ridiculous as she hid in the privy, but there she had privacy and quiet. As long as she didn't breathe deeply, the outhouse provided respite from the bickering, the accusations, and the complaints. To bolster her spirits on warmer winter days, she cracked the privy's door for light and read the Book of Mormon.

Several days after their wedding, Washington had brought home three short planks, remnants of a cabin roof, to place over Aveline's trunks. The trunks stood as the legs and the planks made a fine, but tiny table where she laid out her tatting material and tatted the edging for handkerchiefs. The trunk nearest to the fireplace held her small bolt of linen.

Nestled beside the butcher paper-wrapped linen stood the small, but long, mahogany box her father built. The box held an ivory shuttle; her number three tatting pin; two knitting needles, one very thin and one a bit thicker; a roll of delicate number 18 cotton thread; and her treasured roll of white silk thread.

By the fire's dim light—or the oil lamp when Dorris slept, she hand-stitched a handkerchief and tatted a lacy edging with tiny, even knots. When Washington vetoed Dorris' demand for the lamp and allowed Aveline to move it to her side of the cabin, the welcoming glow gave off enough light she could see her work with clarity.

She ignored Dorris' snide remarks at her expense, although since living in the Avery cabin she had never ripped out so many knots or unraveled so many twisted threads in her tatting.

In her little space, shielded by the curtain and comforted by the lamp's glow, she could almost ignore Washington and Dorris' complaining and fighting. The growing stack of completed handkerchiefs she would barter for goods that her new family needed.

After the first week of marriage, Washington spent the nights in Dorris' bed. This arrangement made her not as angry. Twice that week, while Aveline lay in her bed, she covered her head to block out the soft grunting from the other side of the quilt.

Dorris, now assured of her primary place in the household as first wife, took delight in ordering Aveline to perform all chores: wash dishes and clothes, iron Washington's shirts, bake bread, make meals, sweep the packed dirt floor, gather firewood, in addition to her regular chores to empty the chamber pot and slop jar, and fetch water.

Throughout the unending daily tasks, Aveline had one small victory: she had scrubbed Dorris' apron enough to get out all the stains. *I cannot abide the stain blossoms on this garment.* After she beat the cloth, Aveline studied her chapped hands. *My hands will heal from the lye, but at least I won't have look at grease stains.*

Alone one morning after Dorris left to shop at Bishop Whitney's store, a knock on the door sounded. Dorris had taught Aveline the hard way that she may not open the door if she were alone; the visitor would have to go away.

Aveline peeked through a crack in the door. "Frances!"

She threw open the door and hugged her panting sister. She pulled her sister indoors, out of the driving rain. Aveline whipped off Frances' shawl and brushed off the wetness. She drew back from her sister and recoiled at the sight.

Frances was skinny; her face sallow. Fear darted from her tired eyes.

"Come, let me make you some tea." Aveline tugged Frances' hands toward the chair.

"No. It's Carissa. She's very sick. Can you come with me to fetch medicine for her and her coming babe?"

Chapter 5

Frances shrieked as she slipped in the muddy street. She pulled her shawl tighter over her head as if the sodden fabric would shield her from the torrential rain. Behind Frances, Aveline jumped to avoid stepping in the same puddle. Splashing rain was loud in her ears. Water poured off the cabin roofs in sheets and spattered mud into the streets. No one else was about; everyone was indoors to escape the storm.

Fear for Carissa spurred them toward the store. Between gasps for air, Frances spoke how Carissa's time came fast. The birthing pain was more than midwife Ma and Carissa's sister-wife Em had ever seen, and she weakened quickly. Ma and Em feared for not only Carissa's life but also for the babe's.

Frances stopped at the door of the trading store and gasped for breath. Aveline caught up to her sister, pressed the pain in her side, and wheezed.

"Ready?" Frances asked.

"Oh, yes," Aveline said as the girls moved in unison when Frances threw open the door to the store. As one, they dashed in and slammed the door closed to prevent the driving rain from flooding the cabin. Each exclaimed at the warmth and drier air. They peeled off their dripping shawls and hung them on nails near the door. The girls shivered as they hugged themselves to warm their soaked arms before stepping up to the plank counter held up by two barrels.

"Girls, what brings you out in this rain? You'll catch your death." The fat woman behind the makeshift counter shook her finger at the girls. "But since you're here, what can I do for you?"

"Our ma sent us to get some composition powder. There's a woman who is very ill." Frances rubbed her upper arms hard to raise some heat. She leaned closer to the woman and whispered, "Newborn."

The woman knew. "Ah. You'll need some of this." She reached behind her and pulled down a tin. The herbal mixture would help relieve Carissa's pain and give her strength, Ma had said. With a small spoon, the woman measured out a portion of the powder onto a square of paper. She carefully folded the paper. "Laced with lobelia. Five cents, then."

Frances tugged a little bag from her wet skirt's pocket and counted out the five coins. "Thank you, Sister." Both girls chimed and curtsied in unison. They grabbed their shawls before dashing out into the deluge.

Frances knocked lightly on the Paddock family's cabin door then pulled it open. Panting quietly so as to not disturb her mother or the bedridden woman she tended, Frances held out the medicine. Aveline hung their shawls by the door.

Carissa Clarke lay beneath a mound of quilts. The sweat on her face had dried, but tears flowed down her red cheeks while she cuddled the tiny bundle wrapped in a thin blanket. Carissa's sister-wife, Em Paddock, sat on the bed's edge and wiped off Carissa's tears.

Aveline admired the love between them—much like her own parents, only with two women. Separately, Em and Carissa had told Aveline they had initially been afraid of the revelation of plural marriage, but once married, they and husband Hamish were determined to welcome the new relationship and be faithful to each other for the Lord and for the promise of heaven. Now, Aveline celebrated Carissa's baby, her second, but she also prayed this baby would survive.

Aveline clasped her hands together, quietly, pleased to be a part of the new life after witnessing so much death in camp.

Ma stroked Carissa's hair and placed a soft kiss on the wet cheek. She laid a gentle hand on Em's shoulder as she slipped past toward her girls. Frances still held out the package of powder.

Ma shook her head. The powder wasn't needed.

Aveline and Frances looked from their mother to Carissa's tear-streaked face. Realization flooded their large eyes.

Ma whispered, "Come. Let us leave them in peace. The bishop is on his way." She reached for her shawl and shepherded her girls out the door.

All three women ran through the downpour to Ma's cabin next door. Ma pulled it open and the women rushed in. Pa took their shawls and hung the sodden masses. "I have tea water boiling, if you want some."

"I would love a cup of tea, Royal." Lyda collapsed in her chair while Frances and Aveline dragged their old cottonwood stumps closer to the fire. Aveline ignored the water trickling through the roof and splashing into puddles in the cabin's corners.

Their father poured the boiling water over the Imperial tea leaves in the cup and offered the cup to his wife. "Thank you," she murmured. Pa sat on his chair, placed his hand on her shoulder, and waited patiently for news.

Ma looked up knowing everyone wanted to know. She shook her head. "A little girl. The babe did not live but for a moment." Tears formed in her eyes. She blinked hard. "I don't know why she didn't live. She was perfect, beautiful. The Lord must have wanted her in heaven more than He wanted her on earth."

A sob escaped. "This is the second child poor Carissa has lost at birth." Ma's chin quivered. "Carissa named her Hope Em Paddock to honor her love for Em."

Pa patted his wife's shoulder. He watched his daughters wipe the tears off their faces. His voice choked. "I'm sorry, my dear. You did all you could. Let us pray for the infant Hope's soul and peace for the Paddocks." All four bowed their heads while Pa murmured a soft prayer.

"Amen." Ma reached up to touch her husband's hand lingering on her shoulder. The softness in her eyes glowed with appreciation for his consideration.

No one spoke as she sipped her tea.

Frances said, "At least we have the composition powder if anyone needs it. We might be able to help someone in need a bit quicker."

Ma nodded. "I wish I could have done more," she whispered as tears trickled down her face. Pa, Aveline and Frances held their mother as she sobbed.

~*~

Aveline pushed her cabin's door open and felt relief that Dorris hadn't yet returned. She hurried to fill the kettle with water and set the kettle over the low flames. Frances scurried in and hung their shawls on the hooks by the door. Both women had work to do, but their need for comfort in their sorrow gave them the strength to chance a scolding from their sister-wives for their idleness.

Frances sat on Dorris' rocking chair and Aveline sat on Washington's chair. If Dorris caught Frances sitting in her rocker, Dorris would wait until after Frances left to "correct" Aveline for allowing Frances to commit the sin of sitting in her rocking chair.

The glint of tears on Frances' cheeks caught Aveline's attention. Aveline reached out to hold her sister's hand and felt the bones through the thin skin.

Frances burst into tears. Huge sobs wracked her body. Frightened, this was more than sorrow about Carissa's lost infant. Aveline knelt in front of her, then held and rocked her until she cried herself dry. The water in the kettle boiled. Aveline spooned Imperial tea flakes into two mugs and added the water. She didn't pry, but waited impatiently for Frances to talk.

Fearing Dorris' return and the spoiling of a sisterly moment, Aveline stepped to her nearest trunk and lifted the trunk lid. She pulled out the handkerchief she had finished the day before.

In front of Frances, she knelt again and held out the cloth. "I want you to have this right now. I may be vain to say this, but I finally perfected the scallops and the rings in tatting. I want you to have the first one."

Frances smiled a sad smile. "That is so kind of you." She examined the tatted lace. The tiny knots were even, the rings, flawless. "You did perfect it. These rings are so tiny they look like seed pearls."

"Look, your embroidered initials: F, C, B, B. Frances Cooper Bowmore Bates."

Frances lowered the handkerchief to her lap, leaned over and grabbed Aveline in a strong hug. Sitting back, Frances smiled again, a brighter smile as she studied the craftsmanship. "This is beautiful. You'll keep making these to trade?"

"Yes, but not all of them. I made one for Mister Avery. I haven't given it to him yet. I'm deciding whether to make one for Sister Avery. I think I shall. Perhaps a small gift will warm her heart toward me."

"A small gift! You can sell these for a lot of money. They are that exquisite. The lace is so delicate it seems as if the linen should float away."

Aveline pushed back on her heels. She rubbed her sister's knees then sat on Washington's chair. "Please tell me. How are you?"

Frances looked at her hands. She fingered the handkerchief as if trying to decide what to say. She looked Aveline in the eyes. "I don't know if I can remain in the Bates household."

To Aveline's shocked expression, Frances shook her head. "Sister Eliza is angry … all the time. I can't do anything right. If I make the slightest mistake, she throws things or she'll come up behind me and slap me. Mister Bates and Eliza fight all the time. They throw things and scream and curse. He has taken to striking her. Eleanor—Eliza's sister—is just as evil. She'll come over, and she and Eliza will just sit and watch me. They criticize everything. The more they criticize, the more mistakes I make, and the more punishment they dispense. My stomach hurts all the time. I can't eat. All I do is pour my sorrow into the journal you bought me. I don't know what else to do."

"I'm so sorry, Frances. I only know a little how you feel. Dorris is angry all the time, but at least she usually ignores me. She and Mister Avery fight all the time too, but they leave me alone when I'm in my bed space." Aveline reached for her sister's hand. "You know what Ma says, that we must submit to God's will. Our reward will come in the highest reaches of heaven."

Frances' chin trembled. She gulped in a deep breath. "I'm trying. I really am."

Aveline patted Frances' knee. "What do you think about us visiting the Paddocks when Carissa is recovered? The three of them get along so well. Perhaps they could give us ideas or at least give us the strength to keep us going."

Shaking her head, Frances said, "I started work at the braid shop on Cahoon Street that Mister Bates built. He employs only sisters. He says women work harder than the men. I'm getting better at the braiding, but I do not care for it." Frances fingered her handkerchief's tatted edge. "At least the other women have a gay time talking and gossiping whilst we work, and I'm away from Eliza and Eleanor. I am most grateful for that, but when I return home, even when I have worked all day, Eliza still expects me to do all my daily chores while she has done nothing all day except to concoct criticisms about me with Eleanor."

Aveline opened her mouth to speak, but jumped with guilt when the cabin door opened.

Dorris came in, drenched and with her arms laden with wet packages from the store. She froze, surprised at having a visitor, and stared at them both. "Are you going to help me or do you have to wait for your sister to tell you to help me?"

Aveline gave Frances an "I know what you mean" look. She stood to take the packages from Dorris' arms.

Frances understood the situation. To lighten the mood, she stood from Dorris' rocker and asked, "Are you all going to the dance next month? It'll be at the Council House—to celebrate its opening. Will you go, Aveline?" Frances looked at each woman. "Sister Avery?"

Taking in Frances' tear-stained face, Dorris gave Frances a "wouldn't you like to know" shrug before turning away. Aveline looked to Frances behind Dorris' back and shrugged.

Frances slipped the handkerchief into her left sleeve. "I'd better get back to my chores." She took her coat and shawl off the nail then reached out her arms for a goodbye embrace. "We'll talk again soon," she whispered into Aveline's ear.

Aveline pulled the door closed as Frances walked away. As she turned, a sharp slap knocked her head into the door.

"How dare you let someone in this house when I told you never to let anyone in!" Dorris screamed into Aveline's face.

Aveline shook off her shock. Anger and anguish simmering below the surface boiled over from Frances' and her own abusive treatment and Carissa's heartbreaking loss. "This is my home too! My sister needed me and I needed my sister!" Aveline screamed back. Without realizing it, she pulled back her fist and let it fly. Knuckles hit Dorris' cheek with a crack.

The sharp sound masked the sound of the door opening. Arms outstretched to grab Dorris' hair, Aveline's wrists were suddenly pinned by strong hands. Her face stung from an unseen blow. She slammed onto the dirt floor and she lost her breath.

Washington stood over her, his face red with fury. "How dare you strike my wife!" Lightning-fast, he backhanded Aveline across her cheek. "You will yield to her! You will obey her! Do you understand?"

Hot blood ran from Aveline's nose as she nodded and fought to keep from weeping.

"Go to bed. You forfeit your week with me."

Aveline nodded, careful to not jar her throbbing head and grateful not to share her bed with him. She staggered to her feet but tripped over her dragging skirt. Gathering her skirt in her fists, she collapsed onto her bed.

Chapter 6

Aveline threw back the quilt at what she guessed was first light. The flames had died, and the glowing coals cast a dim light across the hearth. Her head ached. Her cheek and nose hurt from where Washington backhanded her. Wincing, her right shoulder twinged as she pulled on her dress. Hitting the floor must have damaged her shoulder. Ashamed of her lack of restraint concerning Dorris the night before, she wanted to be the first one up to warm the cabin and start the coffee brewing to atone for her sin of screaming at and striking the first wife.

She poked the dying coals then added thin sticks of wood she had collected the day before. The wooden water bucket was empty. Pulling her shawl tightly over her head, she pushed the door closed behind her then lugged the bucket to the well. She shivered against the still-frigid air. The cold's icy fingers scraped her bruised face, spiking her pain. As she wound the windlass, she took a moment to watch the rising sun cast its red glow on the thin clouds skittering to the east. A white ring of breath puffed from her open mouth was perfect for her to poke a finger through. The bucket full, she staggered back under the weight, careful not to splash water onto her skirt.

Grateful to be back in the warm cabin, she ladled the water into the coffee pot, hung the pot from the long trammel and pushed the crane above the small flame. She added a thicker wood stick on the fire. As quietly as she could, she measured out the coffee beans onto the skillet. With her foot, she nudged the spider over the flames and placed the skillet on it. As she stirred the beans to prevent them from burning, the aroma made her stomach growl. She watched in the fire's flickering light as the beans roasted to a rich brown. Aveline reached for the coffee grinder and ground the hot beans as quietly as the churning gears allowed.

With the coffee pot suspended over the growing flames, Aveline sat on her stump to wait for Washington and Dorris to rise. Murmuring announced they were awake. The curtain moved with every head and knee bump.

Washington emerged. He stepped behind his chair. Then he stared at Aveline as if deciding what to say. Tired of the turmoil, she stood, hands clasped. "I apologize for my conduct last night, Husband." She choked on saying "husband". "I beg your pardon. I'll try harder to be in accord."

Washington grunted. "See to it." He sat on his chair. Dorris appeared from behind the curtain, adjusting her skirt and pulling her shawl around her shoulder. A light bruise blossomed under her left eye. She ignored Aveline, stood behind Washington and placed her hands on his shoulders. He placed his hands on hers. Both stared into the fire.

Aveline cleared her throat and took a deep breath. "Sister Avery, I wish to—"

"Be silent." Dorris tossed her head and sat on her chair.

Flush with anger and embarrassment at her rebuffed attempt to make amends, Aveline sat on her stump and breathed heavily. She felt like a pouting child, which only made her angrier.

Not moving his eyes from the flames, Washington leaned his head toward Dorris. "You must know I leave for a mission in January. I don't know when I'll return."

A small gasp escaped from Dorris. Her eyes grew wide. "Oh, no. Why now?" she asked softly as she reached for his hand.

"This mission is a test of my skills. I'm sure of it. Since the council did not see their way to select me as a member when they replaced several last week, perhaps the High Council will judge me from this mission. My success will make them see me as a possible member or select me as a bishop. After that, if the council cannot see the value of my work," his voice trailed off as he threw up his hands. "Otherwise, their judgment of whom to select is lacking," Washington said with a sneer in his voice.

"I fear they do not take notice of your skills, Washington," Dorris said.

"Where will you go? What will you do?" Aveline asked, wanting to feel like a member of the family as well as to lessen the tension.

A pall fell over the cabin. Washington stared into the fire again. "A man's mission is of no concern to you."

Embarrassed by the rebuke, she wanted to shrink into the walls. Aveline crossed her arms and chewed her nails. She glanced over to her bed. She had too many chores to perform before she could hide herself behind the quilt curtain and tat.

"How may I help you prepare for your mission?" Dorris asked softly, yet loud enough for Aveline to hear.

More thinking out loud, Washington nodded as he spoke. "I am to broker an agreement between merchants to supply the Saints in Mount Pisgah for travel to Zion. I'll need my best shirt and trousers. Likely, I'll assist in building wagons to trade for beasts so I'll need all my field clothes."

The coffee finished percolating. Aveline slipped off her stump and grabbed the rag to lift the pot. She poured the coffee in two cups and delivered one to Washington and to Dorris. Neither spoke as they accepted her offering. Aveline poured a mug for herself and hurried back to her stump.

"But," Washington said loudly, "I have plenty of time to prepare for this mission. There is not much for me to do right now." He sipped the coffee and flinched as it burned his mouth.

"January will be a disagreeable month to travel to Pisgah, but April shall arrive before we know it, and we must be ready. Our companies of Saints will begin the trek west to our new home in Zion, away from the reach of the American government."

No one spoke as each sat in silence. Dorris flicked her eyes in Aveline's direction as if to say, "This is how you find out information."

With a sigh, Washington glanced in Aveline's direction. "Prepare a big breakfast for me." He looked back to Dorris. "Today, several of us will attach the roof on Brother Richards' place. I'm not looking forward to it. It's two stories tall. Getting the roofing materials up to that height, in this wind, will be hazardous."

"His place is the big house with eight sides, isn't it?" Aveline asked brightly as she headed toward the larder box. "I watched them build it and wondered what he was going to use for. It is intriguing."

"Pretentious, I'd say," Washington muttered before he took a sip of coffee. "Saints are dying every day from want and sickness, yet he builds this blight in the town. It looks like a potato pile."

Aveline sliced the pork chunk into slabs then placed them in the skillet. She wiped off the carving knife on her rag before she set it toward the back of the table, sharp edge to the wall. "Poppy said the building will house a great deal more than just Doctor Richards' home. It'll be a post office, his surgery—"

"Piffle." Washington said, effectively ending the discussion as he held up his cup for a refill.

After he finished his breakfast, Washington tossed his plate and coffee cup onto the makeshift table. Without a word, he grabbed his wool coat off the nail. He wrapped his scarf around his neck and hesitated, then looked back at Dorris. "I don't know when I'll be back," Washington said with a sneer. "If the good doctor could see fit to feed and house the workers for the night, I shall remain there."

He yanked on his coat. "It'll be good to get the roof attached. Brother Paddock said there's a storm coming. Can feel it in his left knee. After showing my respect to the good Saint Richards, I've got to check on the feed for the oxen. No matter what happens with Richards' roof, I may not be back for a few days." He flung open the door and disappeared into the overcast day.

~*~

With a groan, Aveline straightened up and lifted her arms to ease the cramps that seized her shoulder and back muscles.

She stumbled to the fireplace, struggling to keep her knees from buckling and to avoid bumping Dorris sitting in her rocker. With a few more branches in the fire, she held out her claw-like hands, stiff from scrubbing the week's soiled clothes, to absorb the flames' warmth. The fresh wood in the fire caught; the sap popped, spewing spark showers onto the hearth.

After warming for several minutes, her strained muscles relaxed. Aveline hoisted the washtub and lugged it outside, careful not to slosh the scummy water indoors. Any wetness on the cabin's hard-packed dirt floor took days to dry out. Mud would be dragged everywhere. No matter how careful she walked, small clumps of the muck ended up in her bed.

She ignored the horse-drawn wagon creaking down Russell Street as she concentrated on balancing the tub and keeping her legs churning in a smooth manner. Snowflakes gently poked at her eyes. The wet splashes on her face stung in the cold breeze.

At the corner of the cabin, with a quick thrust, she chucked the tub's contents away from her and stepped back quickly to escape the splash of wash water and muck.

She backed into a solid object: Lucas Bates. Aveline gasped at the surprise and stepped away from the big man. His lips were tight and his eyes squinted in his fury.

"Sister, I was just comin' to fetch ye. Would ye be so kind as to come to ma house?" His eyelids squeezed in anger. Aveline flinched as snowflakes and spittle pelted her face.

"Brother Bates, you startled me. What's wrong? Is something wrong with Frances?"

"They're fixin' ta come ta blows, the two women."

Aveline hurried to the cabin door, lugging the empty tub. "Let me get my coat." She stepped into the cabin and slid the tub in its place under the table. Lucas followed her into the cabin. He saw Dorris and tipped his hat, "Sister Avery."

"Brother Lucas, what a surprise." Dorris had a cheery lilt to her voice that Aveline had never heard before.

"I came needin' the sister here. I'm ashamed to say my wife and," he motioned to Aveline, "her sister are fighting something fierce. I'm hoping she can help calm them down."

Dorris' cheery face fell as Lucas spoke. Her lip curled as she watched Aveline don her coat and grab her shawl from the nail. Knowing what Dorris thought, Aveline said, "My chores are done. I'm going with Brother Lucas." She was out the door before Dorris could say anything.

"Brother, what happened?" Aveline asked as she trotted to keep up with the big man's strides. Fumbling the coat buttons, she gave up and pulled the shawl over her head. The snowflakes grew in thickness. At the bluff to the west, low dirty-white clouds hid the hills.

"My wife took exception to yer sister sleepin' in this morn. Complained yer sister's not doin' her chores. Yer sister said she'd been up all night helpin' her mother—yer mother—with the sick Sister Fagan. Said she had gotten back only an hour ago."

A small pack of dogs approached, their legs stiff, their noses in the air. Sensing a game with the hustling duo, the dogs broke into a run alongside.

Lucas threw a kick in the direction of the nearest dog. That one sank back, but another took its place. Lucas didn't break stride as he whipped off his hat and swung it at the cur. Sensing a lack of sport, the pack lost interest and skulked behind a cabin.

Aveline and Lucas turned up Pratt Street as an oxen-drawn wagon made them skirt the edge of a cabin. Aveline started to pant; her short legs couldn't keep up with Lucas' long legs and ever-quickening pace.

Before they reached Cahoon Street, screams rent the air. She broke into a run, followed by the thumps of Lucas' boots.

The two women fought in the street. Grappling, each clenched the other's hair in their fists. Frances screamed. Curses poured from Eliza's mouth between gobs of spittle. Cloth gave way with a tearing sound.

Frances kicked; Eliza leaped over the foot. Another woman joined in the fray and pummeled Frances. Forced to release Eliza's hair to defend herself, Frances covered her head with her arms.

Both Eliza and the other woman beat and kicked the shrieking Frances. Passersby ran to join the crowd and barking dogs ran between legs. A few men and a woman shouted their encouragement.

"Stop it! Stop!" Aveline screamed.

Before she reached the writhing pile of womanhood, an arc of water flew through the air and struck the grapplers. The wet shock stopped the women's motion.

The unknown woman shoved Frances to the ground and ran in the opposite direction. Aveline bent over Frances and held her as she wept.

Blood dripped from her nose and the swelling corner of her mouth. She pulled the edges of her torn bodice together. Deep scratches from her throat down to her chest seeped blood. A bruise sprouted on her left cheek. Hanks of mud-glopped hair draped across her face.

"Cease such ungodly behavior!" The bellow stopped all motion and sound of the passersby. As one, they turned to see who threw the water and barked the command.

"How dare you foul the scent of womankind with this stench of evil!" Brigham Young's eyes bulged with a white-hot rage as he shoved his way through the crowd to the wet combatants. Trembling with anger, he looked from Eliza down to the stooped Frances. "What manner of woman would behave with such wickedness?"

"Brother," Eliza pointed down to Frances, still huddled weeping on the ground, "she refused to do her duty today. She is derelict, and she refuses to maintain her station as a second wife."

The "second" sneer infuriated Aveline. She patted Frances and tried to help her stand.

Young turned his head and jammed his fists on his hips. "Is this abominable behavior true, Sister?"

Frances stood, supported by Aveline. Frances couldn't speak so she shook her head. Aveline tossed her head toward Lucas. "Brother Young, Brother Bates is the husband of these women. He told me what happened; he can tell you truth."

Young turned to Lucas. "This is *your* wife?"

"Aye, Brother. I have no excuse for their behavior, and I'm ashamed." He shoved his hands into his coat pocket. "This one," he pointed with the toe of his boot toward Eliza. "Is ma primary wife, as ye know. This one." He pointed to Frances. "Is ma second wife. She's been a bit slow learnin' the instructions and the ways of the plural wife."

Aveline gasped, as did Frances, at Lucas' betrayal. "You told me moments ago Frances spent the night helping to birth a baby and just returned! In your household, Brother, at what time may your women rest? Or do you just expect them to faint from fatigue?"

The crowd held their breath. As one, they turned to look at Young. His mouth creased to a thin line and his face turned dark red. Seconds passed as his mouth worked.

Aveline didn't speak; she had already said too much. A woman must never publicly or privately chastise a man, a member of the priesthood, but someone needed to defend her sister.

"Silence, Sister!" exploded Young. "Take her home." He turned to Lucas. "Perhaps, Brother, you should instruct your wives—both of them—on the proper behavior required of women in this settlement." He faced the crowd. "Go back to your labors."

The crowd disappeared in response to the command. Young glared at Aveline, Frances, and Eliza in turn. He disappeared into the fog of falling snow.

Eliza stepped into her cabin. Aveline guided Frances toward the door. As Lucas approached the door, Aveline slowed Frances so he could enter first. Frances lurched for the cabin wall as her legs gave way. Grabbing her weeping sister's arm, Aveline yanked the arm over her shoulder to keep Frances from falling. A cry erupted from the battered woman.

The stink from unwashed clothing, bedding, and an unemptied slop jar wafted from the cabin. Aveline held her breath. She and Frances started forward to cross the threshold, but Eliza blocked their way. The blaze from her eyes bored into Aveline's. "You may not enter my house. You will leave this … baggage here."

"My sister is not baggage. She is your sister-wife. You should learn manners, *Sister*." The sneer came through her words, and she regretted it. Her blatant disrespect to the primary wife of the house would only make things worse for Frances.

Eliza grabbed Frances' arm and whipped her into the house. "Go to your husband's house. He would do well to provide *you* with instruction." She slammed the door closed.

Frozen as stiff as the snow-covered ground, Aveline stood in the cold and listened to the snowflakes hitting the ground. No one was in the street, no beasts, no dogs. The unknown woman who helped beat Frances was gone, hiding in her cowardice.

She pulled her shawl over her head and turned to head home. A resounding slap followed by a cry came from the Bates cabin.

Chapter 7

Boom!

Aveline jumped at the concussion that shook the cabin and dropped the skillet filled with coffee beans. "Indians?" Frozen with shock, she looked to the curtain for an answer.

A few weeks earlier, word had spread throughout the camp about Sioux Indians massacring a band of Omahas across the Missouri River. A few weeks before that, an Omaha chief living in Winter Quarters at Brother Brigham's request had been ambushed. The chief and four other Omahas had been wounded.

One of the wounded was an Indian woman whose arm had been so badly damaged in the attack it was amputated.

Boom!

"What *is* that?" Dorris cried out from her bed.

"Cannon. The artillery is recognizing this most holy day, Christmas," Washington announced to Dorris as he pushed off the bedclothes.

Tension flowed from Aveline's body. She felt foolish, but relieved that no coffee beans had spilled onto the dirt floor.

Boom!

Washington emerged from behind the curtain as he pulled on his waistcoat.

"Happy Christmas, Mister Avery," Aveline said softly so as to not enrage Dorris so early in the morning. She held out a small package for him.

Washington glanced at her as he unfolded the tiny bundle. By the firelight, he examined the gift, Aveline's handmade handkerchief with her perfect tatted lace edge.

"See? I embroidered your initials, W, J, A. Washington. John. Avery."

"Lovely, my dear, lovely. You are most generous. Thank you." He leaned over and brushed a quick kiss on her cheek.

Dorris left her bed space and stepped to the fire. She tossed a tiny object toward the fire, but it fell short of the coals. Aveline looked at the object: another tooth.

"Happy Christmas, Sister Avery." Aveline held out a package to Dorris.

"Do I want that?"

"I wish to share this gift with you."

Dorris snatched the packet from Aveline's hand. Flipping the handkerchief back and forth, she inspected it. She blew her nose with great noise into the fabric and stuffed the treasure into her left sleeve's cuff.

Washington glared at Dorris as she sat and stared into the fire. "Dorris," he chastised with a soft voice. "It is a holy day. Be considerate of her gift."

Dorris said nothing, but continued to stare at the fire.

Aveline gulped to dampen the rising fury. "You're welcome." She sat on her stump, shaking from anger at the insult, forcing herself to act respectful to the first wife.

Dorris rose for battle, but Washington pulled her back to her seat.

"Enough. I demand we have peace in this house. A man must have shelter from storms without and *shall not* have to weather storms within."

He looked to each woman, puffing from the exertion of containing his temper. "Now, we must be ready for the gathering here this evening. What food and drink will you prepare?" He looked from Dorris to Aveline and back.

"I shall make a cake," Aveline said, quicker than Dorris.

"I must go to Bishop Whitney's store. I shall make a pumpkin pie. If he has brandy, I prefer that to rum in my warm slings," Dorris said.

The hot and sweet drink with rum or brandy was bound to liven any gathering.

Washington considered the planned refreshments and nodded his approval. "Ward members will be here tonight, including Bishop Lang. I'm told the Twelve shall grace my home with their presence. Everything must be perfect."

Aveline's heart rate quickened. Apostles from the Quorum of Twelve — in her home! The settlement's leadership would see how she lived and how she served her church. This was an opportunity for the Avery household to rise in stature in their eyes.

She glanced around the tiny cabin crammed with furniture. She imagined the tight fit, all those people pressed together. Perhaps the chairs could be set outside. A film of sweat broke out from her brow just thinking of the crowding and the pressure of the leadership coming to her home — to her husband's home.

Washington continued. "I want everything immaculate. This night, the church leadership will see that I may be of great service to the Saints."

~*~

Body heat from the several ward residents, Willard Richards — First Counselor to Brigham Young and the sole member of the Quorum of Twelve Apostles who appeared — and the roaring fire in the hearth overheated the small Avery cabin. Compounding the warmth inside, the temperature outside was the winter's highest. No one complained of the heat or minded the overcrowding, and the dancers jigged in place, in time to the clapping hands. Aveline waved her hand to cool her burning face. This was the warmest she'd felt since winter had begun. She dabbed at her sweating face with her handkerchief.

Washington and Dorris had been difficult all afternoon. Tension from the pressure of church leadership coming to the gathering, likely to view how Washington managed his household, made them argumentative and quick to criticize. Aveline wanted a successful evening for her husband.

Perhaps he wouldn't be so difficult should the church leadership give him the approval he so desired. Aveline daydreamed he would rise to Bishop, perhaps eventually ascend to the High Council. The stress of the party preparation eased from her body as she watched the laughing Saints.

Aveline pressed through the crowd to her parents. "You've lost weight," her mother remarked as she stroked her youngest daughter's face. Aveline nodded. In Winter Quarters, everyone suffered privations.

Lucas Bates, his first wife Eliza, and Frances squeezed in through the door. Aveline skirted the crowd and grabbed her sister. Aveline pulled her to their parents. Her mother cupped her eldest daughter's face in her hands. Fine wrinkles in her forehead deepened as she pulled her close. When she released Frances, Pa pulled her to him in a bear hug. The pearls in Frances' hair comb rocked in time to her father's swaying hug.

As the dance concluded, Bishop Lang called for attention. When the clamor died down, he said, "Let us take a moment and pray for the safety of our brave men serving in the Mormon Battalion." Aveline glanced at her mother as the bishop continued. "You will be pleased to know, from Ward Nine, our man defending our nation is Private Bedford Bowmore. The last contact from the Battalion was a letter from Captain Daniel Davis, captain of E Company, received just hours ago. They were then in the territory of Arizona. As promised by Brother Brigham, they have not seen combat. Although they suffer from lack of food and suitable clothing, members are in good spirits."

Aveline squeezed her mother's arm and gasped. Her mother clapped her hands to her face in silent relief. Her father's lips tightened as he reached for his wife.

"Let us pray for Brother Bowmore's safe return, for all of our brethren's success and their safe return."

Aveline reached for her father's hand, Frances held her mother's. While the bishop prayed, Aveline tried to remember how her brother looked—tall, skinny. She smiled at the memory of his pranks against his sisters. Her father would scold Bedford for tormenting them, but Aveline doubted her father really meant it.

"Amen," Bishop Lang intoned. "Let us uplift our hearts and rejoice by singing *Come, Come, ye Saints.*"

The group sang, in various tones and quality, and Aveline felt the spirit move through her. She sang as loud as she could. At the line "All is well, all is well," everyone sang as loud as they could. Fists pumped the air.

"Let us remember our brethren away from us in the service of the Saints in far-off lands. Let us pray for the safe return and mission success of Caleb Abernethy, laboring in France, and other Saints serving the Lord."

Aveline bowed her head and prayed for Brother Abernethy's return. Upon learning how dire his wife's health had deteriorated, the church leadership sent for him to return home. Last week, after she had finished her chores, Aveline spent the day tending to Sister Edwinna. The black canker had moved up her thin body, blackened her legs, and attacked her face. Her pain was fierce, and Edwinna gulped constantly, as if trying to swallow her pain. Aveline tried to be strong for Edwinna's sake. Thankfully, her three boys were old enough to hire themselves out for odd jobs and were absent most of the day. They didn't have to witness her suffering. Edwinna's four-year-old girl struggled to understand what was happening to her mother. Aveline prayed hard for Caleb's return, hopefully in time to see his wife before she died.

"Amen. Cherish our time on the Lord's earth, but prepare for heaven's glory. Think, this day, of our families who have passed on before us and remember them. I dismiss you with the blessings of the Lord."

As the group thinned, Aveline responded to departing wishes of "Happy Christmas" with a kiss on the cheek. Poppy Wallace, Aveline's girlhood friend, and her husband, Anson, with son Levi draped over his shoulder, praised Aveline's peach cake. Hamish Paddock eased his way out the door with unabashed slaps on the back for Washington and Dorris. His three young boys drooped and dragged their feet from sleepiness. His wives Em Paddock and Carissa Clarke gave long hugs to Aveline and whispered support into her ear.

Ma and Pa lingered to be near their daughters. Aveline felt the glow of a successful gathering and felt relaxed and happy. Frances stayed close by Aveline's side as if she needed the comfort that emanated from her sister. Aveline stood with her arm around Frances.

"It is time." Lucas shook Washington's hand and bowed to Dorris. Eliza stood beside him. As the crush lessened, Aveline saw Eliza, truly for the first time. The only other time she had seen her was when she was dripping wet from the water Brigham Young had thrown on her and Frances. She resembled her husband: tall, stout. Her round shoulders stooped; rolls of belly fat bulged below and above her corset. Frizzy hair framed a fleshy face. Eliza did not acknowledge or thank Aveline. Frances gave Aveline a knowing look and shrugged. Lucas steered Frances out the door.

Except for the Averys, the cabin was empty, its vitality sucked from the room with the last guests' departure. Its three occupants gave a relieved sigh. From under the beds they retrieved the chairs and log stump from where they had been pushed out of the way. They sank into their seats. Aveline felt a joyous high. "That was fun. I enjoyed having the gathering here. When may we do it again?"

The tension rose. No one offered to answer her question. Confused, Aveline stood and asked, "Right? Didn't it go well?"

"Simpleton. You don't understand," Dorris snapped.

The silence was thick. Aveline sat on her stump. No, she didn't understand.

Washington stared into the fire. "Only one from the Quorum showed up."

"I noticed," Aveline said in her defense. "Maybe they couldn't come. Perhaps they — "

"Imbecile!" The hiss came from Dorris. "The remainder didn't show up — on purpose. It was a slap in the face to Washington."

Washington shook his head. "I don't know what more I can do to please the church leadership and impress upon them my sincerity and devotion."

Chapter 8

Pulling up the covers on her bed one evening, Aveline bid farewell to the Year of Our Lord 1846 and, pushing them off in the morning, welcomed 1847 as the promise of a better year for herself and for the Saints. The bright promise of a new year dulled as the days' mind-numbing chores dragged into sameness. Hours passed like the evaporation of a water puddle on a humid day: slow and unnoticed.

Throughout January, the tedium of daily chores never varied. Water, fetch and dispose; collect firewood, dump ashes; stamp at rodents scurrying to find the flour and sugar bags tucked on a shelf over the beds; dishes, cook to soil and wash to clean; dab the finger's bleeding gash from the washbasin's split rim; dump buckets of water that dripped endlessly through the shake roof.

The only change in routine was the occasional blizzard that drifted snow outside the door. With luck, the drift stayed outside. Aveline was forced to shove the door as hard as she could to nudge the door open before slogging to the outhouse or the well.

Beside the daily chores, Aveline and the Avery household settled into another routine. Dorris would provoke Aveline with insults until Aveline responded in kind. Washington, when he was home, would demand they desist their arguing. "A king expects peace in his castle," he would roar. When he could take no more bickering, he would grab his coat and stalk out the door.

Aveline would complete her daily chores and collapse in fatigue on her wood stump; Dorris would stare at the fire. In the strained silence of the evening, Aveline would escape to her bed to stitch her handkerchiefs into squares and tat the lace edging.

Once a week, even during the frigid blast that chased everyone indoors for several days, Aveline bundled up in her coat and shawl and fought against the bitter wind and snow to join the quilting bee at Brother Paddock's house on the other side of the block. Aveline, Em, Carissa, and Frances—on her day off from the basket factory and when Eliza allowed her to attend—met to stitch a quilt. Spending quiet time with her sister and two plural wives who enjoyed each other's company was a welcome respite for the two blood sisters. The crowd of four adults and three little Paddock boys in the small cabin, the squeals of laughter, the boys' underfoot activities, and even the stink of feces and urine from diapers crammed in the overflowing slop jar were more enjoyable than the elbow room and freshness of the Avery cabin.

This day, Em and Carissa had the quilt rack prepared with their latest patchwork, a bright Flying Geese pattern. The green triangles of the "geese" contrasted to the pure white cotton squares. The women selected their favorite needles and settled to stitch. Aveline watched the door, hoping Frances would appear.

"Brother Caleb Abernethy returned from his mission in France." Em squinted to pierce the needle's eye with a point of thread. She stabbed at the tiny hole, missing every time. Carissa stood, reached for Em's needle, licked her thumb and forefinger, swiped the thread and drove it through the hole. Em made a face. A slight smile crossed Carissa's mouth as she pulled a length through the hole and handed the needle back to Em.

Aveline stopped her stitching to watch Em. "How sad he did not arrive in time to bid Edwinna farewell before she passed from the black canker." With her left hand, she pushed the quilt fabric up from below to poke the needle down with her right hand. "If only he'd returned a week earlier, she could have been comforted by him until they meet in heaven."

"Yes, poor soul. Brother Caleb has two living children—"

"Three," Em said firmness in her correction.

"Three," Carissa leaned toward Em. "But if I were allowed to finish, Luke is still so sick with the fever. Bishop Riter goes every day to lay on the hands and pray. If Luke survives, we don't know how he will fare in life. The heat from that poor boy is such that it warms the whole cabin, near about. I just wish for his suffering to be over."

Em craned her neck to watch her three napping boys, piled like a heap of puppies on their mattress in the cabin's tiny loft. She watched them for a moment and turned back to her stitching.

"How does Brother Caleb fare?" Aveline asked.

Carissa shook her head. "Like all the life is out of him, as if his very soul lies on top of that bluff." The needle hovered above the quilt as tears welled in her eyes. "I see his children trying to cheer him, but it makes no difference."

The poignancy of the image, that Caleb's source of life was buried with Edwinna in the Winter Quarters cemetery, tightened Aveline's throat. Welling tears blurred the spot where she was to poke the needle. She cleared her throat to ease the tightness. "At least he had a love that sustained him. I confess an envy of him, loving his wife so much, though I am sorry he grieves so."

With no father present at their mother's burial and to support the children, Aveline joined other mourners from the community to trudge up the steep hill to the cemetery that overlooked Winter Quarters to pray for Edwinna's happiness in heaven. Gale winds buffeted the bluff. Trees swayed and moaned in time with the mourners. Tiny snowflakes stung their faces, but not one person left the gathering early for the sake of Edwinna's children. Bishop Riter's wife remained with the boys and cared for Luke until their father returned from his mission.

The cabin fell quiet as the women poked their needles into the fabric. The wood in the fireplace popped, spraying embers onto the hearth. Occasionally, one little boy would snort a snore or roll over. Each time, Em stopped her needlework to look up and watch. She blinked back tears and poked the quilt again with her needle.

The women jerked in their seats when the door opened. Snow fell into the doorway before Frances entered, noticed the working women and sleeping boys, then pulled the door closed quietly. She gave a quick wave and allowed her shawl to slip down around her shoulders. "Hello, Sisters," she said quietly.

Em and Carissa helloed back. Aveline stood to give her sister a lingering embrace. As she stepped back, she saw the purple bruise and the swelling of Frances' left eye. Aveline opened her mouth to speak, but Frances held up a hand. "I don't wish to discuss it." She pulled up the only remaining chair in the cabin and dug for a needle in Em's sewing basket.

The other three women stared at Frances, not moving. Without a word, Frances threaded her needle, pushed up her hand on the quilt, and stabbed the material. One by one, the other three women began to stitch.

"We were discussing how touching it is how deeply Brother Caleb loved his wife," Aveline said. She knew such sentiment would prod her sister to speak.

"And Edwinna for him," Em added.

"'Tis touching to see such love between a husband and a wife," Carissa said.

The women stitched in the peace. Moments passed and a tear glittered down Frances' face. She gasped in a sob and collapsed in a heap against the quilt stand. Aveline dropped her needle and reached for her. Em and Carissa poked their needles in the fabric and abandoned their stitching.

"I'm sorry," Frances mumbled as she wiped her running eyes and nose. She gulped in air to calm her weeping.

"Let me get you a cup of tea," Em said as she hustled to the fire for the kettle.

Carissa moved beside Frances. "Would you like to tell us what happened?" She rubbed Frances' shoulders lightly.

"Oh, that witch," Frances said too loud then glanced at the boys. They hadn't budged.

"Eliza?" Em asked.

A quick laugh burst from Frances. "Her too. Her sister Eleanor. She has to be the meanest woman on earth." She turned to Aveline and waved her hand to fan her hot face. "She's the one who joined in the abuse a few weeks ago when we fought in the street. She is a widow and has only Eliza and a brother left in her family. I am grateful she doesn't live with us. I try to be patient with them because they have experienced such horror and torment in Missouri at the hands of a Gentile mob, but I believe it has distorted their reality."

Frances turned to look up at Carissa. "They act as if everyone except Mister Bates is the enemy. They trust no one except him. She and Eliza put their heads together and whisper. The next thing I know, I have transgressed against them." Tears flowed down her cheeks. "Thank you," she whispered at Em's offered cup of steaming tea.

"Did Eleanor give you this?" Em pointed at Frances' bruised face.

Frances nodded. "This one was because I left a piece of bone in the stew. Eleanor bit down on it and broke out one of her few remaining teeth. She accused that I placed the bone in the stew purposefully. I said the bit could have gone into anyone's bowl. She said I ladled it into her bowl knowing it would break her tooth." Her hand shook as she sipped the tea. "Oh, that's wonderful," she sighed.

"I cannot believe that the revelation of plural wifery meant a woman must endure such abuse," Em said. "Have you talked to your bishop? He should instruct Eliza and Lucas on how to live together in harmony, and he should instruct Eleanor to mind her business and stay out of yours. On your behalf."

"I went to Bishop Rolfe two weeks ago. He must have said something to them because when they returned home, they acted better. Even Eleanor was quiet." Frances took another sip. "I'm not surprised the truce didn't hold."

"We can hope you will find happiness, can't we?" Em asked. "Of course, to be fair, you must do your part to hold the peace. While you have a gentle and considerate manner, Frances, you must ensure you do not antagonize them, even when you're at the end of your rope."

"Yes, but I'm not sure what more I can do." Frances sipped her tea. "Something has to change."

~*~

The day's quilting finished, Frances embraced Aveline for a long time then pulled away. Aveline waved goodbye to Em and Carissa and reluctantly turned toward home.

As Aveline walked from the Paddock cabin, a wicked thought popped into her mind. If Hamish Paddock could rise higher in the church than Washington and Lucas, she and Frances could simply move in with Hamish and become his third and fourth wives. With all the trouble she and Frances seemed to cause Washington and Lucas, all the men would have to do is agree to the move. No divorce would be necessary. With Em and Carissa being such dear friends and Hamish so loving to his wives, then perhaps she and Frances could be happy. Horrified by her lack of faith, she shoved the disloyal thought from her mind.

She pulled open the door to her cabin. Dorris sat in her rocker sipping tea and didn't look up or acknowledge Aveline's presence. As Aveline hung up her shawl, she noted the rumpled quilt on Dorris' bed. Washington alternated weeks with each wife, and this week was Aveline's turn. Whenever he slept with Aveline, Dorris complained louder and nitpicked at everything; she never straightened her bedclothes. Aveline learned to appreciate the relief when Washington slept in Dorris' bed. Dorris' temper was not as foul, she was not as quick to anger, and the neat beds satisfied Aveline's sense of tidiness.

The past several mornings, Dorris had been sick, throwing up the small amount of food in her stomach. Washington insisted that Aveline complete Dorris' few chores. "She needs her rest," he had said. Dorris never spoke to Aveline about her illness, but she would whisper to Washington in the evenings and they would smile.

Aveline sat on her stump and chewed her nails.

Dorris stared into the flames. "The Lord has chosen me to present Washington with his first heir." She looked over to Aveline, superiority shown from her eyes. "A glorious surprise fulfillment and duty for the first wife."

Aveline admitted to herself she felt relieved she would not be the first with child, yet spite rose within her. "A surprise, yes, for someone so old and toothless." She immediately regretted the words' cruelty and disrespect.

Dorris shot out of her rocking chair and grabbed the nearest pot. She heaved the utensil at Aveline just as Washington opened the door. The pot hit him in the chest, and he let loose a roar.

"She insulted me, your primary wife, your wife with child!" Dorris screamed as the pot thumped to the dirt floor. She pointed at Aveline.

Washington turned to affix Aveline with a furious look. She cringed as he raised a shaking finger. "Repent. Repent or be damned for causing such strife in this household! Beg, on your knees, for my forgiveness, or else you will be taught a most serious lesson in humility."

Chapter 9

Aveline removed her best dress from her trunk and smoothed the ruffles. Looking down as she held the red cotton dress up to her chest, she imagined how the dress would fit. Likely, the dress would sag on her thinning frame.

Now March had arrived, the cold wind didn't seem so bitter, so relentless, as it blew spring toward Winter Quarters. She laid the dress on the bed and stepped to the makeshift table that held the wash basin and a water pitcher. Glancing at Dorris, who had turned her back to Aveline, she pulled down her bodice and slipped her arms out of her undergarment. She squeezed out a wet rag and gasped as the icy water hit her chest and her underarms. Chasing after the soap scrap in the cold water, her teeth began to chatter. Her shaking hand scraped a jagged edge; the soap scum stung the open flesh. She quickly soaped her torso, rinsed from the pitcher's icy water, and dabbed her apron to dry off. Her undergarment top felt warm as she slipped her goosebumpy arms in the sleeves. She crossed her arms and hurried to her side of the quilt curtain to pull on her red dress.

The dance tonight would be a joyous occasion. Brother Brigham allowed the Saints to hold a dance in the new Council House. The one-and-a-half-story log building was the settlement's social center. One of the largest buildings in the settlement, each member of the church's leadership, from the Quorum of Twelve to the ward bishops, supplied a twenty-five-foot log toward its construction. Many people were expected to attend, a grand time to throw off the winter's shackles of gloom and celebrate the coming of greener times.

Even Dorris seemed to be in a high mood as she pulled out her best dress, a green brocade gown, from her trunk. A tune Aveline had never heard before hummed from Dorris' mouth. Neither woman spoke as each dressed then combed and pinned up her hair. The dress sagged on Aveline's skinny frame, and her sacred undergarment peeked out of the dress' drooping bodice. She poked the garment's top to hide it below the edge of the bodice. Frustrated, she pulled out a handkerchief from her trunk and tucked the linen in the top of her bodice. The protruding tatted lace hid the top of her undergarment. In the cracked mirror on the cabin wall, she admired the effect.

Aveline sat, nervous, on her stump. Dorris sat on her rocking chair. Dorris wearing her green brocade dress reminded Aveline of an engraving of Queen Victoria: perfect posture adorned with a round angel's face punctuated with full lips. "That dress looks very pretty on you." Her compliment was met with a stare into the fire.

The women had been especially nervous all day. Tomorrow, Washington would leave for his mission to Mount Pisgah in Iowa. That settlement was about one hundred and twenty miles away, three days in good, dry weather.

His trunk was already packed and on the wagon so he could leave at first light. He told Dorris he expected to return from the mission a week before the first company headed west in the spring.

The cabin door opened. Washington entered. The women stood and presented themselves for his approval. "Lovely," he purred.

Washington offered an arm to each wife. The three walked arm in arm in silence to the Council House. As they approached, light streamed from the doorway and windows. Laughter and the band's music reached out to them, seducing them forward on an ethereal carpet. Aveline hung back as Washington entered, followed by Dorris.

Candles lined the walls; their smoke trails streamed upward into a dark cloud at the ceiling. The fires in the fireplaces danced brightly. Rows of benches filled with Saints faced the fireplaces. The air felt charged with excitement.

The Averys squeezed into an open section of a bench while Patriarch John Smith called for silence. As he delved into his sermon, Aveline fought to remain still and focus on the speaker's words. When the patriarch finished, Brigham Young stood to speak to the crowd.

Those seated and those standing against the wall listened to the sermons and tried to dampen their squirms to a polite level. Aveline's interest in Young's words dimmed. Moving her eyes, she looked around the room and inspected other women's gowns.

Satin and lace contrasted sharply with her cotton. Some women who were converted to the Latter-day Saints in Europe wore their native dress. Her inspection was interrupted when the crowd stood. Everyone pitched in to push the benches aside; the scraping of the benches against the wood floor added to the cacophony of laughter and talking in various languages.

Aveline caught a glimpse of Frances and squeezed her way toward her sister.

"Aveline!" Frances hugged her as though they hadn't seen each other in a long time, although only three days had passed since their last quilting bee. The bruise beside Frances' eye had faded.

Aveline poked at a couple of the dangling pearls in her hair comb. The jewelry's pearls highlighted the white beads on Frances' red bodice. "Beautiful," Aveline said.

Frances laughed and flicked the tatted lace protruding from Aveline's bodice. "Beautiful!"

They stood with their arms around each other as they scanned the crowd.

Behind them, a strong voice called out. "Good evening, Sisters." Aveline and Frances turned to face Brigham Young. The Saints' tall, clean-shaven leader looked from one woman to the other. His long hair curled under his ears; the long nose gently sloped to its tip. If not for the import of his station,

Aveline thought he looked rakish, as if he were ready to spring a practical joke. He tucked his hands into his waistcoat and patiently waited for their response.

"Good evening, Brother," Aveline stammered, her eyes wide to be so near the leader of the Saints. Only a gurgle escaped from Frances' mouth as both women curtsied.

"I trust all is well in your husbands' households," Young said, studying them intently.

Aveline squirmed, remembering the brawl between Frances and Eliza. "Yes, Brother. We have been given proper counsel by our husbands." She resented the words as she uttered them, as if she and Frances were trained children capable of performing on command.

Young gave a slight bow, one arm bent at the waist, the other behind him, before moving on.

The sisters turned to each other. Aveline covered her mouth with her hand to stifle the giggle. "He spoke to us. I couldn't think of anything interesting to say. All I could think of was when he stopped the fight with Eliza."

Frances pulled Aveline's hand away from her mouth. "At least you said the appropriate things. I couldn't think of anything to say! After the fight with Eliza, he must think I'm an incorrigible halfwit." Both women looked in Young's direction and giggled.

"What did Brother Brigham say to you?"

Aveline started and spun. Washington stood before her. She hadn't seen him approach. "'Good evening, Sisters'. That was all he said before he moved on."

"What did you say to him?"

"'Good evening, Brother.'"

Washington's brow furrowed. "That was all?"

Frances touched her forehead in remembering. "That was all *she* said. At least your wife thought of the right thing to say. I was so embarrassed by what Eliza and Eleanor had done, forcing me to brawl in the street, I couldn't say anything!"

Neither sister glanced at the other and neither admitted to the remainder of the conversation.

Washington studied Frances. His face softened and he turned to Aveline. "May I have this dance?" He bent in a slight bow. This would be Aveline's first dance with her husband. With a big smile, she curtsied. Pride flowed through her as she slipped her hand on her husband's arm. He led her to the center of the room, and Aveline's pride was dashed to see Dorris standing as she awaited their arrival. Washington held out his other arm, which Dorris grasped. Tucked in the crush of other dancers, the three paraded around the room three times, calling out "praise the Lord" as they marched.

During the march, Frances marched beside Lucas. Her face was expressionless. Eliza held onto his other arm and glared in Frances' direction.

As the dance concluded, the dancers clapped their appreciation to the Quadrille Band. Washington bowed, in turn, to his two partners. Dorris returned his bow as Aveline curtsied. Washington, followed by Dorris, walked away.

While Aveline searched the crowd for Frances and her parents, someone tapped her shoulder. "Good evening, Sister. May I have this dance?" Hamish Paddock grinned down at her, his hand outstretched to her.

Why, Brother Paddock, I'd be delighted," Aveline said. She smiled as she curtsied deeply. He led her to the floor. Hamish reminded Aveline of her brother, Bedford — tall, wiry, a wide smile split the long face. His wavy black hair curled in front of his eyes. He constantly flipped away the curl as it fell back. Nearby, Hamish's wives, Em and Carissa, danced the schottische with other partners. As Aveline caught their eyes, they waved. Aveline and Hamish laughed, breathless, when the music ended. They clapped in appreciation for the band's effort. A tune of a waltz rose above the chattering crowd.

Hamish held out his arms, an invitation for a slow dance. Aveline curtsied then grasped his left hand in her right. He pulled her, snug, to him.

In the center of the mass of dancers, Aveline saw Washington dancing. Looking past Hamish's shoulder, she saw his partner: Frances. Aveline felt pleased that Frances danced with another man beside Lucas until another sensation swept Aveline: jealousy. It was a surprise feeling, a possession toward Washington she'd never felt before. Grateful Frances was his partner, Aveline set aside the envy to concentrate on Hamish. He was an elegant dancer, although Aveline twice stepped on his foot. Each time, Aveline apologized. Each time, Hamish threw back his head and laughed an open-mouthed belly laugh that made Aveline giggle.

Near the end of the waltz, Aveline looked over to Washington. Still in his arms, Frances' face had paled; her eyes were wide and red as if she were ready to burst into tears. The pearls in her head comb jerked in time to the trembling of her head. The dancers shifted, blocking Aveline's sight. As the tune ended, Aveline clapped and curtsied to Hamish's bow. The band stuck up another schottische.

She turned from Hamish and was engulfed in a hug. "Aveline! I haven't seen you since you married!"

Aveline returned Poppy Wallace's embrace, then reached for Poppy's husband, Anson. "How beautiful you look tonight," Aveline exclaimed to Poppy, who wore a red silk gown trimmed with white lace.

"Why, thank you, most kind." Anson tugged on his lapels and turned to his side to show off his jacket.

Poppy nudged her husband as Aveline smiled. Her attention was diverted. "Who is that?" Poppy shouted over the music and pointed. "I have never seen them before."

Aveline and Anson craned their necks to see. A short man danced with his equally short wife. Each was beautifully dressed in the latest fashion. She wore a green silk dress rimmed with white lace. Her green silk headdress was spiked with long white feathers. His silk brocade waistcoat would have popped open except for bone buttons straining to contain his ample belly. Both laughed and waved to their fellow dancers.

"That's Mister Keegan and Missus Keegan. He owns that massive mercantile in Kanesville. I suspect he was invited since he supplies us with goods," Anson said.

"They are Gentile?" Poppy asked.

"Yes. I've dealt with him many times. He's an honorable businessman."

Leaning toward Poppy's ear, Aveline whispered. "I have a gift for you." She had made a handkerchief for Poppy; the gift was tucked inside a hidden pocket in her dress. She fumbled the cloth from the pocket and handed it to Poppy.

"How thoughtful!" Poppy cried as she glimpsed the tatted silk lace. Anson laughed and pulled her to the dance floor.

Aveline made her way toward the spot where she last saw Washington and Frances. The Quadrille Band struck up a waltz. The music's tempo and the dancers slowed, the good-natured shouting and laughing dimmed to match the quieter music.

"Sister Bowmore, will ye grace me with this dance?"

Aveline turned to see Lucas Bates, Frances' husband, in a slight bow. His left arm bent behind him, his right arm extended toward the dance floor. Aveline tried to think of an excuse to decline. He seemed to read her thoughts and grasped her arm as if to prevent her from escaping. She bobbed a slight curtsy before he pulled her to the dance floor.

She tried not to place her nose too close to his waistcoat. The stink of grease, manure and smoke emanated from the fabric. His exhalations surged over her head, and she tried not to breathe.

"I have a proposal for ye, Sister." The low rumble of his voice vibrated from his chest.

She squinted in confusion into the blurred depths of dancers. "What might that be, Brother?"

Lucas hesitated. He stepped Aveline in a circle. With Lucas' bulk so close to her face, she could see little. At her vision's outer edges, the room spun. Dizziness washed over her. His leading slowed and the room came into focus.

"When we reach Zion, and our temple is built and consecrated, the ordinances for sealing may begin again."

Aveline nodded, understanding, "Yes." As with a Gentile's marriage, a Mormon marriage was for time only—

"until death do you part." A ceremony that allowed a Mormon marriage to transcend time and continue through eternity was called sealing and could only take place in a consecrated temple. Winter Quarters was so temporary, it didn't have a temple, consecrated or otherwise.

The rumble in Lucas' chest throbbed. "I wish for ye to seal to me, not to Brother Avery."

Her shock was so strong at his unexpected request, Aveline tripped over her own feet. He pressed her to him, tight, to keep her from falling. "Ye and yer children would be mine for eternity. My kingdom in heaven would include yer children and yer sister's."

Her mouth opened, but no words came out. A woman could seal to only one man, any man, regardless of whether or not he was her husband. Any children she would have with Washington would not belong to him in the hereafter, but would belong to the man to whom she was sealed. A man could have any number of women—and men—seal to him, an extended family intertwined throughout eternity.

Only a gurgle dribbled from Aveline's mouth.

"I fear I have disturbed ye with my request, Sister." Lucas' voice vibrated around her. "My request is most sincere and based on respect for ye and yer sister."

"Does Mister Avery know you asked me to bestow this honor?" Aveline found her voice; she felt angrier the more she talked.

Laughter rumbled from Lucas' chest. "Nay. He knows nothing of what I seek."

"I shall tell him tonight of your request." She leaned her head back to look at Lucas full in the face to let him see her anger. She stopped moving her feet and tried to pull her hands away from Lucas, but he gripped them in his steel vise.

A snort of grease and smoke blew into Aveline's face. "I beg of ye to keep silent of this request. I fear that with Brother Washington's temper, blood would spill."

"What should I care that you make such a request then expect to continue bruise-free."

Aveline spoke a little too loud for Lucas. He pulled her tight to him. "I should care what yer sister thinks. She's a sensitive sort."

Aveline's eyes grew wide. Frances was already upset all the time. She struggled in her new life as a plural wife, terrorized by a malevolent first wife and her sister. Now she had an insensitive husband seeking to expand his place in heaven.

"Attention! Attention!" Patriarch John Smith held up his hands. The music stopped. To the still-conversing Saints, he introduced Brother Brigham Young. Silence was immediate.

Aveline whipped her hands from Lucas' and hurried for the back wall, away from him, his stink, and his proposal.

"We have enjoyed this evening of frivolity and each other's company. We end with a song and prayer in gratitude for our Lord's protection and sustenance."

In myriad tones, the Saints sang *Come, Come, ye Saints* as loud as they could, as if their voices would rise above their earthly log homes to heaven. Brigham Young led the group in a prayer then dismissed the gathering with the blessing from the Lord.

As the gathering broke up, excited voices bade farewell and goodnight. Aveline tried to hide her anger as she waved to the Paddocks on their way out the door. Washington stood near the other door, and she made her way to him. Looking around, she asked him, "Have you seen Frances?"

His eyes glanced around the room. "It appears she left."

"Without saying goodbye?" Aveline continued to search the thinning crowd. Clumps of excited dancers who didn't want the fun to end blocked her view. Her parents stood at the other end of the room. She went to them.

"Did you enjoy yourself, my dear?" Her father draped his arm over her shoulders. Aveline could only nod, afraid if she opened her mouth the secret Lucas demanded she keep would spill out.

Pa reached for her mother. "I did. She had me spinning like a top! I haven't laughed this hard in a long time."

Ma laughed. "He nearly wore me out dancing. I think everyone danced their feet off. Even Frances said she was worn out."

As Aveline turned to head back to Washington, she knew Frances had left. *Odd.* Lucas and Eliza were still at the dance, but Frances slaved under the Bateses' rule. Frances must have been exhausted to leave early. Aveline headed toward Lucas and Eliza, although she didn't want to see or talk to either of them. Ever.

"Good evening, Brother Bates, Sister Bates. Did you enjoy the evening?" Aveline fought to keep her voice even and not betray the anger she felt. "Is Frances here?"

Lucas and Eliza returned Aveline's fake warmth with genuine icy glares. "Do you see her anywhere?" Eliza's voice matched the coldness in her eyes.

"No. Good night." Aveline spun on her heels and walked away. Tomorrow she'd find her sister.

The room was nearly deserted. Across the room, Brigham Young listened as Thomas Keegan's arms waved during his lively discussion. Aveline approached Washington as he explained to Dorris how he had ward business to conduct before he headed home that night. He turned to Aveline. "I'll be home shortly, before I leave on my mission."

A chill escaped down Aveline's spine. She knew from his look that when he returned home, he would spend the night in her bed. She nodded in understanding.

"You won't spend your last night with me?" Dorris hissed.

Washington leaned toward his wife. He stroked her face and smoothed a loose hair behind her ear. "We cannot chance losing *this* child."

His response startled Aveline. She'd never heard spoken that Dorris had lost a child. Aveline wasn't sure how she felt about the news.

His touch and his answer satisfied Dorris, although she shot a hated look at Aveline. Dorris turned to leave the Council House.

Washington looked at Aveline. "Follow her. Make sure she gets home safely." He walked out the other door.

Hurt, Aveline wondered who would see *her* safely home.

Chapter 10

A small cloud blocked what little light the waning moon shed on the earth. The darkness pressed against her as Frances pushed open the braid shop's door. The squeak from the wooden hinges only spiked her nervousness. Inside, straw dust hanging in the air tickled her nose.

A small fire danced in the fireplace; a trace of its smoke lingered in the room. *This makes no sense. One of us always makes sure the fire's out at the end of the day. With all this straw, if that fire got out from the hearth ...*

In the flickering light, nothing seemed out of place. Nothing was broken or spilled. Baskets and hats, in various stages of construction, lay scattered on the workbenches. Completed pieces, stacked high in the corner, waited for her and Mister Bates — her husband, she reminded herself — to haul them to Kanesville. Beside the fireplace, Frances lifted the lid of the tin box that held coins — empty. But then, her husband would have taken the coins when the shop closed for the day.

What's the real reason I was ordered here? I can't believe what I was told.

Although she wasn't cold, she pulled her shawl tighter. The evening was still warm, and the fire burned brightly. She stared into the coals as if the fiery glow held insight to her life, now and beyond. Was her decision last week the right decision? For her family — her blood family? Only her blood family existed for her now.

Crackling straw broke her reverie. Maybe a mouse searched for a warm place to spend the night, or a pack rat sought something shiny to steal from its landlord. She glanced toward the corner, expecting a glimpse of a scurrying fat rat, and gasped. Her face grew cold as terror streamed down to her feet. Her head shook in shock and blurred her vision. In reflex, her arm struck the tin coin box. It hit the fireplace hearth with a loud clank.

Beyond the straw pile, past the fire's glow, a black ghost rose from the dimness. From the depths of the hood, the face stared at her. The black mass drifted around the pile toward her. Disgust-filled eyes never left her face.

Frances' trembling hand pressed to her mouth. *Think.* "You startled me," she stuttered as she gasped for air. She hesitated to make a joke, but cracked wise to relieve her fear. "I thought perhaps you were a pack rat seeking its next treasure." She exhaled quickly with a weak laugh. The edges of her lips flicked up into a quick smile. The smile vanished.

The silent figure drew closer. The flames' light reflected the growing smile.

"I have tried ... I am trying ... very hard to be a righteous woman," Frances said, brighter than she felt. She gripped the edges of her shawl and turned slightly to lean against the fireplace opening as if to embrace the fire's warmth and comfort. "Why do you wish to meet me here, at this time of night?" The grinning face before her never wavered. "Please, I beg you to tell me how I can make amends."

The smile faded. Hate from the squinting eyes bored into hers. A hiss leaked from the hooded face. "Sinner."

A flash of anger shoved aside Frances' fear. She spun to face the shadow. "*Never!* I obey all God's laws. How dare you accuse me of such?"

"I dare!" The cry burst forth as the figure rushed forward, arms outstretched to seize Frances by the throat.

She couldn't scream for help. The tight grip around her throat closed off her air. Panicked, she kicked her feet and flung her fists. She gripped her assailant's sleeve. Muffled by the roar in her ears, she hardly heard the tear.

Agony from the vise grip around her neck spread to her chest. Her head felt like it would explode. The assailant dragged her to the straw pile. Fingers outstretched, claw-like,

Frances scratched at the savage's face. The hate-powered steel grips loosened. She gulped welcome air. A scream erupted from her open mouth.

Frances shoved aside the reaching hands. She ran for her life, but tripped over a wood bucket hidden in the shadows. A wave of water splashed her skirt. The drenched fabric sagged. She tripped into the straw pile, flailed, unable to find leverage in the thatch to push against to get to her feet. Her assailant pounced and drove her deeper into the straw.

A renewed stranglehold severed any chance for a breath. Legs, too weak to kick, arms, with no strength to push, Frances' muscles relaxed. As her vision faded, her last sight of life was the flames dancing in the fireplace.

~*~

My forearms are burning. *Don't let go. She deserves death. Her actions brought her to this.* My arms tremble from the strain. I slack off. *Any movement? Any breathing?* The only thing shaking is my body.

Calm yourself. This had to be done. Take slow breaths. I push off the body and watch for any sign of life. A smell drifts over us that seems to have come from the depths of hell. Whether it's her or me, I don't know or care. To soothe my cramping fingers, I flick off straw from her dress. It's something to do while I wait to make sure.

My cloak has twisted in the fight, and precious seconds pass as I fumble in the fabric to find the knife. I untangle the handle and pull it from its pouch. The knife doesn't feel right in my grip. The handle seems too big for my hand. The knife tip gouges her throat, but I stop. *This must be done. Do it!* I re-grip my knife and draw the blade across the white throat. *One unbroken line.* My palm's too sweaty. The knife slips again.

"That music was so uplifting!"

My chest beats in panic at the woman's voice outside the door. *They're right outside the door! Where to hide?* I catch sight of my earlier hiding place in the corner. *One twist of the door handle and I could slip there unseen.* A man's voice, muffled in its bassy depth, answers and recedes into the night.

My heart slows. I catch my breath. *How untoward if I'm caught. A person in my position ...* I look toward the ceiling. *Get this over with.*

I lean forward and tighten my grip on the knife handle. *Press deeper. That's it. Drag it straight.* At the gullet, I pull up the knife and twist my wrist to start on the other side of the neck. I press in the tip. *Drag to the center.* The knife tip flicks out from the skin. A drop of blood flies into the darkness. *Deeper, pull even.* My arm muscles quiver from the strain, but the cuts meet at the center. I sit up to relax my back.

Thin lines of blood ooze from the lacerations carved into her smooth skin. My stomach heaves. *Swallow hard! Deep breath. The worst is over.*

I lift a segment of the departed's skirt, wipe the knife clean and slip the knife back into its pouch. I tug a cloth from another hidden pocket in my cloak. My hands cramp as I twist the material into a rope. My knees sink deeper into the straw as I crouch to press the fabric into the bloody slits. I stifle a chuckle as I imagine how the message will be received. Pulling the cloth taut across the throat, I tuck the ends under the neck and take care not to touch the flesh.

I study the corpse. How obvious it appears, sprawled across the yellow straw. I flip stalks onto the body. Some strands land on the face. I pick them off. The open eyes reflect the dancing flames in the fireplace. *They're staring at me.* I reach out to place my fingertips on the eyelids to press them closed. My hand freezes, unable to touch her skin and block the window to her soul that now reveals frozen terror.

Instead, I stroke the treasure, the only thing of value, the gold comb decorating Frances' hair. *It's mine.* I wriggle it, trying to release the priceless piece. The teeth dig deeper into the mass of black curls. I tear at the hair, but every tug only entangles the locks and the dangling pearls more.

Soft clomps of a horse's hooves grow louder and slow outside the shop. My heart races. *Will they stop here?*

I hurry and fumble at another pocket for a cloth. I whip the cloth flat and drape it over Frances' face. *Your reward.* I hurl straw by the handful over the body.

At the door, I listen for the horse or other people. Only wood popping in the fireplace breaks the silence. With a quick look around the room, I decide to make a mess. I push over a table and shove the stacks of completed baskets and hats. With loud crackling, the baskets roll across the dirt floor.

Good. I tug open the shop door and peer out into the darkness. The streets are deserted. I slip through the opening, latch the door tight, and run into the night.

Chapter 11

Aveline hugged her arms to ward off the cooling night air after she left the Council House. Warm during the day, when the sun dropped in the west so had the temperature. The lingering laughter and conversation sounded far away. Dorris must have walked fast; Aveline could not see her.

A roar of rage stopped Aveline in her tracks. She looked around the deserted street as her heart rate quickened. Shouting came from behind her. She lifted up her skirt and ran in that direction.

In the splashes of light spilling through the Council House's open doorway, Washington and the Gentile Mister Keegan grappled. Aveline covered her mouth with both hands to stifle a gasp.

"She's a thief," Keegan yelled. He pointed at Lucas Bates. "And he is a cheat!"

Washington punched Keegan in the nose, but before Keegan could stagger back, Washington grabbed him in a bear hug and hit him in the stomach. Each time Washington struck, he pulled Keegan back to him to strike again. Keegan swiped at Washington's face.

"Stop it!" Missus Keegan screamed as she reached for her husband when Washington allowed Keegan to lurch to his knees. Blood poured from Keegan's nose and dripped onto his white shirt and brocade vest.

Washington's face contorted with rage. He breathed heavily, his jaw jutting in triumph. His plait had loosened, the wavy hair draped over his heaving chest. Scratches gashed across his face. Blood trickled from a corner of his mouth.

Lucas stepped forward and slapped Washington's back. A triumphant smirk creased his ogrish face. Lucas spied Aveline and pointed with his chin in her direction.

Washington turned and recognized her in the dim light. He pointed in the direction of their cabin. *"Woman, go home!"*

She shrank back, terrified, turned then ran. At the cabin, she slammed the door behind her. She tried to catch her breath, but her corset squeezed her chest in its viselike grip. Alerted by Aveline's sudden entrance, Dorris had spun in her chair to face the door. She said nothing, but turned back to stare at the fire.

Aveline staggered to her bed. She'd never seen a fist fight before. The ugliness of it repulsed her. That Washington had been involved in this brutality shocked her to a deep level. *She's a thief,* echoed in Aveline's head. Who was this thief? *Her?* She shook her head to rid her mind of that madness. She'd never stolen anything in her life. Dorris? Possibly. Dorris was a lot of nasty things in one skinny, toothless package, but Aveline had never thought of her as a thief. Aveline shuddered, wondering what this disgraceful business was about.

Dorris' voice rang in her head from a lesson weeks ago after Aveline had asked Washington about a mission he'd been ordered to perform: "A woman does not concern herself about her husband's business."

Aveline settled on the edge of her bed while she calmed down. Likely, Washington would not arrive for some time, so she tried to relax as she prepared for him.

Moments later, Aveline lay in bed and shivered. The bed felt warmer now, but she couldn't get the brutal fisticuffs out of her mind.

Dorris retreated to her bed and, within moments, snored softly on the other side of the quilt. Aveline relaxed and felt herself drift toward sleep.

The cabin door flung open. Washington yelled, "Get up!"

Aveline sat up. Her fear spiked at her husband's fury.

"Dorris, wash my shirt. It must be clean before I leave this morning." He looked at Aveline. "You. Fetch her the water," his voice adamant as he stripped off his coat, then his waistcoat, then his shirt.

Aveline obeyed without hesitation. She flung back the quilt, but in her turmoil and the dim light she couldn't find her robe. Dressed only in her nightgown, she reached for the water bucket and filled the washbasin.

Dorris yelled, "I need my rest!" With a growl, Washington yanked the older woman from her bed and pushed her in Aveline's direction.

"I can do this, Mister Avery," Aveline said. "Sister Avery should stay in bed. I must wash the shirt in cold water anyway, and I have enough." *We cannot chance losing this child* echoed in her memory.

"Just get it clean."

Aveline looked to Dorris and nodded her head as Dorris sank back into bed. Aveline plunged the shirt and waistcoat into the wash tub then added lye soap. She pulled Dorris' chair to the table and sat. She avoided looking at Washington by focusing on her fingers stirring the icy water.

He sat in his chair while he pulled on another shirt. With a rag, he dabbed at the seeping gashes on his mouth and cheek.

For some time, Aveline beat the shirt and waistcoat on the washboard and worked in the soap. By the fire's dim light, she squinted to gain the best visual advantage to ensure all traces of blood were gone. The cold water stiffened her hands, but she ignored the pain. Occasionally, she glanced at Washington. He never turned in her direction or said anything.

Convinced all the blood was out, she left the garments to soak as she searched for her robe, pulled on her boots and grabbed the wood bucket. In the darkness, she tiptoed to the well and filled the bucket. She gasped as the water sloshed from the bucket, soaking the lower part of her robe and nightgown.

Teeth chattering from cold and jittery nerves, she pulled the shirt and waistcoat from the tub, squeezed out the bloody water, and plunged the garments into the water bucket. Too late, she realized this bucket contained their drinking and food water. Oh well, she thought and dunked the garments to rinse. Her hands fumbled, squeezing out most of the cold water without introducing wrinkles. Finally, with the garments draped over Dorris' chair, she rested for a moment. Holding her hands as close to the flames as she dared, pain radiated up her arms. Shivering turned to quaking.

"Have those garments ironed by morning," Washington said, quietly.

Aveline nodded, too cold to speak. The iron would need more heat; she added more wood to the fire and hung the iron from the crane over the flames. She sat on Dorris' chair while she waited to warm up along with the iron.

They both stared at the fire. With a quick motion, Washington stood, grabbed Aveline by a hand and pulled her to the bed. He stripped her robe and nightgown then almost tore her undergarment as he yanked her legs out. He threw his trousers onto her trunk and pulled a leg from his undergarment. With his full weight, he lay on Aveline and stabbed into her. She bit her lips and winced while he grunted softly above her.

After he groaned, he pushed off her, pulled on his garment leg, and rolled over. He ignored Aveline. Within moments, a low snore rattled from his mouth.

Numb, she tried to catch her breath. Her legs felt like weights were attached as she slipped her legs back into her garment. She lay still, fending off shock, and covered her face with her hands. Weariness and the past hours' nightmare washed over her. She choked back sobs. To resume her duties, she'd have to climb over her husband, something she'd never done before.

Tentative, she sat up and leaned over to hear his snores. *Don't wake up.* Throwing a leg over his waist and stretching to avoid touching him, she gave a quick hop and jumped. She gathered her nightgown and robe and shivered into them.

~*~

After what felt like hours, Washington's crisp shirt and waistcoat hung over his chair's back. Exhausted, with hands in pain from the cold water and hot iron, Aveline hopped back over Washington. She pulled the quilt over her head, and concentrated to relax enough to sleep. Her husband's body had warmed the bed, and the warmth emanating from him felt delicious to her aching muscles.

Washington stirred. Buried under the quilt, Aveline pretended to sleep. He threw back the quilt. She peeked from the quilt's edge to watch him pull on his pants and freshly ironed clothes and step behind the curtain. He spoke to Dorris in a soft, rumbling voice. After a moment, he emerged from behind the quilt, tugged on his overcoat and left.

Aveline blinked back tears. There was no appreciation for her efforts in the night, no thanks for caring enough about his pregnant wife to do her chore, no farewell. She rolled over in bed and stared at the wall.

Chapter 12

Bang, bang, bang, bang.

Aveline shot up in bed. The pounding on the door matched the pounding of her heart. Dorris, already fully dressed, ran to it. She pushed open the door and stared out. No one spoke.

Aveline flung back the quilt, grabbed her robe and pulled on her boots. She didn't bother to lace them, but pulled the robe tight around her. She stood behind Dorris and peered around her.

Police Chief Finis Cane stood at the door, his dirty hat floppy in his hands. His long wavy hair was flat where his hat had clamped down on his head, highlighting the gray streaks. Hunched, his wool coat hung on his skinny frame.

Behind Cane stood Pa, who leaned against the police chief for support. Both men's eyes were wide from shock. Pa's were red, his mouth slack jawed.

"Ma?" Aveline cried out, terrified.

Pa shook his head.

"Bedford." The worst had happened. He had died in combat, serving the country that condemned his faith and his people. Pa shook his head again.

She's a thief. Keegan's words rang in Aveline's head. Terrified she might have done something wrong without realizing it, she reached around Dorris to push open the door further and motioned for them to enter. She sat, quaking, on Washington's chair and hugged herself.

Dorris stepped aside and sat on her chair.

Pa knelt before Aveline and burst into tears. He laid his head on her lap and sobbed. A wail ripped open his soul. Almost faint from fear, Aveline laid her hands on his head and wept with him. She looked up at Chief Cane. The croak escaped from her mouth, "What is it?"

Cane gripped his hat, his knuckles white. "It's yer sister."

"Frances?" Aveline felt her face grow cold.

Cane nodded. He took a deep breath and laid a hand on Pa's shoulder in comfort. "In the braid shop." Cane took another breath. "She was found this morn." He took another deep breath. "Someone took her life."

~*~

The wet rag provided no comfort as Pa wiped Aveline's face. She lay on her bed. "No. No. God, no," she moaned.

Pa and Finis Cane pulled Aveline from the bed, and Pa tugged a dress over her nightgown. Cane knelt and laced her boots. "Come home. Your mother needs you," was all Pa could repeat.

Cane and Pa steadied Aveline by wrapping their arms around her. They took her out the door, half carrying, half dragging her up Second Street, then over Woodruff Street. They ignored the stares of those who stood outside their cabins to watch.

At the Bowmore house, Chief Cane nudged open the door. The two men took Aveline to her mother, prostrate on the bed. The two women clung to each other and howled in their anguish. Pa draped himself over them and wept.

Chief Cane stepped to the other side of the cabin, respectful in his distance for the family's grief. After a moment, he moved closer and cleared his throat. In a quiet voice, he said, "Forgive me, Brother, Sisters, but we must discuss this."

Pa pushed himself off the two women, wiped his face with his sleeve, and nodded. He leaned over and pulled Aveline off her mother. "He's right," he whispered. "We must be strong, to do what we can to help."

For the first time, Aveline became vaguely aware of her surroundings. She noticed another woman melting into the wall of her parents' cabin. Sister Ann Cassell worked at the braid shop with Frances. As head of the braiders, she would have been the first to open the shop that morning. She must have discovered Frances and notified the police.

Ma moaned on the bed, her eyes swollen shut.

Aveline nodded. "Where is she now?" she whispered.

"In the braid shop," Cane said.

"You *left her* there?" Aveline cried out.

"Aye. I have police there, keeping watch." Cane shuffled his feet. His calloused fingers worked the edge of his hat. "I wanted to notify the family before moving her. I wondered if someone from the family might come with me and help me figure out who may have done this deed."

Ma moaned. "I can't. I can't."

"I'll go," Aveline said quickly to end her mother's agony of witnessing her daughter at the place of her death. Her voice caught. "It'll be the last thing I can do for her." She gasped and began to weep again.

~*~

Aveline and Chief Cane approached the braid shop. He gripped her arm to steady her. Other women who worked in the shop lingered outside. A policeman stood at the door. Aveline's mind refused to work. She barely realized anyone else was near. At the door, her legs shook and grew weak. She whispered, "Brother Cane," and held out her hand. Cane took her hand and placed his other hand on her back to help her through the door.

In the dim light from the open door and the fire in the fireplace, she could make out a large mound of straw in the back corner. A dark form, half covered in straw, draped the stack. Aveline realized the form was Frances. She moaned and felt her legs go weak.

Cane held her up. "Be strong, lass. Yer sister needs ye." The poignancy of Cane's words struck Aveline. Tears flowed down her cheeks. The truth of the words forced her to allow him to lead her to the body.

She knelt beside her sister. Frances still wore the red gown from the night before. A cloth covered her face. Breathing deeply, Aveline held her hands together in silent prayer and implored God for exaltation of her sister's soul in heaven.

"What do you need me to do?" Aveline whispered.

"Do you recognize the veil?'

Aveline seemed confused. "Veil?"

"The cloth covering her face."

She leaned closer. The white cloth was a wedding veil. Plain stitching marched in straight edges. She shook her head, "No. It can't be her veil. I laced the edges for her before she married Lucas." Mentioning Lucas' name brought him to mind. "Where is Brother Bates? Does he know?"

"He's at home with his wife. Aye, he knows."

"A woman's wedding veil left over her face at death …" Aveline dared not continue.

"Aye," Cane stammered. "If her veil is left over her face, she cannot be resurrected."

Fury flared in Aveline. "Damn whoever covered her face! Frances was good. She tried to be a good wife!" Clasping her hands in prayer, Aveline looked skyward. "In the name of the Lord and all that is holy, she shall be resurrected!" She gripped the veil and whipped the cloth off Frances' face.

Frances' terror-filled eyes stared into Aveline's.

A scream sounded from far away.

Chapter 13

Frances' body lay on her old bed in the Bowmore cabin. Aveline stood beside the bed and unbuttoned her sister's red bodice and skirt.

Ma and Pa lay on their bed, separated from their girls' former bed by the faded sheet hanging from the purlin. Aveline refused Ma's offer to help with this task for Frances. "A mother should not have to remember her daughter this way," Aveline said.

Sister Hulda Cane, the chief's stout wife, stood beside Aveline. Hulda's calmness and practical demeanor steadied Aveline's nerves. Every time Aveline fumbled the clothing or she hesitated to look at the marks on Frances' body, Hulda kindly took over.

Hulda must be a great help to her husband, Aveline thought. Hulda had asked many questions earlier, trying to help figure out who may have murdered Frances. In a gentle voice, Hulda asked, "Do ye have any ideas who may have done this? Do ye know why the veil was placed over her face?"

At the braid shop, Chief Cane had taken the veil. Hulda had draped another cloth over Frances' face before a couple men placed her in a cart then moved her to the Bowmore cabin. The cloth remained in place while Hulda and Pa gently moved her body onto the bed and as the women undressed her. Aveline lugged the full water bucket to wash her sister's body. She lifted the bucket onto Frances' old stump-chair.

A quizzical furrow on her brow, Hulda stared down at the pile of removed clothing.

"What's wrong?" Aveline whispered, frightened that Hulda found something incriminating. Both women kept their voices low out of respect for Frances' parents a few feet away.

"Something's missing," Hulda whispered back. She gathered Frances' clothes and inspected each garment, one at a time. She stopped and, eyes wide, looked to Aveline. "There is no sacred undergarment."

"There has to be." Aveline reached for the clothes. "I know she wore it. She complained how it didn't fit well." She shook out each cloth: Frances' underskirt, corset, another underskirt, undershirt, blouse, skirt, sash, stockings, shawl. Aveline stared at the pile. *No undergarment.* She looked to Hulda. "I don't understand."

"She was devout?" Hulda asked, low.

"She was a plural wife!"

Hulda shook her head in confusion. "Let me see her wound." She looked up at Aveline. "Do ye wish to step away?"

"Thank you for your kindness, Sister." Aveline took a deep breath. "No, I want to know everything."

Hulda lifted the cloth that draped Frances' head and neck. She hefted the oil lamp and leaned in for a closer look. Now Aveline, slowly, looked back at Frances. Hulda pressed Frances' eyelids closed with her fingertips. She studied the grisly neck wound, jagged from being hacked.

"Husband said her throat was cut, but I don't reckon I see that much blood." Hulda spoke matter-of-factly. Gingerly, she poked a puffy part of the throat. "What *is* this?" Hulda tugged at the puffiness and peeled off a stringy, blood-soaked mass.

Aveline gagged and ran outside to the street. She fell to her knees and retched on the side of the cabin, barely aware of watching passersby.

Carissa Clarke and Em Paddock ran to her. They held her until her stomach stopped heaving. Em wiped Aveline's mouth with a cloth. Carissa clutched her tight while Aveline gasped in rasping breaths. Sobbing, whispers of "I'm praying for you" and "Godspeed" pressed into Aveline's hair.

Unable to speak, Aveline nodded her appreciation. Numb, she let them lift her to her feet and support her as she staggered back into the cabin. She didn't want her parents to rise from their bed, see Frances, and understand why Aveline had been weak.

Letting her eyes grow accustomed to the dim light, she heard Hulda whisper. "Can ye manage?"

Aveline nodded, still unable to speak.

The white beads stitched to Frances' dress reminded Aveline of the gaiety of that dance. They also triggered a memory. "There's something else missing."

"What is it?"

"Frances' hair comb. Do you see it?"

Hulda bent over Frances. She ran her fingers through the hair's tangled mass and felt under Frances' head. Hulda straightened. "It's not here."

"It couldn't have fallen out. I know how she attached it. It couldn't have just dropped off."

"Could whoever did this have taken it?"

"Possibly." Aveline shivered at the image in her mind's eye of her sister's killer bending over her body to steal the comb. She steeled herself to look at Frances' neck. Hulda had wiped off the dried blood from the slender throat. The cuts across her neck weren't as gruesome as Aveline expected.

Hulda noticed Aveline's focus. "I think the cuts were inflicted after her death. They're not deep."

"Cuts? Not one slice?"

"Several. Not one clean through. Several slight cuts." Hulda's finger made light slashing movements. "Like someone didn't know how to slice, like a woman who might have been afraid, or someone afraid to dig, or the knife was dull. See those tiny, jagged edges?" Hulda paused. "I'm sorry to tell ye this. If I trace all the cuts, the cuts went from ear to ear."

Aveline gulped. Rumors floated around the camp about the meaning of a throat cut from ear to ear, but her mind spun too fast to remember them. It was a sign, but what was the message, and why Frances?

"While ye were outside, I washed this off. This cloth was coiled very tight, like a rope, taut against her throat. Choking or this cloth is what killed her, not the cuts," Hulda whispered. "It soaked up the seepage. Can ye identify this?"

Hulda's question distracted Aveline from staring at her sister's scored neck. Hulda held out the wet thing. Aveline pressed her hands to her chest, unable to reach for or touch the object.

"Here, ye don't have to touch it," Hulda said softly. She laid it on the table, stretched it out with her fingers and set the oil lamp on the table.

Aveline studied the flattened material. *It can't be.* She looked closer at the cloth on the table: a white linen square, tatted lace edging, embroidered initials *WJA*: Washington John Avery.

Aveline sank to the floor.

~*~

When she awoke on Ma and Pa's bed, Ma was wiping Aveline's face with a damp cloth. Pa stood over them both, hovering. Hulda stood off to the bed's side, leaned over and stroked Aveline's hair.

Confused, Aveline looked around, trying to get her bearings. Then she remembered. She covered her face with her hands. She wanted to cry but felt cried out. Her hands dropped to her chest, and she stared into her father's face.

"Sister Cane told us what you found." His lips were tight. Tears spilled from his wide eyes. He ignored them. "And what you did not. I don't understand."

Unable to speak, Ma shook her head. She helped Aveline sit up as a knock sounded on the cabin door. Hulda opened the door and spoke some words to the unseen visitor. She leaned back and said, "Brother Allred is here with the coffin."

Ma moaned in despair. Aveline held her while her mother's shoulders shook. Pa stepped to the door and told Allred to come in. "I expected you some time ago."

The skinniest man Aveline had ever seen entered the cabin. Allred had a sallow complexion, probably, Aveline thought, from too much death from the sickness rampant throughout Winter Quarters.

Allred took off his bowler and made a small bow towards Ma. "My condolences. I met the Sister Bowmore a couple times. A fine lady." He turned toward Pa. "After I was fetched, I stopped by the Bates house, figuring she was there. Brother Bates said she was here. The woman of the house said she," he gestured toward Frances' body, "wouldn't be allowed back in the house."

Pa turned red, furious. "That witch wouldn't know a good woman if one—"

"Royal." Ma's voice was small, tired. "Please."

Pa laid a hand on his wife's shoulder. "I set up two chairs. I think that will work."

Allred looked at the chairs and nodded. He stepped outside. In a moment, he hefted in a long wood box and set it over the chairs. "Do you need help in moving her?"

Pa shook his head. "I will move her."

Allred nodded his head. "As you wish. I'll prepare her grave. When would you like for me to take her?"

Ma wailed at the question. Hulda stepped in. "Perhaps I should fetch Husband. I'll tell him what I saw and what I know. He may need to see for himself before she is taken." She took her shawl and left.

"A few hours." Pa said. "That should be enough time for Brother Cane to do any of his business and for us to … pay our final respects."

Allred bowed. "As you wish." He stepped close to Pa. "The coffin is three dollars. Burial and the burial fee is four dollars more. The fee includes the sexton's fee for the grave digging and record keeping. If you can't afford the fees, we'll set up a payment; just don't sneak her into the cemetery."

Pa, tightlipped, waved Allred out the door.

Aveline wiped her face of tears. "We need to prepare Frances before others arrive."

"I've already taken care of her, with Hulda's help," Ma said. She looked down at her hands. "It's the last thing I could do—" She brought her handkerchief up to her mouth and fought back tears.

Aveline shuffled to the other side of the curtain. Frances lay wrapped in the quilt she and Aveline had stitched as girls years before. It had been their first attempt. The quality wasn't good: the stitching was uneven and the cloth squares didn't line up, but the quilt had been their first and Frances and Aveline had been proud of their efforts. She burst into tears at the thought that she never imagined their first shared venture would be Frances' burial shroud.

Pa picked up Frances. He held her body close as he turned to lay his daughter in the coffin. The quilt shifted, exposing one of Frances' hands. He shifted her hand under the quilt and tugged the fabric taut and busied himself tugging the blanket smooth along her body. He placed his hand on her head, closed his eyes, and prayed.

Ma went to him, encircling his waist with her arms. Aveline wrapped her arms around them. They stood together, lost in their sad embrace until Pa said, "It's time for others to say farewell."

Chapter 14

The morning after Frances' burial, Aveline woke with a start. Disoriented in the dark, she realized she was in her old bed in her parents' cabin. Memories of yesterday evening swam in her mind: trudging behind the rattling wagon up the knoll to the cemetery; the prayers; her mother's collapse as her sobbing father shoveled the first clump of earth on Frances' coffin; the jolting ride home in the empty wagon; the silent evening staring at the fire.

Aveline threw back her mother's quilt and shivered into her dress. The fire had gone out, and her boots were stiff from cold. She hurried to light the fire before her parents rose. After burying their daughter, they didn't need to wake to a frigid house.

She glanced at the bulging quilt on her parents' bed. They didn't stir. As quietly as she could, she coaxed the fire higher. Reaching for the water bucket, she halted. Was this the bucket she used to wash Washington's bloody clothes? Her grief-stricken and sleep-deprived brain was slow to think. No, that was the Avery bucket. She grabbed the handle and hustled in the cold to the well. Heading back into the cabin, this time she didn't care if the water sloshed on her clothes. She just wanted to return to her parents.

Aveline pulled open the door and heard some muffled talk behind the quilt curtain. "Hello," Aveline said softly so as to not jar them from any sleepiness, yet gently remind them they were not alone. She set the bucket on the table, remembering this time not to set the bucket too close to the edge, where a plank had a habit of tipping. As she ladled water into the coffee pot, Pa stumbled from behind the curtain, tucking his shirt into his pants. He didn't say anything, but kissed Aveline on top of her head and collapsed on his chair.

How old he looked this morning.

He looked up at Aveline. "It's been a great comfort having you here … a great comfort to your mother, to me."

She knelt in front of him, her arms folded across his knees. With her head on his knee, he stroked her hair.

"There's no place I'd rather be than with you and Ma."

Ma staggered on unsteady legs into the room and crumpled on her rocking chair. Her eyes had a sunken, hollow look. Aveline hugged her from behind, and Ma laid her hands on Aveline's arms.

"I'll have the coffee going in a minute. You just rest and let me take care of breakfast."

Ma gave a weak smile as she patted Aveline's arms. "I don't know how you have the strength."

Aveline thought about her own condition—exhausted, numb. She didn't have the strength, but she had more than her parents. "I just want to make things easier for you both."

No one spoke while Aveline prepared the coffee and breakfast. Stomachs growled at the scent of the sizzling bacon and eggs. She served Pa, then Ma breakfast and pulled out her old stump to sit on while she ate.

"I will talk to Chief Cane after breakfast," Aveline said. "I want to know what's being done." She didn't want to say "about Frances' murder".

"I will go to Chief Cane," Pa said. "Man to man, he'll tell me more than you."

Aveline wanted to argue. His insinuation that a policeman would divulge more to a murdered woman's father than to her sister infuriated her, but she didn't have the strength to debate the injustice of it.

"I'll talk to Lucas and Eliza then," Aveline said. "She was a member of their family. They should take some responsibility for her."

"From what Brother Allred said yesterday, I doubt that they will," Pa poked at his eggs with the fork.

"Then they can at least pay for her coffin and funeral. I heard what Brother Allred told you, Pa," Aveline said, flatly.

"Aveline." Ma's voice sounded like a tired little girl's. The exhaustion in it reminded Aveline this woman had buried her daughter yesterday, and the remembrance shamed Aveline for her spite. She could not comprehend the sorrow her mother was feeling.

"I'm sorry, Ma."

~*~

The sun set behind the hills. A pink glow reflected off the clouds and onto the rows of cabins and the parked wagons. The air was calm, and silence hissed in her ears. The warm sight and peace were lost to Aveline as she stood before the cabin door of Eliza and Lucas Bates.

Staring at the door, she couldn't decipher her feelings: anger at their desertion, fear of what they might tell her, contempt for their tormenting her sister when all she wanted to be was a righteous plural wife for the Lord. Aveline didn't want to hear what they had to say about denying Frances the dignity of her burial preparation and wake in her home, or what they had to say about heaping abuse on her while she lived under Lucas' roof. She didn't want to hear why they didn't attend her wake or her burial.

She only needed them to hear her disgust for them, for their neglect during the last, worst day of Frances' life. She beat on the door. Her heartbeat ticked off the seconds. She beat again.

The door flung open, and Lucas filled the doorway. A grease-spotted rag tucked into his collar draped over his bulging belly. His oily hair dragged across the rag. He stood, smacking his lips from the meal, and stared down at Aveline.

Taken aback by the reality of Lucas' sudden appearance, her mouth didn't work and her mind froze. Her nose twitched from the stench of fireplace smoke, old sweat, and an unemptied chamber pot.

Lucas seemed content to look at her. Aveline remembered her manners and bobbed a slight curtsy. "Brother," she croaked. "I want to know what you're doing about Frances' murder."

Lucas worked his tongue around his missing teeth to get at any food remnants. "I'll pretend it's yer business to ask. I told all I will to Cane."

Aveline wondered about the information Lucas could provide to the Chief of Police Finis Cane. "Which was?"

"Not yer business."

Anger rose in Aveline. "You refused for Frances to be prepared for burial in her own home."

"Aye."

"Why?"

"Not a woman's business what a man does."

"You're her husband. You didn't attend her burial!"

"Was her husband, and aye." Lucas' eyes narrowed in anger. Aveline thought she saw a flicker of pain. Perhaps he did feel something for Frances' death. "I wasn't allowed to bury my Esther, murdered years ago." His shoulders drooped as his body relaxed. "She was innocent. I have nothing to say about yer sister."

Aveline wasn't sure what to say next, but Lucas didn't seem anxious to get back to his dinner or for her to leave. If anything, he seemed content to stand there, like he was enjoying a debate with an old friend. She recognized Lucas' shirt as the one he wore to the dance; it bore the same grease stain pattern on the same frayed collar. Now, two dark spots that appeared to be dried blood had dribbled on the left chest and a slight tear gaped at the seam of the arm and the chest. She wondered what other violence had taken place at the Council House.

"I'm here for Frances' belongings. She had clothing, a few books, and a quilt that belonged to the Bowmore family for decades. Her journal and writing implements—those treasures would bring great comfort to my parents."

Lucas made sucking sounds between his teeth, still trying to remove leftovers stuck between them. Aveline made the effort to not curl her lip at his coarse ways. He kept his eyes on her while he turned his head to spit. A dribble coursed its way down his chin. In her mind's eye, a flash of him lying on top of Frances caused her stomach to turn. Sympathy and understanding spiked for the conditions Frances endured.

"Nay. Even when she was alive, her things belonged to me. I am her next of kin. Her things stay here."

The fury almost bubbled out of her mouth. *How dare you deny her parents the last vestiges of their daughter?* Aveline knew he had the right to keep her things. Struggling to keep her temper, a swinging lantern attached to one cabin down the street reminded Aveline of a question that had been bothering her. "Where's Frances' hair comb?"

Lucas blinked, his face went blank, and his tongue stopped its probing. He shrugged, "Maybe the police took it. They are the rowdiest quality of Mormons."

Aveline had heard stories of their gatherings where they drank confiscated whiskey. When they caught offenders committing minor infractions, some officers dispensed corporal punishment before the bishops in their courts could rule on the cases and decide proper punishments. While some officers were undisciplined, the sadistic murder of a reverent Saint was not in the same category as a drunken brawl or an owner throwing a fit over being fined because his cow had gotten loose. She doubted the police would have helped themselves to Frances' hair comb from her dead body.

"I do not believe they'd take it," Aveline said.

"Then ask your parents."

Now it was Aveline's turn to blink. "My parents don't have it, and they don't know what happened to it."

Crossing his arms and widening his stance, Lucas pulled himself to his full, great height. "Ye and that Cane woman took yer sister to yer parents' house. It's either there or the Canes have it."

Aveline stood tall, ready to defend her parents and Sister Cane. "Don't you dare accuse my ma and pa or Sister Cane, the wife of our chief of police. Shame on you!" Aveline's voice rose to a scream, "Don't accuse good Saints!"

Lucas leaned toward Aveline, his face close to hers. Through his missing teeth he whispered, "Then the killer took it."

He shut the cabin door.

Chapter 15

In the darkening evening, Aveline trudged to her parents' cabin. She needed to be near them. With Frances forever gone and Bedford away in the Army, she didn't want her parents to be alone. Going to her cabin, the Avery cabin, flashed in her mind, but that place held no warmth or comfort.

Recalling Lucas' demeanor about the murder of his wife, he would have grieved more over the loss of a hunting dog. Would a Mormon man think so little of his plural wife? At times Aveline thought Washington only cared that she was available to him on a weekly basis. Beyond that, she was as useful as the slop jar to him, all duty and function.

The Paddock family never made Aveline believe the second wife, Carissa, was an annoyance. An evil jealousy flooded Aveline at times during their weekly quilting sessions.

Em and Carissa acted toward each other like Aveline and Frances had: loving, teasing, helpful. Hamish treated each of them the same way. He was free with his hugs, pats on the back, compliments, and gifts when he could afford them or make them. No, the revelation wasn't evil; it was the participants in the practice.

"It takes all kinds." Ma's voice popped in her head, a favored saying meaning not everyone thought or acted the same way. "What a dull world it would be otherwise."

Aveline dragged open the door to her parents' cabin. Ma and Pa sat on their chairs in front of the fire. Ma didn't move, but Pa looked up. Aveline leaned over and gave him a hug. She kissed the top of her mother's head and leaned in for an embrace. Ma didn't move except to lay a weak hand on Aveline's arm.

A Dutch oven filled with stew stood beside the fire in the hearth. Aveline pulled bowls and spoons from the cabinet and ladled out the food. She gave one bowl to Ma, one to Pa and sat on her stump holding her meal and watched her parents. Pa took a spoonful and slowly chewed like he had forgotten how to swallow. Ma just held the bowl.

Aveline waited. In a gentle voice, she urged, "Ma, please try to eat. You need to eat."

Ma nodded and ignored the tears pouring down her face. Aveline set aside her bowl and picked up the edge of Ma's apron. She dabbed at her mother's wet cheeks. "I know, Ma, but please eat."

Pa swallowed his mouthful and cleared his throat. "I spoke to Brother Cane this afternoon. He said he'd asked around, but had no idea, no information why such malice was done to Frances. Even with the knowledge from Sister Cane, he could not understand the reason for this evil deed. He cannot fathom the purpose of Brother Avery's handkerchief as the mechanism of her death. He said he must delay his investigation until Avery returns from his mission."

Aveline sat at her father's feet. "Did the chief find the hair comb?"

Pa shook his head. "Cane returned to the braid shop to search, but found nothing. He can only conclude she may have been murdered for that jewelry and the evil doer has it."

Lucas' voice echoed in Aveline's head. *Then the killer took it.* She shook her head. "I cannot understand such a purpose for this act. Many of our women have finery and jewels." The hair comb was a magnificent piece. Was it worth a young woman's life?

Aveline realized she owned no finery or jewels. Neither did Ma. "Did Brother Cane question Lucas?"

Chewing another mouthful, Pa looked at Aveline. He swallowed. "I inquired. He refused to divulge what Lucas and Eliza said. I wanted to scream at him for withholding information from me, but I settled for him being a professional officer and keeping the information to himself. Cane can be a powerful ally or a formidable enemy." He looked to his wife. "I chose the former."

"You chose wisely, Royal," Ma said softly, her first words all evening. "I expect he'll tell us everything when he figures it out." She spooned the stew into her mouth.

"I stopped at Lucas Bates' house," Aveline sat on her stump and picked up her bowl. Ma and Pa looked up, expectantly. "I only spoke to Lucas. He refused to invite me in. He told me nothing we didn't already know." She took a bite of stew. "Odd though, when I asked him about the hair comb, he accused you two and Sister Cane of taking it."

Pa slapped his bowl on the table and rose. "That bullock, I'll thrash him myself—"

"I did that, Pa." She placed a calming hand on his shoulder. "I lost my temper, and my mouth …" Aveline appeared sorrowful before her face changed to defiance. "I shan't apologize."

"Aveline," Ma said, her voice weak. "A good Mormon wife does not question or chastise a man, a member of the priesthood." She slowly stirred her stew.

"Frances was a good Mormon wife. Her obedience did her no good."

Ma rose stiffly from her rocking chair and faced Aveline. "Her trials have placed her among the stars in the highest level of heaven."

Aveline hung her head, shamed. They had not broached the unbroachable: Frances was not wearing her sacred undergarment. Who removed it and why?

A sick feeling in Aveline's stomach hinted that Frances was not in the highest level in heaven.

Chapter 16

Aveline closed the door to her parents' cabin. Glancing at the brightening sky, she tugged her shawl tighter around her to ward off the morning's chill. Her boots crunched through the thin frosty crust that appeared during the night. The awakening sounds of the Camp of Israel grew louder. An ox-drawn wagon pulled past; the beasts' hooves' thuds and the wheels' creaking echoed off the cabins. She curtsied to the brother who walked beside the lead beast. Smoke bubbled from chimneys, stoked to warm the cabins against the morning's cold. Bleary-eyed, she barely noticed the puffs of white air from her exhalations.

She hesitated before opening the door of her own cabin. Seeing Dorris or hearing her sarcastic mouth held only aggravation. *Please, Lord, not this morning.* No fire burned in the fireplace. The cabin was dark. A damp chill seeped through Aveline's clothes. In the light cast from the open door, Aveline could see clothes strewn about and could smell the soiled dishes and full chamber pot. Aveline had stayed away only two nights, and in that time Dorris allowed the clean cabin to revert to filth.

The cabin was quiet. Amazed and relieved, Aveline lay on her bed. She didn't bother to pull off her boots, but dragged her quilt over her. In the silence, a slight rustle of fabric sounded from the other side of the cabin. Opening her eyes in the dark, she concentrated on the sound. She heard it again.

"Where have you been?"

Dorris' harsh voice, loud in the dark, caused Aveline to sit up. She groaned inwardly, lay back down and pulled the quilt toward her head.

"Answer me."

Aveline answered by rolling onto her other side and pulling her quilt completely over her head. Her eyes popped open in shock. Proddings jabbed at her back.

She's *poking* me! Aveline sat up, threw off her quilt and swung her arm, hard. Her fist connected with something solid and round, like Dorris' head. That something gasped—a satisfying sound. Aveline yelled, "Leave me alone, *Dorris!* Touch me again and I'll strike you harder." She flung herself down and yanked the quilt over her head.

Through the quilt, Aveline heard a soft weeping. She ignored the distress. She didn't care if Dorris was upset; she just wanted her to shut up or go away, preferably both. Aveline knew she should be more caring and patient, but being a caring and patient second wife hadn't helped her sister. Right now, she felt too low to care.

The weeping grew louder. A wail pierced the darkness. Dorris was pregnant. She might need help. Aveline sighed and threw back the quilt.

She stepped over the figure on the floor and groped her way to open the door. Using the light beaming in, she prepared the fire and closed the door. In the growing flame's glow, she stood over Dorris with her hands on her hips and stared down at the weeping woman.

"Come on, Dorris." There was resignation in Aveline's voice. She reached down to pull Dorris' arm to help her up.

"Don't touch me. You're mean." It was a petulant child's whimper followed by a sniff.

"You haven't seen me mean yet, Dorris, but you're fixin' to." Again, Aveline reached down as Dorris swung and slapped Aveline. "How dare you strike me. Wait until my husband returns. He'll beat you," Dorris hissed.

Exhaustion from burying her abused and murdered sister made Aveline immune to Dorris' threat and mistreatment. She screamed down at the prostrate woman. "You cow! If *my husband* lays a hand on me again, I'll kill him in his sleep, maybe even you too."

Aveline snatched her coat and shawl from the nail and stalked out of the cabin. She strode up the knoll west of Winter Quarters. Gasping for air, she flung herself on the frosted grass and let the ice chill her red-hot anger. Rocking, she hoped the movement would ease her fury.

Behind her at the western horizon, a line of dark clouds shielded the earth. More snow was coming, a smothering white blanket to conceal another cold injustice.

To her right, on the bluff beyond, lay the cemetery. Another family trudged that sorrowful trek this morning. A long row of mourners were burying another Saint. A few days ago, she'd made that journey to bury Frances. She pulled the shawl down to cover her face as if to block out the world and her grief.

The veil! Covering her face caused her to remember a piece of information about Frances' death. The cloth that covered Frances' face was some woman's wedding veil. Find the woman the cloth belonged to and that woman might lead the police to the killer.

Her anger forgotten, Aveline took off running down the slope toward the police chief's home.

Chapter 17

Racing down the knoll, Aveline looked for Chief Cane's house. He and his wife Hulda and family lived in the corner cabin on Cahoon Street, fifteenth ward. The warming sun melted the thin coat of ice wherever the rays hit the earth, and Aveline's boots stuck to the soft mud. She pulled her boots up with every step. Her skirt dragged as the mud clung to her hem.

The children outside the corner cabin indicated this was the one. Six of the seven Cane children were forever outside, oft times unruly. They chucked dried horse manure at passing wagons.

Sometimes they acted as if they were smaller versions of the more corrupt police officers in the department. Today, they scuffed their boots through the mud where the sun had melted the ice and skidded into the cabin's shadow where the ice was still solid.

Breathless, Aveline ran up to the oldest boy. "Hyrum, where's your father?"

Hyrum pointed toward the settlement's center, toward the police department.

"Is your mother here?"

He pointed to the cabin. A younger child watched the exchange, then dragged open the cabin door for her.

She placed her hand on the child's shoulder in gratitude. Aveline stood in the doorway, willing her eyes to see in the dark. "Sister Cane?"

"Sister Bowmore. Come in, child. Mind the baby on the floor so ye don't step on her. So what brings ye here all breathless as if the devil hisself is after ye?"

Aveline stepped forward, tentative, blinking hard. A slight movement, an arm, revealed she was squirming in the corner.

"Sister Cane, may I talk with you about my sister? I had a remembrance and thought you may know some information." Aveline's night vision opened, and she could make out Hulda preparing vegetables on the far side of the cabin. A large three-legged black pot stood on the table, half-filled with water. One shriveled potato lay next to it. Two small carrots, one with a large dark spot on the end, were beside the potato and a large, handsome turnip.

Aveline stepped forward, picked up the knife on the table and began to chop the soft potato. With a heave, Hulda picked up the child from the floor, an action that informed Aveline that the child took after Hulda's heft. Aveline asked, "Why don't you sit for a spell while I cut these vegetables?"

"I supposin' I'd rather enjoy that," Hulda said as she sat. The rocking chair squeaked in protest at her weight. "Umph, this feels right nice."

"Do you cut out the eyes or how much of this bruise do you keep for your stew?"

"With this lot, I keep it all. It would have ta be a lot worse than that for me to waste any." Hulda fumbled with the front of her bodice. She withdrew a huge breast and offered the nipple to her child. The girl ignored the breast and turned her head to watch Aveline. Hulda pulled the girl's head to her chest and pressed the distended nipple in the girl's mouth.

"So, ye had a remembrance?"

"I forgot to ask about the veil draped over Frances' face. I remembered it just now. Would you have any knowledge of whose veil that was?"

"Nay. Husband does rely on me at times to assist, such as with your sister, and times he'll talk about things seekin' my opinion." She started to push the rocker. It squeaked in rhythm to her back and forth movement. "But, alas, he has kept much ta himself about this. I asked him, but he just shakes his head. Yer not thinking of asking him yesself, are ye?"

Aveline nodded. "I want to know all. I believe we need to know all. Think of this, Sister: a killer is in the Camp of Israel."

The rocking stopped. "Ye believe the killer could smite another Saint?"

Aveline slid the carrots toward her and sliced them before answering. "I don't know. Brother Cane has not passed on a concern to you?"

The rocking and the rhythmic squeaking resumed. "He never mentioned such." She didn't say anything for a moment as she stuffed one deflated breast into her blouse, draped her child on the other arm, and lifted the other breast. "I daresay if Husband thought a threat to others was in the camp, he would have mentioned such."

Aveline admired the turnip, a rarity in its hardness and lack of bruises or rot.

"Aye, it's a nice one," Hulda said, watching Aveline. "Sister Richards brought those back from Keegan's Mercantile. She brought several. I'm portioning them to make them last."

"That was kind of her," Aveline said. Sister Mary Richards, a tiny woman, seemed to be everywhere, helping those in need or providing a welcome diversion to those who weren't. Aveline finished chopping the turnip and scooped the chunks into the pot. She hesitated to ask if Hulda had spices to add. If Hulda had no spices, she might be embarrassed to say so.

Hulda must have sensed the pause. "There's salt in the bag next to the sugar. I have a beef in the salt bin. It's a chunk. I'd be obliged if ye'd chop that."

"I'm happy to help you, Sister. I'm certainly obliged to you for helping us with Frances. I'll never forget your kindness." Aveline opened the salt bag, scooped a small portion with her hand and tossed it into the mixture. She opened the bin and pulled out a hunk of beef bigger than her hand. "That's nice beef, Sister."

Hulda laughed from deep in her ample chest. "Brother Andrus' cow busted its pen. Broke its leg. Rather than pay the fine for his cow getting loose, he butchered it on the spot. Gave a lovely piece to Husband."

Aveline smiled to herself. "Good luck for you. Bad luck for Brother Andrus." Andrus lived in a dugout with a curtain for a door and a sod roof of dubious protection. The shelter, west of the settlement, was shared with his wife and seven children. The loss of a cow was a severe hardship. Theirs was a hardscrabble existence, but they hadn't lost one child, a miracle by the standard in some wards where a child's passing was a daily occurrence.

Looking down at her suckling child, Hulda understood. "We'll feast on the brother's loss. At least good can come out of it. I am blessed as are the Andruses. Like them, we have seven babes." She smoothed the child's hair. "We are blessed to have them all."

The blood oozing from the beef and Hulda mentioning Keegan's Mercantile reminded Aveline of the scene the night of Frances' murder. "By chance, did Brother Cane mention the fight after the Council House dance? The fight between Mister Keegan, Brother Bates, and my husband."

"Oh, aye. Husband was quite angry about it. Mister Keegan is well thought of in the Mormon community — fair in business, doesn't condemn us. By the by, I have heard terrible things of Lucas Bates." Hulda leaned forward and lowered her voice. "Husband hinted of the brother being a Danite."

This last tidbit caught Aveline's attention and she tensed. "A Danite?" she whispered to the darkness.

"Aye. Even when Husband speaks of it, he speaks low."

Danites were hinted to be the enforcers for the Saints, dating back to the time of Joseph Smith, Junior. Their intent was to protect the people and the faith from harm, using whatever means necessary. Rumors were passed on in the dark that Brigham Young continued the group. A few of the men were thought to be so devoted to Young and the Saints they would kill to avenge any wrongdoing or at the suggestion of it.

"Your husband fought with Mister Keegan because Mister Keegan called Lucas Bates a cheat, that Bates cheated at faro. It cost Mister Keegan a lot of money." Hulda stopped rocking and looked at Aveline. In the dim light, Aveline could see Hulda's wide eyes. "Husband said in that game, Mister Keegan also lost a hair comb to Lucas."

Chapter 18

The sun's warmth melted the frost coating on the dirt road and the cabins' roofs. Water dripping off the roofs' eaves splashed into puddles and threw mud up the cabin walls. Aveline ignored it all. She felt confused by the information Hulda gave her: her brother-in-law, Lucas, may be a Danite; he cheated a respected Gentile out of money; and her husband started a fistfight with that Gentile. Mister Keegan lost a hair comb to Lucas, a hair comb that may have cost her sister her life.

Aveline stopped in her tracks at the shock of her thoughts. Could Mister Keegan have killed Frances for her hair comb? Thanks to his store, Keegan was wealthy, and he could afford several hair combs for his wife, but even if he could afford it, was he a man who would allow someone to swindle him without exacting some revenge? Why would her husband take such a violent exception to Lucas being called a cheat, if he was one?

Apparently, Keegan told Chief Cane that Lucas had cheated him, but an accusation didn't make it true. Gossip in Winter Quarters flowed like the winter wind: cold, fast, cruel, and from all directions. One could not believe the gossip except for what was blowing around the settlement at that instant.

She slogged to the chief of police's headquarters cabin, down Cahoon Street from his home. She scraped off her muddy boots at the iron bar beside the door. An ox-drawn wagon struggled up the street. The wheels sank almost to its axles in the soft mud. Two men leaned into the rear wheels and hollered at the straining oxen.

Standing at the door, Aveline hesitated, took a deep breath, and knocked.

"Enter."

Pushing open the wood door, Aveline peeked in. She'd never been in the cabin that served as the police office.

"Come in, lass, come in." An officer with a stubble beard, likely in his thirties, sat on a chair, one leg propped on the makeshift desk: a wood plank supported by a whiskey barrel.

Aveline stepped in and gave the officer a slight curtsy.

"Sister Bowmore."

Turning toward the direction of the voice, Finis Cane, the chief of police stood. As he came around his own makeshift desk, he pushed the officer's leg off the desk. The officer stood.

Brother Cane indicated Aveline, "This is Sister Bowmore, sister of Brother Bates' wife." The man immediately understood the connection and nodded to Aveline. Cane did not introduce the officer to Aveline.

"How may I be of service ta ye, Sister?" Cane pointed to a chair. He stood, poised to sit, until Aveline sat on the offered seat.

"Brother, I want to talk with you about Frances' murder."

Cane looked at the man. "Officer Younger, don't ye have a patrol?"

"No. I patrolled already."

"Do it again."

With a slight grimace, the officer grabbed his coat and headed out the door.

"I appreciate your presence at my sister's burial, Brother. I apologize for not saying so then."

"Sister Frances was a kind woman," Cane said.

"Do you have any information as to who did this?"

Cane shook his head. "As of yet, I have nothing I feel should be told."

Not wanting to put Hulda in a tight spot with her husband, Aveline admitted to Cane about her visit with his wife and what Hulda said. "I pray, on Sister Hulda's behalf, she did nothing wrong by telling me these things." She was aware that Hulda may have spoken out of turn and violated her husband's confidence.

Cane's lips widened into a small smile. "If I wish for information to stay secret, I keep it secret. Many things I tell the wife. She knows what she may tell and what she must keep secret."

Aveline wondered if Hulda knew more than she said, but she had seemed open with her information.

"Do you have anything you may share?" Aveline asked. "Do you know whose wedding veil was over her face? Why was she in the braid shop so late and after a dance? What became of her hair comb? You do know Mister Keegan lost his hair comb to Lucas Bates in a game of chance?"

Cane leaned forward and waved his hands back and forth in a sign for Aveline to slow down her questioning. "Most of the information ye seek I do not know. Some I do, and I will tell you. I know of the skullduggery with Mister Keegan. As far as yer sister, Brother Bates said some devil broke into the braid shop. The front door was kicked in."

She shook her head and stared out the only window. The ox cart was still stuck in the mud. The driver was digging out the wheels.

Tears formed in her eyes. "Do you know what she was doing in the shop?"

"I do not know."

"Can you tell me more?"

Cane shrugged. "I will tell what I can. Right now, I do not know what I can or cannot tell. I do not have all the information to even decide that."

"What information are you waiting on? Can you tell me that? Perhaps I can help you find out that information. Is Mister Keegan involved in this?"

Cane sighed at the mention of Keegan. "I have not questioned Mister Keegan of the incident involving your husband or the murder."

"Have you found out the owner of the veil that covered Frances' face?"

This time, Cane hesitated then nodded. "Aye. The veil belongs to the Sister Eliza Bates."

"Eliza?" Dizziness sweep over her.

"Aye. Sister Bates denies knowing why or how her veil came to be placed over her sister-wife's face."

"But the veil had to have come out of Bates' house! How could she not know how it came to leave the premises? What did Lucas say?"

At the mention of Lucas, Cane squirmed in his seat. "I have spoken to Brother Bates. He assured me he knows nothing of how the veil came to be placed over your sister's face."

Her eyes narrowed; doubt flooded through her. She shook her head. "I cannot fathom that any stranger would enter Brother Bates' house, take the wedding veil of the woman of the house, and place it over a murdered girl's face."

Cane made a gesture Aveline read as "who knows?" He picked at a knot on the plank desktop. "Do ye think that Frances herself took Eliza's veil, and the killer mistook the veil as hers when he or she placed the veil over her face?"

Stunned, Aveline shook her head. "Frances would never touch such a thing. Never! She was not so ill-bred as to allow her curiosity to rifle another's trunk, like a, like a, common pirate. Even if the veil were sitting on a table, she'd never take it."

"Was your sister happy in Brother Bates' household?"

Her throat tightened as she recalled how Frances suffered at Eliza and Eleanor's hands. Aveline shook her head. "She was ill-used. Frances told me Eliza could not abide having another wife in the house. Frances said sometimes Lucas and Eleanor would join in abusing her."

Cane dug deeper at the wood knot. For several seconds he concentrated on it. "In the braid shop's fireplace, a fire had been started. Even when I was there later in the morning, I was told the fire was easy to start. Do ye think yer sister may have started the fire with the intent on burning the veil? She had access to the trunk where Eliza kept her veil, and may have taken it to burn as a symbol of her hatred for Eliza."

"No. No. That would be a hateful thing to do. As much as Frances suffered and as much as she loathed being in the Bates household, she would never do such evil." Aveline ignored the tears of anguish and rage flowing down her cheeks.

"She did not wear the sacred undergarment." Cane looked at Aveline full in her face. The accusation in his voice made Aveline burst into tears.

A symbol of their devotion, a Mormon would always wear the undergarment. Aveline shook her head and wailed. "She was a plural wife. What more did she have to do to prove her devotion?"

Chapter 19

Aveline stood outside, her back against the police chief's door. She wiped her wet face with her hands and pulled her shawl tighter as if the cloth would shield her from the world's wickedness. She took a deep breath and looked up.

Sister Ann Cassell's portly figure sloshed through the mud into the braid shop, diagonally across the dirt street from the police office, and slammed the door closed. Squinting in the bright sun, Aveline stared at the closed door. Behind that door, Frances was murdered.

She squared her shoulders, marched across the street and pushed on the door. Leaving it open to shine some light into the dim space, Aveline blinked to focus her eyes.

From somewhere in the darkness, she heard the rustle of straw being woven into baskets and hats. A voice melodic with an Irish lilt called from the depth of the cabin. "May I help you, Sister?"

Aveline stepped forward. Sister Cassell's figure loomed out the darkness; she stopped as she recognized Aveline. "I am so sorry for what happened to dear Frances. She was a kind soul." Ann reached for Aveline to lead her to a chair.

"Thank you, Sister; that's most kind of you to say so." She settled into the chair and noticed the other women in the braid shop staring at her. In a low voice she asked, "May I ask you some questions about that night? That morning?"

Ann sat next to Aveline and leaned close. "Of course. I do not know much, but I will reveal what I can. Though, I must ask you to keep what I tell you to yourself. The Brother, Lucas Bates, said not to discuss it, especially with you." She leaned back to study Aveline's reaction.

"I am no threat to him. I don't know why he would forbid you to say what you will to me, Sister."

Ann shrugged. "I follow my orders." She glanced at the other women bent over their work pretending not to listen. "Frances was a sweet child, kind, and worked hard." Ann made a sign of the cross, a Catholic blessing. Both Ann and Aveline froze at the movement. Ann shook her head. "Old habit. My parents are Irish Catholic. I am a new Saint. So, for Sister Frances' sake, I'll answer your questions."

"You found her?"

"Yes. I came to work in the morn. I opened the shop as I always do."

"Did you notice anything untoward?"

Ann stared into the darkness. "Mostly I thought it was all as it should have been, except the ashes in the fireplace were still hot, like someone had spent the night in here. It was easy to start the fire that morn. Later, I heard about the shop being broken into, the door being kicked in and all, but when I arrived that morning the door was closed."

"How did you find my sister?"

"I didn't know she was here for the longest time. Oh, I was bent on preparing for the day: starting the fire, lugging the water bucket to fill, lighting the oil lamps. I saw some clutter, a small table knocked over. 'Odd,' I thought to myself. I straightened it up. A stack of finished baskets had fallen over, but that happens. I think the pack rats look for a home, and they knock the stacks over. I even wove a bit on a hat. I went to the pile to fetch some straw."

Ann stopped her talk and picked at the tip of a finger. "I went to the pile. There was a dark patch on the straw and some straw strewn on top of the darkness, almost as if it was covered up, but yet not. I started to sweep it away, tossing it to the top of the pile."

Ann paused and made another sign of the cross. This time both women ignored the movement. "I saw a hand." Shaking her head hard, her voice lowered as if she were ashamed, "I stared at it. I couldn't understand why a hand would just lay there. I, I am ashamed to say I picked it up. Her hand was cold, stiff. That's when I realized … I ran screaming from the cabin, across the street to fetch Finis Cane."

Aveline sat quietly, imagining Ann's movements and the horror of her discovery. She swallowed hard and hugged herself to stop shivering. "How was Frances' demeanor while she worked here?"

"Oh, very quiet. Very unhappy. Often she had bruises on her face. Brother Bates is not an easy man to work for." She leaned closer to Aveline. "I cannot imagine having to live with him too." Ann sat back upright. "Though I must say she seemed happier this past week, like something had changed. Last week I heard her laugh for the first time." She looked at the floor and kicked some straw with her toe. "'Tis a sad thing to work alongside someone for so long yet never hear her laugh."

The grabbing of the door handle caused both women to jump. The door flung open and Lucas Bates' huge form filled the doorway. He stepped inside and headed toward the back. He couldn't see in the darkness, his eyes unaccustomed to the dim light, Aveline knew. She didn't move, afraid he would see her. As he passed, Aveline silently touched Ann's hand in thanks and slipped toward the door.

"What brings ye here, disrupting the sisters' work?" The bellow pulled Aveline around to face him. "And ye? Are ye talkin' when ye should a been workin'?"

He approached not Aveline, but Ann, the glower in his face clear. Aveline tensed, prepared to see Lucas strike Ann.

Instead, Ann rose, her hands folded in front of her rounded belly. Her bulk almost matched Lucas'. She cocked her head. "Why, Brother, what makes you think Sister Bowmore is disrupting our work?" The sweetness in her voice seemed to lessen Lucas' anger or confuse him.

He stuttered with fury. "I don't want her here, an' I tol' ye not to talk to her."

"Brother," Ann's voice was soft as if speaking to a child. "You instructed that I couldn't talk with her about her sister.

You didn't say I couldn't converse about her sibling." Leaning over to peer around Lucas' bulk, Ann called out to the women working, "I didn't talk to Sister Bowmore about her sister, did I?"

Almost in unison, the other three women exclaimed, "Oh, no, Brother, she only conversed about a sibling. She didn't do what you told her not to."

Lucas' eyes narrowed in concentration. He nodded and grunted. "See that ye don't again." He looked at Aveline's silhouette in the doorway. "And ye can just git on out."

As Lucas stalked to the rear of the cabin, Ann spun toward Aveline. A satisfied smile crossed her fleshy lips. Aveline blew her a kiss in thanks and waved as she escaped out the door.

Chapter 20

The light from the open door illuminated the disarray in the Avery cabin. Clothing draped over the chairs. Aveline wrinkled her nose at the stench. Decayed food? No, it was the unemptied chamber pot and slop jar. The fire was not lit. Cold, dark, and stink again filled the cabin.

Aveline left the door open to let in some fresh air. She sat slouching on the edge of her bed feeling as tired as she'd ever felt in her life.

Fabric rustled on the other side of the curtain. She buried her face in her hands and ignored it.

"The chamber pot is full. The slop jar needs dumping. Do your job."

"No," Aveline said in a soft voice, too tired to scream.

The bedding on the other bed was thrown back. Dorris' head bumped the curtain as she pulled on her shoes. Aveline daydreamed about whacking the bumps.

Dorris whipped the quilt curtain out of her way. "I am not well." A moan of emotion escaped her throat. "I expect you do to your duties. Now."

Hulda Cane with seven children to feed and care for popped into Aveline's head. It was doubtful Hulda lay around whining to whomever might be near. "No."

The instant Dorris' hand touched Aveline's shoulder, Aveline pushed it off. "Don't you touch me. You get your toothless, skinny carcass back to bed if you can't stand being up, but do not touch me. Dump your own slop jar. Dump your own chamber pot. I may be the second wife, but I am *not* your slave."

Dorris seemed unsure how to proceed. She struggled with herself to maintain her dominant position in the household, but wasn't sure how. "Washington instructed you to obey me."

"Well, he is not here now, is he?"

"He will return, and when he does—"

"And when he does, what? Will he beat me? Throw me out? If he does, I will make sure everyone knows what manner of husband he is. If he wants so much to rise in the Church, let him be a good Mormon husband, like my father, like Hamish Paddock."

"Whether he's good or kind or mean, it is of no matter to anyone outside this household, or inside this household. You belong to him to do as he sees fit," Dorris said. "Or do you wish to end up like your sister?"

A chill of horror raced through Aveline. She stiffened in shock and anger. "Do not—ever—speak of my sister again." Exhaustion prevented Aveline from throwing a fist at Dorris. She stood and pushed Dorris slightly, just enough to make her off balance.

Dorris staggered and groped her way to her rocking chair. She pushed back in the chair to start rocking. "You could leave, like Phineas Richards' second wife did."

Aveline had heard of Brother Richards' second wife. His first wife, Wealthy, was so nasty to the woman that she ran away. "I try to be a good plural wife to earn the Lord's grace and salvation." She paused. "I should hope you would too."

The rocking stopped. Dorris stared at the fireplace, comprehending Aveline's words. This was their longest conversation. Perhaps Aveline had broken through Dorris' cruel shell. She stepped beside Dorris and sat in Washington's chair. She said nothing, but stared at the fireplace.

Moments passed. Occasionally, a small explosion from a burning log sent sparks onto the stone hearth.

"I am not happy in my life," Dorris said in a voice very small, a little girl's voice, an admission that stunned Aveline with its honesty. Her eyelids drooped and she fought to keep them up.

Aveline said nothing, hoping for more.

"I remember when I used to be happy with Washington." There was a long pause. "I remember when he used to be happy with me. Then we received instruction on the revelation of plural marriage. I felt sick over it. Washington was sick over it too. He could not abide it. One day, Brother Heber Kimball came to him, and instructed him that he must do this, for his salvation ... and for mine." Dorris' voice had dropped to a whisper at the effort.

Dorris said nothing for so long Aveline thought that was all she'd hear.

"Washington used to be a quiet man, a giving man, a kind husband." She shook her head, weariness weighed her head down. "After his instruction from Brother Kimball, all he could think of was rising in the Church and marrying another woman."

The rocking chair began its motion. A glimmer of light from the flames caught a slow tear as it slowly traced its way down her cheek.

Shame swept through Aveline. She waited longer in case Dorris had more to say, but no more words were offered. Aveline whispered, "Sister Avery, I humbly beg your pardon. I shall try to do better. For you. For your child."

Dorris said nothing, but the rocking came faster. Her chest heaved. The rocking stopped. Throwing her head back she wailed, "God in heaven!" She flung herself to the dirt floor, weeping.

Thunderstruck, Aveline threw herself beside Dorris and wrapped her arms around the wailing woman. Heat radiated from Dorris. She stroked Dorris' hair. "Let me take care of you and your child."

"The Lord took the babe," she wailed. "There is no child."

Aveline closed her eyes. *Dorris suffered alone.* Aveline hugged Dorris tighter. The two sister-wives crouched on the dirt floor, one holding the other.

~*~

That evening, Aveline rested on Washington's chair. The cabin smelled fresh again since she rid it of the filled chamber pot and slop jar. Aveline retched as she dumped the contents of Dorris' miscarriage and her bowel's reaction to an infection.

Behind her, Dorris slept in Aveline's bed. In her illness, Dorris had soiled her sheets. While Dorris rested, Aveline had stripped the soiled bed and washed the bedding. It now draped the back of Dorris' rocker and on the table to dry by the fire. Aveline could feel the heat radiating from Dorris' body as it fought an infection.

Throughout the day, after coaxing Dorris to eat a bite of stew Aveline had made, Dorris vomited most of it. She couldn't keep down any water Aveline dribbled from a spoon into her mouth.

Openly worried, Aveline sat on the edge of her bed and leaned over Dorris. "I'll be right back. I'm going to fetch my ma." Dorris didn't react. *Please let her be sleeping.* Aveline grabbed her shawl and ran into the night.

~*~

The washbasin filled with cold water didn't slosh as Aveline balanced it toward Em Paddock. Em sat on the edge of the bed, dipped a rag into the water and squeezed it out, then wiped Dorris' burning face.

For the fifth time since she had arrived, Em straightened Dorris' nightgown collar. The movement was something to do, something Aveline had performed several times herself before she left the cabin last night to seek help.

Aveline had run to her parents' house, wanting her mother's help with Dorris' raging fever. "She's not here," her father said. "She's been at Caleb Abernethy's cabin for two days now. His two littlest ones are gravely ill. Luke and Carrie, they have the fever. I have been praying hard for them."

Pa poked at the fire. "You remember Caleb lost his wife to black canker a few months ago, just before he returned from his mission in France. He has four living children. He had lost two children before then. And now ..." He rose from his chair. "I'll find Bishop Lang and send him to Sister Dorris."

As Aveline ran to the Paddock cabin she prayed for Luke and Carrie. "They are so little, Lord."

At the Paddock house, Em answered the door. Within a minute of Aveline's hurried explanation, Em had grabbed her shawl and hurried after Aveline. Carissa stayed behind with the three children. Em had directed Aveline to run to the trade shop for horseradish for a plaster to place on Dorris' abdomen. The heat would help draw out the infection, Em said.

Now, Aveline and Em stared at Dorris, watching her chest rise and fall in a shallow movement. Fear for the older woman's life and fatigue made Aveline begin to weep. Em patted her shoulder and leaned toward Aveline. "Shall we pray?" Aveline nodded and both women sank to their knees. After a few moments, Aveline stood and leaned over to kiss Dorris' hot forehead.

"Should I get Bishop Lang?" Em whispered.

"That might be wise," Aveline whispered back. "But my pa said he would find the bishop and send him here."

"That was yesterday."

With a start, Aveline realized Em was right. Worry had blurred time. The cabin door closed as Em disappeared to find the bishop.

Alone again with Dorris, Aveline decided to talk to the unconscious face of her sister-wife. "Sister Avery, may I call you Dorris?" She paused and pretended to listen for a response. "Thank you, I appreciate that. When we reach Zion and we have a new home, how would you decorate it? Yes, I think your rocking chair near the fireplace would be very nice. I shall stitch a cloth for the back and tat the cloth with layers of lace. That shall look fine. Mister Avery's chair? Do you think he might desire a stuffed chair? Mister Avery shall build us a big home, with separate bedrooms. A kitchen, yes, stocked with the finest fruits and vegetables. I confess I would like a chair—a real chair—by the fireplace." She turned and pointed at it against the wall. "My stump will be ashes by then. It shall make a hot fire, don't you think? I shall enjoy warming my feet with its heat. Perhaps all our children will rest on our knees and we will warm them by the fire."

The memory of Dorris' miscarriage and her deathly fever now, against the daydream of a small family with children warming themselves by the fire, was too much. The reality did not suit the daydream. "Is it foolish to dream of such things?"

She realized she needed a breath of fresh air and stepped out. Aveline dumped the water basin beside the cabin. She ladled fresh water into it and brought the basin back to the bed. "I do not think such things are foolish. If I may be so bold, why may we not dream of a better future? We struggle so hard today, but can't we wish for a better tomorrow?" A thought popped into Aveline's head. "After all, isn't that why we are plural wives? For the promise of happiness in heaven?"

Aveline untied the string holding Dorris' collar snug, and dabbed the wet, cool cloth at her throat. "It is wise, I think, to work for a better tomorrow, but we can make a better today if we work together. Do you agree?"

I hope so, Aveline thought.

The door opened and Bishop Lang entered. He stood in the doorway, waiting for his eyes to adjust to the darkness. Em walked in behind him.

Aveline rose and curtsied, "Thank you, Bishop, for coming." She stood beside Dorris' head. "Sister Avery is very ill. She has a terrible fever, I fear from the loss of a child."

Bishop Lang sighed. "So much sickness. The sexton has too much labor." He knelt beside the bed, bowed his head and began to pray quietly, his lips moving. Aveline stood beside the bishop and looked at Em. She didn't know if she should join the bishop on her knees. Em didn't move. Both women clasped their hands in prayer and closed their eyes.

After his prayer, the bishop sat on the bed's edge. He placed both hands on Dorris' head and closed his eyes. His lips moved in prayer. Aveline prayed with the bishop.

The laying on of his hands concluded, the bishop stood and looked down at Aveline.

"Would you like a drink of cold water, Bishop Lang?"

He shook his head. "I am to go to the Abernethy cabin with Bishop Riter. He granted me the honor of attending the Abernethys. His family and mine came from neighboring farms in New York. I wish to help them." Sadness passed over his face. "I helped bury his two children and his wife. I do not wish to bury any more."

Before he left, Bishop Lang placed his hands again on Dorris' head and prayed.

~*~

A slight snore jolted Aveline from her near-sleep the next morning. She stirred in Washington's chair that she had dragged by the bed where Dorris lay.

Em had left last night. Save for moral support, there was nothing more she could do. She promised Carissa would come by in the morning to help. Aveline understood Em leaving; she had children, a husband and a wife to care for.

She opened her eyes and rubbed her neck, sore from her head having hung most of the night. The fire had gone out and the cabin was cold. Aveline jumped up, opened the door for the light, and set to start the fire. At the slightest glow, she closed the door to warm the cabin.

She hurried to dip the rag into the cold water and leaned over to dab Dorris' face and throat. Two sunken eyes peered at her below two half-closed lids. Squinting to make sure she wasn't seeing things, she whispered, "Sister Avery?"

A thin croak fell from the cracked lips. "Dorris."

Aveline laughed a half-cry. She choked back tears of joy and kissed Dorris on her cool forehead. She pressed a "praise be" into Dorris' hair.

"Let me fetch you some water and I shall warm some stew. You must be famished." Aveline felt light enough to float to heaven as she dashed around the kitchen to bring Dorris a drink of water and to help her sit up.

She held the ladle so Dorris could sip the cool water. After she eased Dorris back down on the bed, Aveline poked the fire to raise the flame, ladled stew into a small pot, and hung the pot over the flame.

She returned to the bedside and found Dorris' eyes closed. Aveline watched the rise and fall of her chest, deeper than yesterday. She fell to her knees, hands clasped together, to give thanks.

Chapter 21

A week later, Aveline poked the fire, then grabbed the water bucket to fill at the well. She shook out the laundry that had dried overnight while draped over the chairs and folded the clothing. After draping Dorris' clothes on her trunk and her own dress on her bed, she set aside the wood planks Washington brought her to make a table, opened the lid, and slipped in the folded dress. As she knelt, the lace edging from her wedding veil peeked out from under another dress. Lifting it, she studied the cloth and edging and remembered that day — the day she became a plural wife. Pressing the cloth to her cheek, she thought of Frances and her murder. Chief Cane made no progress in solving the killing, or at least he gave her no information. Aveline wondered if the murder had been forgotten.

"I'm going to make a pie today — a pumpkin pie." Dorris was still weak from losing her pregnancy and from the infection she had suffered. She felt stronger every day, but still wobbled when she walked. "I have some dried pumpkin hidden away for just a day like this."

Aveline smiled into the veil pressed against her lips. "That sounds wonderful. Can I help you?"

"No, thank you. It's time I got back to work." Dorris coughed so hard, she had to lean against the table.

"Well, don't tire yourself. I'm here for you." Aveline watched Dorris until she straightened. Aveline placed the veil back into the trunk, dropped the lid, and replaced the plank top.

She still felt the need to tread carefully around Dorris, afraid she would retreat back to that angry, selfish woman.

Since her illness and losing the baby, she had been quiet, gentle, helpful. To her surprise, a couple times Aveline thought that she liked Dorris.

In the first days of Dorris' recovery, Em or Carissa had alternated as they lingered in the Avery household. Aveline had asked for at least one of them to remain to help her. The more Dorris saw how plural wives could help and support each other, the more open to kindness she might remain. After a few days, Aveline hugged Em and Carissa, grateful that Dorris might be easier to live with. So far, her intuition had been right. She worked very hard to clean the cabin, wash clothes, prepare meals, and collect firewood so Dorris could see how helpful Aveline could be. If they worked together, they could have a happy life.

"If you don't mind, I'd like to help Em and Carissa with their quilting. They started several new star quilts. Remember, we're taking them to the Gentile store in Kanesville tomorrow. I'd like to help them get them finished."

"I'm sure they would appreciate the help." She teetered to her chair and breathed heavily from the effort.

Aveline bent and kissed Dorris on the top of her head. "If you don't feel up to baking, I'll help you, or you can wait for a couple days and I'll make you a cake. I'll be back later."

Aveline pulled her shawl over her head and stepped out. She coughed. Taking a deep breath, she coughed harder. The usually incessant breeze blew away smoke from the cabins' fires, but now the air was still and very cold. Like an invisible cap, air pressure forced the smoke down over the town. Winter wind might stir up frozen dirt, but at least the wind kept the air clearer than this smoke-laden pall. The cloud was so thick it felt gritty on her teeth and skin. Coughing, she hurried toward the Paddocks' cabin.

Gravelly coughs sounded from the Fagan cabin, coughs so deep Aveline's lungs hurt to hear it. She stopped. There was a retching sound. If the family needed help, she couldn't just walk away. At her knocks, a raspy "come in" sounded, as if the speaker were being strangled. *Like Frances in her final moment of life.* Aveline dragged open the door and peeked in. "May I help you?"

A form lay in the bed, a figure so slight that the bed still looked made. Standing beside a chair, a skinny young woman leaned on the chair's back and groped her way toward the door. Her cough was as thin as she looked. Ora Fagan croaked, "Good morning, Sister. I never thought I'd wish for a breeze."

Aveline coughed in agreement and nodded. The hacking cough from the bed sounded as if Brother Coal Fagan's insides were being ripped out. Aveline winced at his pain. "Can I help you? Do you need help?"

Sister Ora shook her head and coughed. "My mother will be back soon. She had to go to the bishop's house and the store. She'll be back directly."

"Can I fetch some water for you?" Aveline noted the girl's sallow face.

"Mother filled the bucket before she left. We're fine, Sister." Ora waved a hand, a movement that drained her energy. The hand dropped at her side.

Aveline coughed her acknowledgement. Fireplace smoke roiled into the cabin, not up the chimney. "Is there a problem with your fireplace?" Aveline wiped her tearing eyes, irritated by the smoke.

The woman turned with a stiff body. "It's always smoked. A couple days ago, a brother replaced the canvas roof with a shingle one. It drawed better after that, but today it is worse." She shrugged as if the smoking chimney was another trial to suffer through.

"Call for me if you need help. I'll close the door for you. Goodbye, Sister." Aveline stepped away from the cabin, and rubbed the smoke particles from her eyes.

Blinking fast, she looked over the skyline of the settlement. The sun shone, but a brown light filtered through the dark gray-brown shroud draping the town. The air was too cold not to light the fires, but the cloud trapped every bit of smoke and dirt and forced the haze into living lungs. She looked to the west where most storms materialized and hoped to see clouds building. The sky ended at the horizon. Perhaps the stillness would not last long. Looking back to the Fagan cabin, she wondered how many Saints would sicken from lack of clean air or how many of the sick or weak would not live to see tomorrow.

She slipped her shawl from her head and pressed multiple layers of cloth over her nose and mouth. If she walked slowly, she didn't need to breathe much. No one else was about in the street—no children, no women hanging wet clothes. Except for her, everyone had abandoned the outdoors, although being indoors was not much better.

The door to the Paddocks' stood open and she leaned in. "Hello?"

The three Paddock children and two Paddock wives coughed in response. Carissa motioned for Aveline to enter.

"Do you want the door closed?" Aveline asked.

Em shook her head. "Better to have the door open. If there is a breeze, perhaps it might clear the air." She stood to toss a branch on the fire. "I hate to add to the trapped smoke, but it's too cold for the children and for Carissa."

Aveline looked at Carissa, fearful that she was ill. "Are you not well?"

"Oh, I feel fine, except in the mornings." Carissa laughed and smiled as she watched for Aveline's reaction. Aveline's brow furrowed. She gave a slight gasp as she realized Carissa referred to a morning sickness and was with child. She gave her a quick embrace and asked, "How is this air affecting you?"

"Fine so far, but she will not do as she is told. She's working too hard," Em said as she jumped in the conversation with a pretend fierceness and shook her finger at Carissa. "However, as her time comes closer, she *will* do as she is told when I tell her to rest, even if I have to sit on her."

Em had a half-serious, half-comical look on her face. The image of a woman sitting on a pregnant woman to protect her condition was hilarious. The women laughed until they coughed.

"Will you sit with us? Have some tea." Em placed the kettle over the flame. "Hyrum, take Henry off that chair and put him on my bed."

The eldest son, Hyrum, picked up his little brother in a bear hug and half-carried, half-dragged him to the bed. Henry wailed his protest all the way. He whimpered and looked to the women for comfort but received none. Aveline sat down and glanced about the cabin.

Three adults and three children lived in this cabin the same size as hers. With one husband and three boys to keep clean and in good repair, Em and Carissa fought a continuing battle.

Aveline studied the boys sprawled on the beds. Smoke had collected in the ceiling so the boys couldn't stay in their little loft. She realized she had never figured out which boy belonged to which woman.

Carissa noticed Aveline watching the boys and guessed her thoughts. Softly, she said, "The boys are all Em's."

"This is your second child," Aveline said, remembering that Carissa had lost her infant within moments of birth last fall. She didn't want Carissa to relive the heartbreak, but she was curious how Carissa felt, knowing that one day would be her first time to be with child.

Carissa shook her head and stroked her still-flat belly. "I have two daughters." To Aveline's silence she added, "Faith did not live but four hours. She died two years ago. Hope lived but one moment this past October, which you know about."

"And that is why," Em said loudly to break the painful silence, "Carissa will do as she is told. We hope the Lord will have the 'Charity' to grant us this babe. We shall make every attempt to ensure this child joins the rest of this mob." She swept her hand to indicate the three boys. With all eyes on them, the boys rolled on the bed, giggled, and covered their faces. Carissa held Em's hand and looked up to her.

"We are not quilting today?" Aveline asked. The quilt frame had not been set up.

Carissa shook her head. "We thought it might be too difficult right now. Best to wait until the wind picks up and clears the air. We've managed to finish nearly all the quilts anyway. There are a couple quilts that won't be finished, but, ah, well. We'll still have many to trade. Later this spring, we'll have that many more to trade when we search for exactly what we need for the journey west, so it'll all work out fine."

"I confess I'm looking forward to a night away from Winter Quarters. Seeing something new will be a welcome change," Aveline said.

Em nodded her head. "Something new will be nice. I can't wait to spend some time with my mother and father. That will be wonderful, but I'll worry about this gang o' mine." She lifted her cup to indicate Carissa and the boys.

"We'll be fine." Carissa turned her head and asked loudly, "Won't we, boys? You'll behave so your mother may have a nice time, won't you?"

The center of attention again, the boys covered their faces, snuggled together and giggled. Carissa joined in the giggling. "So, you have a relaxing time, Em. As for now, we can relax for a nice chat. How is Sister Dorris?"

"Oh, so much better. She is still very weak, but she can walk now. She feels strong enough today to want to bake a pumpkin pie." To Em and Carissa's voiced pleasure at the news, she added, "I cannot thank you both enough for what you did for her and me. I'm obliged to you. I hope her seeing how you both work together will cause her to understand how we can live in harmony. She has been kind, helpful this past week."

Coughing, Em walked behind Aveline and patted her shoulder. "I am pleased for you both. We're just happy to make things better for women. We have enough trials."

"Do you know how Caleb Abernethy's children fare?" Aveline asked as she took the offered mug of hot tea. "Thank you, Em. Pa told me the two youngest had the fever. My goodness, that was over a week ago when I went to fetch

Ma to help me with Dorris. I haven't thought about anyone else since."

Carissa sighed and set the cup on her lap. "The fever took the littlest, Carrie. She lost her battle three days ago. Poor child. She would scream with delirium before the Lord ended her suffering." Tears filled her eyes as she unconsciously stroked her still-flat abdomen. "Her older brother, Luke, still suffers. If he survives, we fear he'll be permanently afflicted."

Aveline closed her eyes. "I have been so taken up with caring for Dorris, I haven't thought about anyone else. I feel shame I couldn't do more for the children or Caleb."

Em leaned over and patted Aveline's hand. "Women can only do so much. If the Lord decides the children — or any of us — will go to Him, we shall."

A coughing fit seized Em. Carissa patted her back until Em stopped coughing and caught her breath.

Rubbing her cup's brim, Aveline asked, "Have either of you heard rumors of my sister's murder being solved? Are you aware of any progress?"

A silence as thick as the smoky air hung in the cabin as Em and Carissa studied their cups. They coughed, but Aveline suspected these coughs were excuses to get out of answering. She waited. Carissa caught Em's eye, and Em gave a small nod.

Carissa cleared her throat and sipped her tea. "We heard rumors, not nice rumors. We preferred not to pass them on to you for fear they would hurt you and that they are not correct."

Em took a deep breath and coughed at the effort. "Or worse, if they are." At Aveline's hesitation, Em added, "We don't wish to lose your friendship if we were to tell you what we have heard."

At Em's heartfelt admission, tears filled Aveline's eyes. "I thank you, both of you, for your kindnesses. I wish to know what the people are saying. If the gossip is not correct, I would work to end it. If the gossip is correct …" She became silent, not knowing how to finish.

"Several sisters are saying," Carissa hesitated, "that Frances was a sinner, that only her spilled blood could save her, that the sign of her forgiven sins was the cut from ear-to-ear."

"Blood atonement," Em whispered.

Aveline felt her face grow cold, "Do you believe it?" She whispered back.

"No," Em said loudly. "I heard Frances was not wearing her sacred undergarment when she was found. I know what that sounds like: apostasy, the gravest of sins, but Frances was a plural wife in a marriage to be exalted in heaven. I prefer to think there may be a reason why she was not wearing it. Who knows? She may have soiled it just before the dance and removed it to launder. These things happen."

Em gestured with her teacup. Tea sloshed down the side and spattered the dirt floor. "I know how poorly Eliza treated your sister so perhaps Frances wasn't able to wash it. Add Eleanor to the mix and make the situation worse. Now, *that* I believe."

Aveline nodded, grateful for the approval in how she felt about Frances not wearing her undergarment. *That is what must have happened.*

"Do either of you know Mister Keegan?"

"The Gentile owner of Keegan's Mercantile in Kanesville? Oh, yes. That's who I'm trading our quilts with tomorrow, and your handkerchiefs," Em said. "He is a fair man. Why?"

"I heard Lucas Bates cheated Mister Keegan at a game of chance. Mister Keegan was terribly embarrassed when he lost a great deal of money as well as Frances' hair comb, the comb that we can't find."

Silence hung in the thick air. The dirt tickled Aveline's nose and she sneezed. "Pardon me." Em and Carissa seemed too lost in thought of the possibility of Keegan being the killer to notice.

Em was the first to shake her head. "I cannot hold that thought. Mister Keegan is affluent. I cannot imagine that losing money and a trinket, however precious it may be, would be cause for such a terrible revenge, especially against an innocent wife."

"He may hold a grudge." Carissa appeared to be appalled at her words. She bit her lips, coughed, and took a sip of tea.

"I had considered that," Aveline said. "The money or the comb may not be important to him, but the humiliation of being rooked can drive a man to do bad things."

Except for fits of coughing, the women sat and sipped from their cups. Occasionally, a sneeze erupted from the pile of boys draped on the bed.

"He was at the dance at the Council House before Frances was killed," Aveline offered.

Em said it first. "I heard your husband's handkerchief was found around Frances' neck," her tone conversational, matter-of-fact. She straightened her skirt as if the action were a distraction to keep her emotions in check and the conversation flowing.

Shame washed over Aveline, afraid how such information made her husband look. She nodded. "I cannot reconcile with this. My father said Chief Cane would have to wait until Mister Avery returned from his mission to ask him about it. I have thought about this so long, so often. There was the fight after the Council House. Mister Avery must have dropped the handkerchief." Aveline paused. "If that's true, then it would have been dropped with Mister Keegan there."

Carissa filled the teacups from the kettle.

"Thank you," Aveline and Em said in unison.

Em and Carissa exchanged a long look; their face muscles twitched as they conducted a silent argument. Aveline tensed and tried not to watch too openly as the two women argued over who would say the thing being tossed back and forth in their minds.

Carissa's head gave a slight jerk, her eyelids fluttered and a jerk of her mouth conveyed *No, you say it.*

Em's eyes flared open as if to say *No, you.*

Carissa's lips tightened. *I won't.*

Em cleared her throat. She forced a casual tone in her voice as if she were inquiring how Aveline's bread was rising. "Has Brother Avery mentioned taking another wife?"

The teacup clattered on the saucer in Aveline's lap. Tea spilled onto her dress, but she barely noticed. Her mouth moved, but no words came out.

Em leaned forward and placed her hand on Aveline's knee. "I am sorry to upset you. I heard a rumor —"

"Only a rumor," Carissa chimed in. "It may be false. You said you wanted to know everything we have heard. It may not be true."

"Yes," Em said. "It may be more wickedness from those who wish to add insult to the injury already perpetrated on your family."

The boys wrestled on the bed. Their giggles rose louder until a coughing fit slowed them. "Boys, behave while we have a guest," Em commanded in a stern voice. The silenced boys lay on the bed, draped over each other. Hyrum nudged Henry for more space as they watched the women.

Aveline sipped her tea. She didn't taste it. "I haven't heard anything of the sort. I expect he would approach Sister Dorris of his request first, as required."

A snort erupted from Carissa. "That is the requirement."

"Carissa," Em reproached with soft voice.

To Aveline, Carissa asked, "Have you heard about Sister Eliza Bates?"

"Carissa," Em's voice had a sharp, chastising quality.

"She deserves to know," Carissa protested. She looked at Aveline. "Sister Eliza is not well. Ever since your sister … her health has deteriorated. Sister Beryl Smith lives next door to them. She thinks guilt is weighing on Eliza." Carissa stopped her recitation to judge Aveline's reaction.

Aveline only looked at the dirt floor, not wanting to hear such foul gossip but not wanting to stop her either.

Carissa continued. "Apparently, Eliza and Lucas fight all the time. Sister Beryl said she heard Lucas yelling at Eliza, accusing her of doing the evil deed. Even Eleanor jumped in to accuse her."

"There's a horrifying history there. Eliza and Eleanor are troubled," Em said.

"Deranged is more like it," Carissa muttered and ignored Em's wide-eyed look of chastisement.

This grabbed Aveline's attention. She thought about her last visit to the Bates cabin. "I want to talk to Eliza, but I doubt Lucas would let me. Last we spoke, he refused to let me enter. I don't want to speak with Eleanor. I've never met her, but what little I know, she is frightening."

Em leaned close. "You don't have to worry about Lucas. Mother Young mentioned he left last week on a mission from Brother Brigham. He's not here."

~*~

Aveline pushed the Paddocks' cabin door closed. She had bidden them farewell until the early morning when they would load the quilts and Aveline's handkerchiefs for the journey to Keegan's Mercantile in Kanesville. The lightest of breezes brought a whiff of almost-fresh air. She took a deep, grateful breath. The coughing bout warned her that the thick pall had not yet cleared out, but by moving and breathing slowly, the worst should be over.

Little children toddled past, shepherded by older siblings. Aveline wondered if they breathed cleaner air close to the ground, but a few coughed. She looked to the west. Past the bluffs, small clouds puffed up. Perhaps the wind would rise now. She smiled at herself. Had she ever wished for wind?

As she walked past the Fagan cabin, she noticed Brother Fagan's coughing had stopped.

Chapter 22

Strolling down Woodruff Street, Aveline approached Second Street. She stood at the intersection intending to turn right to her husband's cabin, but with a sudden left turn she walked up Second Street. Squaring her shoulders as she walked, thoughts and accusations tumbled in her mind. She skirted wide around a pack of three dogs fighting over what looked like the remnants of a deer leg.

Right onto Cahoon Street, she made a slight bow to Sister Mary Younger, but did not slow as she walked. "Good morning, Sister, children," Aveline helloed the woman and the three children she herded down the street. Aveline tried not to stare at the woman and children, dirty in their ragged clothes.

The sister did not answer but glared at Aveline. Feeling the staring eyes on her as she walked, Aveline wondered why the woman hadn't responded. She hadn't said anything to anger this woman or made a slight against her. As she got closer to the Bates cabin, she couldn't help but feel the slight was a result of her sister's murder. Could this woman have felt her sister was at fault in her own death?

The thought made Aveline waver in her conviction to speak with Eliza. No matter, Frances deserved to have the truth be told and her killer exposed. She picked up her pace, afraid her bravado would desert her before she reached the Bates' cabin.

At the door, she tried to catch her breath. A slight cough escaped. Before she knew it, her knuckles rapped on the door. No sound. She knocked again, secretly relieved that Eliza was not home. She turned to leave when the door opened.

Carissa had said Eliza was seriously ill, but the stooped skeleton before her was not Eliza. Sunken eyes stared out of a skull's head. A weak cough wheezed from the shallow chest.

"Yes, Sister?" The thin voice cooled Aveline's internal fire to demand information from Eliza.

"Hello, Sister. I am ..." Aveline hesitated to add her name for fear the Bowmore name would anger her. "May I speak with Sister Eliza?"

The woman turned and peered inside the dark cabin. "Liza's not well."

"I heard she is not well." Aveline realized a better excuse to speak with her. "May I see her and if there is something I may do for her? For you?" She realized this was probably Eleanor, the woman who slinked in to assist Eliza beat Frances then scuttled like a frightened cur.

The woman shrugged. "She be afflicted by hay fever, she helped move some straw for Brother Lucas." She stepped backward, slow, and motioned for Aveline to enter.

"May I take over for you for awhile, Sister ...?" Aveline hoped this woman wouldn't answer "Eleanor" and that the woman might leave so she could speak privately with Eliza who might be a murderer or help discover who was. She stepped in the cabin and pulled the door closed behind her and wished she hadn't. The thick stink caused her stomach to retch, but she pretended to cough from the still-smoky air outside. She breathed through her mouth.

"Luddite. Liza's my sister. My—our—father is a member of the Fifties."

Aveline's brow furrowed in the dark cabin. Why would Eleanor ensure Aveline knew their father was high in the church hierarchy? The Council of Fifty was a group of trusted men charged with establishing a new government or in some ministrations. Eleanor must be currying favor by offering such knowledge.

The woman dragged her feet as she led Aveline to the cabin's back corner. The log walls had been neglected. Chunks of chinking were missing. Thin strips of dull light cast jagged dashes of brightness on the room's few furnishings. Despite the drafts of outside air through the large cracks, the stink got stronger as she approached Eliza's bed.

The bed was similar to her parents'. A log frame was wrapped with crisscrossed ropes suspending a straw-filled mattress. The curtain hanging from the purlin to separate the large bed into two spaces had been removed.

Frances had hinted at the stink that emanated from Eliza. Her natural odor must be heightened because of her sickness. A low moan oozed from the bed.

"Hey," Eleanor said with no emotion. She poked at the quilt's long, thin bump. "You have a visitor." Eleanor dragged her feet to the fireplace and let herself fall into a chair.

Aveline realized Eliza hadn't moaned in pain, but had snored. A snort brought quick movement under the quilt. "What?" The question was tiny, almost inaudible.

"Sister Bates, it's Aveline. Aveline—wife of First Counselor Avery, Washington Avery." Aveline stammered, afraid of Eliza's reaction.

"Oh." The voice was weak. The head turned slightly and faced the log wall.

Aveline hiked up her skirt to crawl onto the bed. The ropes groaned from stretching and the mattress sagged from loose ropes. Crouching to get closer to Eliza, she glanced over her shoulder at Eleanor who sat on the chair and faced the fireplace.

Aveline whispered, "I want to know what you know about Frances and her murder."

A small moan came from the head. "Go. I am not long for this world."

Fear ran through Aveline. If Eliza died, there may be no way to solve Frances' murder. But Eleanor said Eliza had a hay fever. "Please, Sister, please find the strength to tell me." She scooted closer to the bed's head, careful not to jostle Eliza.

Several cuts. Not one clean through, but several slight cuts, like someone didn't know what they were doing or was afraid to dig. Hulda Cane's words popped into her head. Aveline sat back and stared at the woman who appeared near death. *Sister Beryl said she heard Lucas yelling at Eliza, accusing her of doing the evil deed.* She shivered at Carissa Clarke's words spoken moments before.

Gulping down a gag from the stench and the thought that the woman who lay before her was her sister's killer, Aveline forced herself to calm down and concentrate on the facts. Possibly a woman made the cuts, too afraid to slice cleanly. Lucas yelling at Eliza that she was a murderess may not mean anything. He could be blowing off his stress. Or would he? Would a man accuse his wife of such a heinous deed if he wasn't sure she had committed it? Aveline didn't know. She had no trust in Lucas' intelligence or self-control.

Would Eliza kill because she hated to share her husband? Would she kill a young wife from jealousy?

"Eliza, if you know anything, please tell me." Aveline waited. The prostrate woman gasped for air. After a moment, Aveline realized Eliza was weeping. Perhaps a certain question might yield real information. "What can you tell me about Frances' hair comb?"

The breathing rose to a higher pitch; Eliza wept harder. She gripped her head with both hands. "My head, so bad."

Why would the hair comb cause Eliza such distress? She touched Eliza. Her fingers burned from the hot flesh. Her fever must be very painful.

Then the killer took it. Lucas' last words rang in her head.

"Do you have the comb, Eliza?"

"No."

"Do you think Mister Keegan hurt Frances?"

"Yes," croaked from the quilt.

Aveline sat back, stunned. She had an answer.

"Why are you making her weep so?" The power behind the words caused Aveline to start. Eleanor dragged her feet toward the foot of Eliza's bed. "I know who you are. You are the sister of the dead Frances." Eleanor sneered the name, a sound that infuriated Aveline. "Leave now."

Aveline turned to Eliza. In a loud voice, not caring how ill they might be, she demanded, "What do you know about the hair comb?"

"Leave!" Eleanor shouted.

"Tell me about Mister Keegan."

"Keegan is a Gentile," Eleanor spit out the words. "He killed our little brother."

"Mister Keegan murdered your brother?" Aveline gasped. *Was he a repeat murderer?*

"Not exactly did he commit the deed, but he is a Gentile. A Gentile split open the head of our brother, just like at Nauvoo, when the hordes were killing our people and slaughtering our beasts. And they did it in cold blood." Eleanor's voice cracked at the memory.

"In Missouri, our brother tried to stop them, the foul-mouthed mob. He tried to reason with them to spare our cow, that we meant no harm to any of them. Instead, they ganged up on him. They taunted him, and they killed him." Tears of anguish poured down Eleanor's sallow cheeks. "He was only thirteen. They left him to die!" Her words ended in screams.

"I cannot fathom how you feel, Sister, but if Mister Keegan did not commit this atrocity to your brother, why are you blaming him now?" Aveline asked, eyes wide and brimmed with tears at the mental image of the boy's murder. She turned to the prostrate woman. "Eliza, just as your family knows injustice, so does mine. You know who did this to my sister. If you did it, just tell me!" Aveline screamed as Eleanor climbed onto the bed's wood frame and grabbed her arm.

Despite her weak appearance, Eleanor commanded the strength to drag Aveline toward the door. The two women grappled, one struggled toward the door, the other to remain in the room.

A wail came from the bed. "I have sinned." Eliza retched. She slumped as she fainted.

Chapter 23

With Eleanor's curses ringing in her ears, Aveline opened the door to her own cabin, hoping she and Dorris were still on good terms. Warm pumpkin scent graced her nose and pulled her spirits from the depths from which they had sunk.

Dorris lifted the washbasin the women used as a sink.

"Let me get that for you," Aveline said as she reached out. "For the scent of that heavenly pie, I'll do the cleaning. You rest and I'll just breathe deeply," she said with a big smile. Beside the politeness Aveline had been trained to exude, she felt she must tread carefully around Dorris. She would work very hard to ensure the woman could comprehend her best intentions.

With a thunk, Dorris set the full basin down on the table, staggered to her rocking chair and fell into it. "I declare I never thought I'd see the day that making a pie would tucker me out." The loss of all her teeth muffled her words. Her gums and cheeks slapped together as she talked. She exhaled loudly and almost panted to catch her breath.

"You're still recovering. You were so sick. I was terrified for you," Aveline said, honestly, as she went out the door. She draped the wood bucket's handle over her left arm and realized she had overloaded her arms by carrying the full washbasin as well. Before she'd got to the door, the bucket's heft dug painfully into her thin forearm muscle. She set the bucket beside the door. "I'll refill the bucket as soon as I dump the basin."

By the time the empty water basin was back under the table and the full water bucket lugged to its place on the stump, Aveline felt lightheaded from the effort. Motionless, she concentrated on breathing slow. A moment passed and with it so passed her dizziness. "I'll make up your bed so you can sleep in your own bedding."

Dorris craned her stiff neck to see Aveline. "I had no idea how much colder it is by the door."

Pleased Dorris had noticed her cold nights, Aveline shrugged and smiled. "Someone must sleep there. It's not your place to sleep there; you're the first wife. You should get the warmer spot." Dragging Washington's chair closer to Dorris, she laid her hand on Dorris' skinny arm. She hoped her words and her movement would convey her acknowledgement of Dorris' superior ranking.

Dorris said nothing, but laid her hand over Aveline's. Both women sat in their chairs and stared at the fire.

~*~

That evening, Aveline removed the three planks that made up a table by her bed. With the trunk lid open, she carefully removed her stack of handkerchiefs she had made since living in the Avery household. She would trade them tomorrow at Keegan's Mercantile in Kanesville. They lay flat in the trunk to prevent any new wrinkles and to make ironing any wrinkles easier. Nervousness bubbled in Aveline's stomach. She had never traded anything as a responsible adult and at a real store.

She had never been to Kanesville, and the trek across Iowa Territory to Winter Quarters was an ordeal that still whirled in her mind. Accidents, deprivations, foul weather, and disease took so many Saints. Now, after months of Winter Quarters' dreary sameness, heading to Kanesville felt like she was stepping out on the town at a new and exotic locale. She took great comfort knowing Em would help her handle the trade at Keegan's Mercantile. A night at Em's parents' home would be a welcome change.

A slight snore filtered through the quilt curtain between Aveline and Dorris' beds. Earlier, the two women had sat for the longest time holding hands, not saying anything. Tears formed in Aveline's eyes in the tenderness that had developed.

She hoped they would continue to be compatible and draw even closer. Sadness stabbed at Aveline's heart as she missed that closeness with her sister.

In the evening, Aveline had heated more stew for dinner, and they almost finished Dorris' pumpkin pie. Even Dorris exclaimed how delicious the stew and the treat tasted. After patting her belly, Aveline made Dorris' bed and insisted the older woman lie down. While Dorris settled into her fresh sheets, Aveline needed to prepare for the journey tomorrow.

Quietly, she stoked the fire and set the iron above the flames … not too close; she didn't want soot on the iron that would smear blackness onto the pure white fabric. She washed the table and carefully checked the wood to make sure no soil or food remnants could stain her cloths. She dug through her trunk for the scrap cotton towel and draped the large cloth on the table to protect the planks and for a smoother finish on the handkerchiefs. One by one, she sprinkled water from the bucket onto the fabric and ironed them rigid. When she finished a cloth, she examined it for perfection. Soon, a stiff stack of lacy handkerchiefs rose over the table.

She pulled out her three dresses from the trunk and selected the brown wool, plain and most modest. Her dress and her handkerchiefs were ready for the morning. She replaced the lid and the planks.

A shuffling sound made Aveline look up. Dorris stood at the end of the curtain, backlit by the fire. The light shone through Dorris' thin nightgown, highlighting her gauntness.

"I watched you iron your handkerchiefs. I have been most negligent in telling you how beautiful they are." She bowed her head. "I shamed myself in how I acted when you presented me with such a treasure at Christmas. I thank you and humbly beg your pardon."

Tears filled and overflowed in Aveline's eyes. She held Dorris, letting herself weep with gratitude and tenderness. Aveline helped Dorris back into her bed and tucked her in for the night.

Chapter 24

Aveline gasped as the cold mist splashed her face. The brisk breeze sucked the air from her lungs and made her lose her breath. She pressed against the wagon wheel. The ferry was a flat log platform with no railing. The thought of falling in the Missouri River frightened her. The platform bumped its way across the choppy river.

The dampness and wind invigorated the two women. Aveline and Em giggled like little girls; they pointed out ducks, and cautiously approached the ferry's edge to squat and dabble their fingers in the wave pushed up by the ferry's leading edge. Aveline turned to look at Winter Quarters, Missouri Territory. The log cabins had a sad quality in their uniform blocks. Wanting a respite from the settlement, she turned her attention to the other side of the river. For a short time, the pain and deprivation of Winter Quarters would not be a part of her life.

Wistful, Em said, "I wish Carissa were here. She'd love to play in the water." Aveline smiled at the thought of a grown woman playing like a little girl, but Carissa's pregnancy was so tenuous she was to remain at home rather than jolt along on a long wagon ride to Kanesville and then on to Em's parents' house. Carissa had wept this morning as they packed the wagon. She would likely never see her adoptive parents again.

The ferry bumped the newly proclaimed State of Iowa. Em led the horses and wagon off and turned the horses south. Aveline hung on to the wagon seat's edge with all her might or risk being thrown from the wagon. Heavy rain the previous week had turned the dirt road into soft muck, and the wheels from the high traffic had caused deep ruts. The wagon wheels slipped into the crisscrossing dried ruts and threatened to turn over the wagon; at least, it felt that way. The sun peeked over the southeastern horizon. The thick frost, almost a hoarfrost, glistened in the early light. She breathed out through her mouth and watched the fog trail behind her.

As they rode past farmhouses, Aveline studied each one. She envied the solid homes, their windows, the farms' distant outbuildings, and Iowa's wide, rolling spaces. Both women fell silent, each consumed with her own thoughts.

While Kanesville jiggled closer, Aveline's excitement escalated to see a new settlement.

Wagon traffic increased and Aveline waved at each passing one. Em had been to Keegan's Mercantile before so she drove there. The business of selling or trading the quilts and handkerchiefs came first.

"Ho, hoss," Em moaned low to her two workhorses as she pulled on the reins. The east-facing sides of the settlement's buildings defrosted under the sun's spring intensity. The other buildings' sides were still frosted. Aveline shielded her eyes from the sun's glare as she stared up at the tall building. The glistening white false front proclaimed in thick black letters *Keegan's Mercantile.*

Em tied the horses to the hitching post and lifted her skirt's hem to step up onto the boardwalk. A thin bell tinkled when she pushed open the door, and Aveline followed her in. Warm air enveloped the women and each took a deep breath in surprise at the warmth. A woodstove in full blaze stood in the middle of the huge room. The stove door's air vents rumbled low and glowed an angry red.

Splashes of color greeted them from the wide array of goods stored on shelves, in bins, on bins, behind glass, on counters, or hung from the walls or the ceiling. Aveline's eyes popped. Even Em stopped in wonder. Her hands brushed the bolts of cloth on a table; her knuckles tapped the metal bowls and her fingers stirred the beans in an open barrel.

"Good morning, ladies. How may I help you?"

The question jarred them from their wonderment. A clerk, likely in his early twenties, stood at the back end of the store where he had emerged from a room. The tall young man had a twinkle in his eyes and sported the shadow of a mustache. Aveline's lips curled in a small smile as she fought the urge to take a wet rag and wipe off the smudge.

"Loyal Keegan, Thomas Keegan's son," Em whispered.

Em introduced herself and presented Aveline, who bobbed a curtsy. He responded with a slight bow and a smile.

"We're here to sell or trade some goods," Em said, getting down to business. "I have quilts of varying sizes and Sister Aveline," Em indicated Aveline, "has the most exquisite handkerchiefs."

"Wonderful! We always look forward to you ladies' quilts. In our experience, your goods have been of excellent quality." To Aveline he said, "I'll clear some space on this counter for you and help you bring in your wares. I'll see what you have. After that I'll get my father; he will confirm the deal."

After four trips lugging armloads of heavy quilts, Aveline left Em with Loyal, and collected her gratefully light stack of handkerchiefs from the wagon. She stood behind Em and listened to her deft handling of her business, then wandered around the store, coveting everything, wishing she could buy it all.

"The pleasure is all mine, Master Keegan." Em's words meant the business of selling the quilts was concluded.

Aveline waited while Loyal moved the quilts to a space across the store. Nervousness spiked at how he would receive her meticulous work. She watched Loyal approach her handkerchiefs stacked on the counter. His mouth opened as he stared at the top cloth. He stepped back to stare at Aveline, transfixed. His eyes widened in disbelief. *He does not appreciate my work*, Aveline worried. She looked to Em who also seemed confused by Loyal's reaction.

"Aveline," he said so low as to be a whisper.

She nodded, not knowing what to say.

His face paled. "Bowmore."

Aveline nodded again.

He cleared his throat and looked at Em. "Ma'am, would you excuse us, please?"

Em nodded, open curiosity in her face. "Certainly." She moved away to the bolts of cloth near the door, but kept watching Aveline and Loyal.

Loyal's mouth worked, but he seemed uncertain how to begin. Finally, he croaked, "I knew your sister. I give you sincere condolences. You miss her, I'm sure."

"Frances. Thank you. Yes, I miss her terribly." Aveline choked back the makings of a sob. "Is she why you asked Sister Paddock to move away? If it is, it wasn't necessary, but I appreciate your thoughtfulness."

Loyal shook his head. With a slow hand, he reached into his jacket pocket and pulled out a cloth. He concentrated on unfolding it as if to conserve a precious artifact.

White linen, edged in tatted lace—tiny rings swayed like little pearls.

Loyal watched Aveline's face as he unfolded the handkerchief to display embroidered initials: *FCB*. Frances Cooper Bowmore. The B for Bates had been picked out.

Aveline's eyes widened. "What are you doing with Frances' handkerchief?"

With level eyes, Loyal said, "Frances gave this to me. I am the one Frances was going to marry."

Aveline gripped the counter's edge. Her brow furrowed. Her throat tightened. "What foulness are you playing at? My sister was already married!" Aveline's voice rose. "Give me that." She made a grab for the handkerchief, but Loyal snatched the cloth out of her reach.

"No. Forgive me, but you may not have this." He glared at Aveline. "She *gave* this to me, freely. Didn't her letter to you explain her feelings?"

"What letter?" Aveline whispered. *She wrote a letter?*

He glanced at Em, who still stood near the bolts of cloth, but now openly watched their discussion.

"Don't mind Sister Paddock," Aveline snapped. On the way home, she'd tell Em everything this boy said anyway. "What letter?" Emotions whirled within her.

"Frances said she wrote a letter to you and to your parents." He paused. "She was leaving the Saints — for me."

His words made no sense as the room darkened and swirled. Her mouth worked, but no sounds emerged.

"You didn't get a letter?"

Aveline shook her head.

"This is the first you have heard of her leaving?"

Aveline whispered, trying to shove away memories of Frances' anguish. "I knew she was unhappy in the extreme …"

Loyal bowed his head and closed his eyes. Seconds passed as he seemed to struggle to collect his thoughts. "I'm sorry that you have to hear about it like this from me. Frances came here almost every other week with her baskets from the braid shop, usually with another sister. Once she came with a man, but he spent the day elsewhere. Then one week, most of the women in the shop had a sickness. Frances was the only one well enough to make the journey. We spent the day talking. Each time she came to trade, after we conducted our business, our lingering stretched longer and longer. We grew to hate her return to Winter Quarters. I confess I loved her. She loved me. I promised to make her happy. I know she was most unhappy in her situation. She had bruises." He focused on the handkerchief as he fingered the lace. In a low voice he said, "She gave me this." He stroked the edging and watched the lace shimmer. He held up the cloth. "She said 'this exquisite cloth is my most valued possession. It is my gift to you'."

"Why didn't she just tell me of her plans?" The whisper tumbled from Aveline's lips.

"She knew how devout you are, how faithful your family is. She was ashamed she wasn't strong enough to bear her situation." He blinked back tears. "She was embarrassed."

Tears flooded Aveline's eyes and poured down her cheeks. A sob burst from her chest. Frances had suffered at the Bateses' hands, so much so she decided to run away with another man—Aveline looked up, horrified. *Infidelity: a sin punishable by death.* She gripped the counter's edge tighter.

Loyal seemed to read Aveline's mind. "Nothing untoward happened between us. Know this: we only spoke of our love. Frances was committed to proper behavior, as I am. She *never* acted inappropriately. I never acted inappropriately." He glanced at Em. "We never even kissed."

Aveline took a breath, relieved and grateful to know the great sin of infidelity hadn't occurred. "Frances was going to leave us and come here. Nothing else happened?"

"I swear on her sweet soul."

"Well, Sisters. Good morning!" Thomas Keegan stepped out with a big smile from behind the curtain and greeted Aveline and Em, arms wide.

His entrance jolted Aveline from her shock. Loyal stood back from the counter in deference to his father. He folded the handkerchief and slipped the treasure into his pocket. Em walked toward the rear of the store toward him. With a business air, she said, "Good morning, Mister Keegan. Loyal has been most generous this morning. I trust he will be as equally generous with Sister Bowmore's trade."

"Bowmore?" Thomas Keegan muttered, trying to place the name. His eyes widened in recognition.

Loyal stammered, "Father, this is Aveline Bowmore, Frances' sister."

Aveline watched Keegan carefully as she bobbed a curtsy. Was he her sister's killer?

Keegan's red face accentuated the healed scrapes across his fleshy cheeks. His lips tightened. A small cut across his nose looked like it refused to heal. *Is that another fresh wound?* Aveline felt the heat of his rising anger.

Why would he be angry at me or my sister? She decided to push the issue. "Mister Keegan, are you angry with me?"

The blunt question seemed to break Keegan from his flush of wrath. "No, my dear, I am not."

"Are you angry with my sister?"

At this question, Em turned to Aveline in bewilderment, but she said nothing.

Keegan's face turned almost purple. "Let me offer my sincere condolences. I am sorry to hear of your sister's death. She was a kind, lovely woman. But yes, I am very angry and disappointed in her family."

His last words unsettled Aveline. "May I ask, sir, why you would be angry at Frances or my family? She never hurt anyone." Her voice trailed off as she recalled her sister was getting ready to do just that by deserting her husband and her sister-wife, her sister and parents, and her faith, for a Gentile.

Keegan looked from Aveline to Em, unsure whether he should answer.

"Sir, you may say anything in front of Sister Paddock," Aveline said. "Please answer."

Keegan nodded. "As you wish. Bates' wife stole from me." He held up his hands. "There it is."

"Never!" Aveline cried. "You must be mistaken."

"I'm ashamed to say I like my game of faro, but it is my only vice. Her husband, Lucas Bates …" Keegan sneered the name. "… is a cheat. He cheated me out of much money and a valuable hair comb."

Em jumped in. "Why, sir, would you blame the wife? A wife cannot control what her husband does."

Keegan snorted. "Mister Bates said he had to cheat. His plural wife ordered him to obtain money and the hair comb she had seen here that she desired above all else. That was the only way she would accept the condition of marriage."

"No Mormon woman can or would order her husband to commit such an act."

Keegan studied Em. "Sometimes a small Mormon woman has a bigger backbone than a big Mormon man."

~*~

Em slapped the reins against the horses' rumps, "Hey, yep." They rode in silence out of town. She occasionally looked over at Aveline.

Aveline's grand adventure to Kanesville had spiraled into a nightmare. A day that started with high hopes crashed in the realization that her sister was an apostate. The only reason for her not wearing their symbol of devotion was that she had chosen to remove her sacred undergarment and to run away. Aveline didn't know what hurt more: that her sister had apostatized, that she was running away from her family, or that Frances couldn't tell her sister to her face about both.

The Bowmores weren't life-long Mormons, Aveline thought. They hadn't been born into the belief. The Book of Mormon had appeared only seventeen years earlier, the year of Frances' birth.

As a family, they had been baptized three years ago. They had been Quakers. Ma and Pa had been particularly drawn to Joseph Smith and the community of Saints. The Bowmore family had been baptized into the Mormon family, sold the Pennsylvania farm, tithed their ten percent to the church, and headed toward Nauvoo, Illinois—then the Saints' spiritual center.

Staring at the rhythmic rolling of the horses' rumps, Aveline realized she couldn't condemn Frances. Of the Bowmores, Frances had voiced the greatest indecision about converting. She had wanted to be a Quaker wife with almost equal standing in a marriage. When Ma and Pa announced they would head west with the Saints, Frances didn't want to remain behind alone. Likely, she wasn't devoted, although outwardly she tried her best. Soon after their conversion, she had been forced to endure her greatest trial. *Polygamy: A salvation to some, an abomination to others.*

Aveline shook her head. No, she couldn't blame Frances for escaping her intolerably abusive marriage and wanting a gentle, young man and the promise of a happier life. Apostasy aside, Frances hadn't deserved her violent death.

Thinking back to Thomas Keegan, would he kill Frances, the reason for his being cheated in a card game? A horrific deed as murder to avenge a loss at cards was unfathomable, yet perhaps the blow to his ego was enough.

His son, Loyal, seemed devoted to Frances. *What did his father think about his son falling in love with a Mormon plural wife? Well, a former Mormon.* Rumors flew in Winter Quarters that Thomas Keegan was a fair man and treated the Saints well, but a business dealing was a different dog than his son marrying a married woman.

A deep rut jolted the wagon so hard Aveline was almost pitched off the seat. She gripped the edge and concentrated on keeping her backside on the bench. She glanced over at Em, who watched her. "You all right?" Em asked.

Aveline shook her head. "I'm trying to reconcile everything that's happened."

"Quite a shock." Changing the subject to a happier thought, Em said, "You were quite profitable with your handkerchiefs. Mister Keegan was very generous."

Aveline laughed. It was a release that felt good. "I am amazed. Two dollars for each cloth!" Keegan paid her a queenly sum. Whether he tried to ingratiate himself or if her pieces were really worth that much, she didn't care.

She'd earned enough money to buy goods for the Avery family's journey west, gifts for Washington, Dorris, and her parents, and would settle the Avery family's tithing to the church. In the spring, she would head west and never see the Keegans or Winter Quarters again.

Em and Aveline said little on the way to Em's parents' farm. They had purchased it after they left Pennsylvania and decided to settle in Iowa. Though they were getting on in years, Em said, they thought they could help the Saints more by setting up a dairy farm to supply traveling Saints and other west-moving pioneers with milk, cheese, and beef.

They turned east off the road that led to the ferry. Ten miles down the road, a two-story house stood, proud with its fresh coat of white paint. The deep porch gave the structure a stature that belied its small size. Outbuildings larger than the house, the barn and myriad sheds, were clustered behind the house. A split-rail fence corralled dairy cows beyond the outbuildings.

An older woman pushed open the door to the house. Her arms flung wide as she lurched down the porch steps. A thin shriek erupted. "Em!"

Em and Aveline jumped down from the wagon. Aveline stayed back as she watched the reunion. Em was a taller, straighter version of her mother. She clung to her mother in a lingering embrace. With a sigh, Em turned to present Aveline, who curtsied deeply. Hannah Rander clasped her hands in delight at the curtsy. Her nose wrinkled in happiness, an imp in a long cotton dress, thin from years of wear.

"Grandmother," Aveline murmured a name of respect with a big smile. Hannah threw open her arms and embraced Aveline. All three women giggled.

"Come, come," Hannah struggled up the steps. Em and Aveline each took one arm and helped her. Hannah led each woman by the hand through the house, pointing out the treasures she and Em's father brought from Illinois. In the back room was her kitchen, a small space sparkling with cleanliness. Hannah turned to Aveline, never letting go of her hand, "Cleanliness is next to Godliness." She wrinkled her nose while she nodded her head. "Yes?"

Hannah pulled the women into a small room. A straw mattress lay on the floor. "I couldn't bring the bedstead." She put her face near Aveline's and whispered, "It wouldn't stay balanced on top of the wagon." Aveline giggled. "You'll sleep in here tonight."

Already prepared, Hannah had set out a sumptuous meal, a chunk of beef as big as Aveline's head, fried potatoes and onions, and a pitcher of milk. Em and Aveline weren't used to seeing or eating such quantity. "Put some of this beef on your bones," Hannah chirped as she gripped Em's and Aveline's arms.

Em's father, Juble, came in just as Hannah set the steaming biscuits on the table. Aveline's stomach grumbled, a noise she hoped went unnoticed. Juble resembled his wife, only taller and he wore pants. His blue eyes sought out mischief, likely his favorite pastime. With an embrace for Em and a bow to

Aveline, he dived into the meal, declaring how famished he was from the long day of chores.

"Eat, eat," Hannah motioned. "I'll wrap up meat and vegetables to take with you." Em perked up. Vegetables were a godsend for her children. They had eaten few vegetables during the hard winter and their bodies were the poorer for it. At least the black canker, or scurvy, had stayed away from the Paddock cabin. "Thank you, Mother." Em reached for her mother's hand.

"Pshaw." Hannah waved her hands, "Them's my grandbabies you're talking about. They need their vegetables. I have apples—a half bushel." She looked at Aveline. "I have some for you too."

By late evening, Aveline's stomach ached from too much food. Used to small portions, the feast was too much, but she refused to groan or complain. Many Saints across the river were hungry that evening. The fireplace blazed, and she sat quietly in the corner of the living room while Em caught up her parents about the Paddock family and the occupants of Winter Quarters. She left out Frances' murder in her litany. From the wagon, Em presented them with a star quilt Carissa had stitched by herself as a gift to her adoptive parents. After Juble and Hannah exclaimed over the workmanship and the fabrics' colors, Juble draped it over their bed. "We'll sleep well with such love keeping us warm," he declared.

As a clock chimed eight, Juble rose. His eyelids and shoulders drooped from fatigue. He wished the women a good night. Em looked with love at her father after they embraced, and he kissed her cheek. He'd be up and out in the field before "you girls" got up. He tottered on tired legs to his room.

Aveline stood. "I'll bid you a good night." She held Hannah's hand in a lingering clasp before she turned to the bedroom. Hannah and Em, mother and daughter, needed private time.

Aveline snuggled into the cold sheets as she scooted close to the wall. She smiled at the darkness; she had forgotten that

Em came from such mirthful stock. As the sheets warmed and her muscles relaxed, she slipped into the deepest sleep she'd had in months.

The next morning, at first light, Aveline slipped out of bed. She glanced over expecting to see Em sleeping, but her side of the bed was rumpled and empty.

~*~

Aveline wished her corset weren't so tight. Hannah's breakfast spread matched the quantity of the dinner the night before. "Allow me, Grandmother." She hurried to her feet to beat Hannah to the coffee pot. Hannah waved at Aveline, "You relax, deary."

Juble had eaten breakfast an hour before Aveline got up from the straw bed. He was already in the field. The girls pushed back from the table with great reluctance. "May I at least help you clean up?"

Hannah waved Aveline away from the table. "Thank you, my dear, but you two have a long way to go."

Em and Aveline assisted Hannah down the porch stairs. Aveline stifled her giggles at Hannah's persistent chirping as she pointed out the now-empty hummingbird nest in the mulberry bush, but she hoped to see it in use in a few months. Hannah nodded in another direction. "That old cottonwood knocked over two weeks ago will make right handy benches for the porch, but at least the neighbor's mongrel won't come over anymore to relieve itself."

At the wagon, Hannah surprised Aveline with a strong embrace. Aveline dug into her pocket to pull out two handkerchiefs to give to Hannah and Juble as a gift for their hospitality. "I hate to leave you and Grandfather," Aveline meant her words with every fiber of her being as she offered the cloths to Hannah. *I love these dear people.*

Gasps of pleasure erupted from Hannah. Her voice rose as she squealed how the lace turned to gossamer in the sun's light, like a white butterfly. Then, her voice lowered as she exclaimed over the workmanship. She clutched the cloths to her chest. Her nose wrinkled and eyes twinkled as she reached for Aveline.

Aveline bent in a deep curtsy, and Hannah tucked her chin down to her chest and gave a wide smile. Aveline stepped aside to allow privacy to mother and daughter, and climbed aboard the wagon. After a few moments, Em scrambled up. She picked up the reins and wiped her pouring eyes. With a gentle "Hey, yup" and a slap of the reins on the horses' rumps, the wagon lurched as they headed home.

Em blew her mother a kiss and Aveline turned to wave. The wagon headed west toward the road to the ferry. Aveline looked away as Em sniffled. Likely, they'd never see each other again. After moments of silence Aveline turned. "Your parents are wonderful. I love them. You must be very happy."

Em gave a quick chuckle. "When I was younger, I used to be embarrassed by them. Yes," she said at Aveline's open-mouthed expression of surprise. "They were always so happy, silly. Nothing got them down. They were supposed to be stern, unemotional, like everyone else's parents. That was the rule. One day they were sick with chills and fever from the pneumonia." Em's eyes filled and overflowed. She whispered, "They were so close to death." She cleared her throat. "But the Lord blessed us and they lived. Ever since then, I treasure their happiness. Now, I wish I could be more like them."

"We must cherish our families, even with all their faults," Aveline said, realizing such a statement included her family and herself. An ache welled within her chest. Frances was gone forever. With a pang, she wanted her parents and Bedford with her.

They rode in silence to the ferry. Em paid the ferryman and led the horses and wagon onto the ferry. Both women knelt at the ferry's edge and stared into the muddy water. Aveline put her arm around Em and leaned into her. "I so appreciate you."

Em smiled a melancholy smile and patted Aveline's arm.

There was no girlish behavior.

Chapter 25

The sun's dying light reflected off the clouds to the west. A pink glow bounced over Winter Quarters, casting an aura of joy over the unbroken brownness of the log buildings and dirt roads. Yet as Aveline studied the Saints going about their business, her heart sank as their faces reflected the same palatable hardships.

Em pulled up the horses at Aveline's cabin. Bumping open the cabin door with her foot, Aveline carried a load of purchased goods into the dark, cold cabin.

"Dorris?"

The cabin was empty. After a few more trips to the wagon to unload treasures, Aveline's adventure to Kanesville was over.

"The boys can help me unload when I get home," Em said after Aveline's offer to unload her supplies.

As Em slapped the reins, Aveline raised her hand. "Farewell, Em, and thank you."

In the cabin, Aveline built and started the fire. Too tired to put away her purchases, a wave of dizziness and overwhelming fatigue washed over her. She collapsed onto Washington's chair.

After a rest, she'd tackle the chore of putting things away.

With a start, Aveline realized she had nodded off. The weariness and excitement of the journey were gone. She poked the fire and added a branch to the blaze. She bent over her trunk to store her frayed wool shawl. Her new wool shawl hung on a nail by the door.

The cabin door opened. "Dorris! Come see what I brought you," Aveline cried out. "You won't believe what Mister Keegan gave me for my handkerchiefs!"

"You went to Keegan's Mercantile?" The deep voice jolted Aveline and she nearly fell into her trunk.

Washington stood in the doorway's light. Behind him, Dorris peered around him.

"Mister Avery. You're home, safe. I'm so grateful," Aveline stammered. Dumbfounded by his surprise appearance, she couldn't remember how to act around him. "When did you return?"

"Yesterday. I expected you here," his voice threatening.

Nervous about Washington's anger and recalling his fight with Keegan, Aveline decided to sidetrack Washington by acting excited about her success. "Sister Paddock took me to Kanesville. Mister Keegan gave me *two dollars* for each of my handkerchiefs." She leaned back to pooch out her stomach and lower her voice to better imitate Thomas Keegan. "He said they were 'the most exquisite I have ever seen'." She looked at Dorris. "You should see what I brought you—"

"Enough!" Washington pulled the door closed. "I forbid you to go there again. Do you understand? You will never go back there. Ever."

Aveline did not expect to go back to Kanesville again, let alone Keegan's Mercantile. "All right." She shrugged, curious about the purpose of his adamant order.

"Do not shrug at your Lord," he growled.

Frightened at his anger and confused about the reason for it, Aveline took care to not move her shoulders. She clasped her hands tightly. "Yes, sir."

Washington stared at Aveline a moment longer. He held out his arms. "I missed you."

Aveline stepped forward to embrace Washington and lightly patted his back. As she pulled away, Dorris cast her eyes to the floor and covered her mouth with her hand. Had the hateful woman returned with her husband?

"Come see what I brought." Aveline grabbed Dorris' hand and tugged her to the table. "Here's a new cooking pot and a new washbasin. See? No jagged edge on the basin. No more cutting our hands! And this is for you." Aveline spun around and lifted her prize. "A bolt of silk for a new blouse." She lifted one end of the dark cloth and wriggled it in front of the flames' light. "The deep green—watch how it shimmers."

With hesitation, Dorris flicked her eyes toward Washington. She reached for the bolt. "This is so beautiful. I should feel like a queen wearing this."

As Aveline leaned in to accept Dorris' quick embrace, she noticed her swollen eyelids. Dorris hurried behind the quilt curtain to lay the bolt on her bed.

Washington sat on his chair and gave Aveline an expectant look.

"Oh. I brought you something too, of course!" She hurried to her trunk to retrieve the gift. With both hands, she held out the knife.

He accepted the hunting knife and fit his hand around the handle. He slowly unsheathed it, reflecting the fire's light off the blade, and flicked his thumb along the blade. "Sharp."

"I saw your old knife. It's been sharpened so many times it's curved. It's a wonder it cuts at all." *Several cuts. Not one clean through.* Hulda Cane's description of the slashes on Frances' neck popped into her head. She shook her head to rid her mind of the words and image.

Washington rubbed the sheath.

"It's buffalo hide. Mister Keegan said buffalo leather is indestructible."

At the mention of Keegan, Washington glanced at Aveline and slid the blade into the sheath. "Yes, this blade can do some damage. A most useful gift. Thank you," he said with a nod.

Aveline nodded. "I take it your mission was successful?"

"Yes."

"What did you accomplish?" Aveline asked.

Washington cleared his throat. "I have instructed you that such things are not the business of women. If it were, likely you would not have the sense to comprehend it."

Aveline's eyes bugged at Washington's chastisement immediately after presenting him with a gift and so soon after his return. An uneasy silence fell over the cabin. Dorris sat in her rocking chair. Aveline sat on her bed, shielded in part by the hanging quilt. She closed her eyes and imagined she was back at the Randers' Iowa dairy farm.

For the remainder of the evening no one said anything. No one moved until Washington stood before Aveline's bed.

~*~

The next morning, Aveline awoke to the scent of sizzling bacon. The aroma caused her mouth to water.

She threw back the covers and winced at her stiffness from the jarring wagon ride. She clambered into her boots and pulled on her robe.

"Dorris, let me help you." She ignored her queasy stomach. "Good morning, Mister Avery," Aveline said to her fully dressed husband who sat in his chair.

"Good morning." He nodded.

Dorris tossed another branch on the fire and turned back to the table. A mound of flour stood tall. Into the hollow at the top, she dribbled buttermilk. Barely glancing over her shoulder, she said, "You had a long day yesterday and a hard week. It's your turn to rest."

Aveline patted Dorris on the back. "I'll make the coffee." After she roasted and ground the beans, she poured them in the pot's strainer.

She turned to Washington. "I have enough money left over from my handkerchiefs to pay our tithing."

She felt a glow of pride in her ability to help the family. "I'll go to Bishop Lang and pay it today."

Washington squinted. "You'll do nothing of the kind. Give me the money. I will pay the bishop."

Aveline shrugged and remembered she wasn't supposed to. She lowered her shoulders even more to counteract the shrug. "I worked very hard on those handkerchiefs to raise the money. I figure I'd like the honor of helping this family."

"It is your duty to work for this family."

"While you were absent, it was our responsibility to pay the tithing," Aveline said, meaning Dorris and herself. "Now we must step aside for your glory after working so hard?"

Washington's face contorted in anger. He stared into Aveline's eyes. "What manner of instruction have you received that you do not know this?"

Aveline didn't know how to answer. His low voice sounded like a dog's growl just before it bit. She feared that no matter her answer, he would strike her. She said nothing and focused on her hands.

"Bring me the money."

In the heavy silence, she lifted the lid of her trunk, retrieved her reticule and rifled the stack of bills. With a glance to ensure Washington wasn't watching, she tugged out three bills, slipped them into a section of underwear in her trunk, and took the purse to him. He pulled out the bills and poured out the coins onto his palm. He counted them then stuffed the money into his vest pocket. He handed the empty purse back to Aveline. She tossed it into her trunk, replaced the planks on the lid, sat on her bed and fumed.

"Bishop Lang wrote me about Frances," Washington said.

Aveline waited for him to say "I am sorry," or "May she rest in peace," but he said nothing. Already angry at not receiving appreciation for what was a triumphant amount of money for her work, then chastised for not obeying his commands, she now faced an insulting silence about her dead sister.

She turned to face Washington's back, "Where is your handkerchief?"

Washington stiffened. He didn't bother to turn to look at her. "I gave it to Keegan."

Aveline swallowed hard and thought about all the care she put into his gift. She fixated on the flame in the hearth. By now, she knew not to question her husband directly on important issues so she chose her words carefully. "May I ask why you would give my gift to you to him?"

Washington shifted in his chair. "Bring me coffee."

Aveline shot off the bed so quickly she stumbled. Chagrined, she pulled a cup from the hook on the wall. She filled it and, with both hands, offered it to Washington.

He took the cup and blew on the hot liquid to cool it. "To sop his blood."

Aveline felt like she'd been slapped in the face. Her hands tightened into fists. "You used my gift *to sop his blood*?" She panted from shock. "Why were you fighting?"

"Aveline," Dorris said, her voice timid in warning.

"I wish to know."

"You are very fortunate I wish to tell you," Washington leaned toward Aveline. "Keegan accused Brother Lucas of cheating at a game of cards. I won't stand for it." He leaned back and sipped his coffee.

"Isn't that an issue between those two men?"

Washington almost smiled at the fire. "We must defend a Saint against a Gentile, in all things, always."

With a supplicant's voice, Aveline asked, "But why would you give him my gift to you?"

"It pleased me to know I had drawn Gentile blood and that it stained my handkerchief."

Her already-roiling stomach churned. She recalled that night of the Council House dance. "When you and Frances were dancing, she seemed very upset, almost crying. Why?"

Washington blew on his coffee. "Your sister sought my counsel about how abusive and insulting Sisters Eliza and Eleanor treated her. She felt she couldn't tell you and she desired that I should. I counseled her to remain with her husband, that it was her duty to submit to him."

Tears formed in Aveline's eyes. "Did she tell you why she couldn't tell me?"

"Frances said she revered you for being a devoted, obedient plural wife, while she failed to be as strong." Washington spoke as if he was dictating his journey's travels rather than discussing the hours before a woman's murder. He spun in his chair and faced her. For several seconds, he studied her. His mouth tightened before he spun back around. "I do not see what she saw."

A chill of dread ran down Aveline's back. *A chastisement? A veiled threat? A promise of divorce?* She considered each possibility … and threat. Her hands trembled as she refilled Washington's cup.

He stared at Aveline's face as if to judge her reaction. "I imagined Sister Eliza would have been arrested for her murder by now."

Aveline was so startled by his comment that she nearly dropped the pot. Even Dorris turned to stare at him.

"When I finished beating Keegan, I was returning here. I saw Eliza running away from the braid shop. It seemed as if her dress was wet … from blood."

Chapter 26

With breakfast in Aveline's stomach, a slight queasiness was replaced by an odd cramping. She ignored the sensation and helped Dorris clean up. She filled the new dishpan with water from the bucket and ignored the puddles that splashed on the table. As Aveline plunged the dishes into the cold water, Dorris stood beside her to dry.

Washington had left moments before to present his mission report to Brother Brigham Young, the rest of the Quorum of Twelve Apostles, and the High Council—the temporary governing body of Winter Quarters.

"You must be more careful with Washington. I fear he has changed much during this past mission," Dorris said, her voice quiet.

"Why so?"

She shook her head and stared up at the wall. "He told me two days ago, the day you left for Kanesville, that he was frustrated with the lack of attention from the High Council." She gave Aveline a hard look. "I strongly recommend you tread lightly around him. Do not push him or—"

"Or what?" Aveline snapped.

"He will beat you … or worse."

Dorris' quiet, simple answer chilled Aveline.

"Remember, it is not your place, or mine, to question or challenge him."

"I know you're right." With the wet rag, Aveline took an angry swipe at a plate. "I just cannot abide that we must work hard to conduct family business while our husband is away on church business, be responsible for his debts, and yet, upon his return, relinquish all authority, and curtsy before him."

"Yet, that is what we must do." Dorris took another rag, picked up the wet plate and wiped it off.

"Doesn't that make you angry?"

Dorris wiped the plate in a slow circle. "I tried to stop being angry a long time ago." With a leisurely movement, she placed it on the table. "Anger will not change things for a woman. Resenting our station in life can only make things worse." She gave a quick laugh, "I especially learned that lesson with you."

"Was Mister Avery always so demanding, so expectant of your services as if you were a scullery maid?" Aveline wondered if her question stepped over an invisible line of privacy.

Dorris stared at the wall as if remembering years past, slowly shaking her head. "No. Years ago, we worked very hard together. He sought my advice." She smiled ruefully. "He even told riddles." She spun toward Aveline. "Would you believe he enjoyed puns?"

At Aveline's shocked expression, she continued in a thoughtful voice. "It is difficult to believe that. Now, no longer. When he was a boy, he lost his parents and siblings to a house fire. The fire haunts him still. Neighbors took him in, but they were not kind. When we married, he was devoted to my happiness. I think he was grateful for love and trust. Then, he met Brother Kimball and he baptized us. Brother Kimball spent hours—days—with Washington, providing council, giving instruction. They became close, so close that Kimball had Washington sealed to him as a so—a father and son in the celestial heavens for eternity." Dorris waved her hand toward the heavens.

"Part of Brother Kimball's instruction was the man rules his kingdom, no exceptions. Since then, he just … does what he feels. Now, he does not deign to ask my thoughts and rarely seeks my help. He did not even ask me for permission to bless his marriage to you, as required." Dorris looked at Aveline. "He came home and said, 'Tomorrow I take a second wife. She and her family have agreed. You will be exalted in heaven. Hang a quilt from the purlin'."

Aveline swept the wet rag over another plate. "How did you feel when he said that?" Her voice was timid, hesitant.

Dorris took a deep breath. "Right after he said it, he walked out the door. I sank to the floor and wept until I could weep no more, not just because another woman was coming into my home, but because I realized our old way of life was gone, never to return." She took the second plate from Aveline's hand.

"After Washington met Kimball, he changed again in Nauvoo. He was receiving instruction on the plural marriage revelation. At first, he was upset, afraid, angry. Then he reconciled to it." Dorris set the plate down. "I think he became excited about it. I could see him study each young woman as she passed him by. Each time he looked, I knew what he was thinking." Dorris' chin quivered. "Each time, a piece of our old life fell away. Now, we have little left."

Aveline blinked back tears at Dorris' sad life. She whispered, "Do you blame me?"

Dorris took the third plate and wiped it in a slow circle.

"I did at first. You, clearly, know how rudely I acted toward you. Now? No. During the ceremony, I didn't feel the promise of heaven. I only knew my beloved was no longer mine. With the command that we cannot deny the principle, I don't know if you could have done anything differently." She stopped wiping. "How did you feel when Washington approached you?"

Aveline fished a knife from the cold water. She rubbed it with a rag. "He didn't approach me at all. He approached my father. The only time we were together was when I met him. Pa brought over Brother Avery to introduce him as our new first counselor—a courtesy. He only stayed a few moments. A month later, he walked into our cabin with my father and Brother Bates. Lucas announced he received a revelation from Mister Avery that Frances was to marry him. She didn't feel she had a choice either. Then Mister Avery said he had another revelation that we must be married."

The morning chores finished, Dorris sat, worn out from the effort. Aveline kneaded bread dough and set it aside to rise, then filled the cast-iron pot with water from the bucket. As she ladled beans to soak she announced a decision. "I'm going to talk with Eliza again."

Dorris nodded her head in time with the chair's rocking. "Figured you might." Then she looked over. "Be careful around Sister Eleanor. She can be mean, quick to fight. With Eliza so ill, she may be even more so. But before you go, please sit down. There's something I have been struggling to tell you."

The seriousness in her voice caused Aveline to tense. She remembered Dorris' swollen eyes from yesterday and her low demeanor since Aveline's return from Kanesville. She fell into Washington's chair, folding her hands as her aching muscles relaxed. Both women stared into the fire.

"There's another thing Washington told me when he returned from Mount Pisgah." Dorris shook her head and blinked back tears. "He brought back a young woman. Right now, she is staying in Bishop Lang's house. Washington will marry her today." A tear streaked down her cheek. "Wife number three will arrive this afternoon."

Chapter 27

Aveline trudged north on Second Street, then turned east on Pratt Street. She felt confused, and she wasn't sure why. A third woman was coming into the Avery cabin. For sleeping arrangements, Dorris said two women would always bunk together. The third would sleep with Washington except when he was absent on Church business. *This is a most vulgar solution. What was he thinking?* Washington was already assured of his place in heaven because of Aveline's marriage to him, so why take a third wife? How high could he rise in heaven? Why here when quarters were corset-tight and food was scarce?

Foul language broke her reverie as she saw a brawl between a small group of men, drunk and cursing, including two police officers. A young lady didn't need to see such things. Retracing her steps, she went north on Second, then turned the corner to head east. She passed the braid shop and slowed to stare at the building where Frances was killed.

She stood beside the corner cabin, Lucas Bates' house, on Cahoon. With no time to mentally prepare to face Eliza, she forced herself to knock.

"Come in." The tiny voice barely seeped through the shake door.

Aveline pulled it open. The voice was as weak as the small flame that lit the first few feet from the hearth. Pausing, Aveline could make out the glow on the quilt that draped the now-skeletal Eliza in her rocking chair. Relieved, Eleanor was not in the cabin.

Aveline considered the vast weight Eliza had lost since the party at her own home only a few months before. She sat on the chair beside Eliza, who said nothing.

After a moment, still staring at the flame, Aveline found her voice. "I trust you feel better?"

From the corner of her eye, Eliza nodded.

"May I have Frances' letter to my parents? It will be a great comfort to them. If not, may I read it?"

The rocking stopped.

Aveline whispered, "Confession is good for the soul." The old Scottish proverb rolled off her tongue.

After a moment, the rocking started then stopped. "Yer sister was an apostate."

Aveline forced herself to stare at the fire and not move a muscle. "I know."

The rocking started. "She wrote as such in a letter to ye and yer parents."

"How did you come to know of this letter?"

"I found it, in her trunk." Eliza tugged on her quilt. "Aye, I looked into her trunk. The letter was tucked into her journal."

"Why would you violate her trust so?"

"She'd been acting strangely, arguing with me, making herself higher than her true position. I am the primary wife. It's my duty to know what's happening in my household. I found her sacred undergarment coiled at the foot of her bed, under her quilt."

"The husband has the primary duty in the household."

A snort escaped from Eliza. "What foolish men and ignorant women say. A smart woman can always find a way around that. The men will be none the wiser. Yer sister had not learned to be subtle, and she refused to submit to her place in this household."

"May I see this letter and her journal?"

"I burned them."

Aveline closed her eyes and fought to keep her temper under control. Her sister's words, her life in ink and on paper, were ashes. Like Frances, they were gone forever. She forced down a sob and blinked back tears.

A teakettle sat beside the dying flame. For something to do other than throw herself on this vile woman and pummel her, Aveline rose, poked the flame and grabbed the last stick of wood. Only small chips remained in the woodpile by the hearth. The kettle was full, and she placed it over the growing flame. She spooned tea flakes into two cups, and sat back in the chair. After a moment of watching the kettle and the growing flames, Aveline murmured, "Did you read the letter and the journal?"

Eliza snorted. "Of course."

Aveline waited for Eliza to speak again, but she uttered no words. Rising steam roiled out of the kettle's spout. Aveline poured the water into the cups. Instead of pitching the scalding liquid in Eliza's face, she forced herself to set one cup beside Eliza and sat in the chair. "May I ask what she wrote?"

"She wrote of her sin, of her weakness. Because she was too weak to be a plural wife, she cursed the Mormon faith. If that wasn't blasphemy enough, she confessed to the lowest depth of wickedness that she loved another. She conceded her damnation and wrote she would flee to Kanesville." Eliza seemed satisfied with the recitation and slurped her tea.

Breathing heavily, Aveline forced the cup to her lips and took a sip. Eliza's voice and words "damnation" and "wickedness" rang in her mind. Frances did not speak or write in such a manner. "Is that exactly how Frances wrote her words?"

"No, but she may as well have written such words."

Aveline gripped the cup handle so tight the china might snap, but she dared not move for fear of throwing herself on Eliza and squeezing the skinny neck. She forced herself to sip the tea. Moments passed.

"To think, she tried to burden her brother, a brave Saint serving far away in defense of this country, with her disgrace." Eliza tsked. "Shame."

"A letter to Bedford?"

Eliza nodded. "Aye. In her journal she wrote she would write her brother of her sins. I expect she had not yet written him of her shame, sparing him."

Aveline paused, relieved her brother would not be burdened with the knowledge of Frances' torment. Bedford and Frances had been especially close as they grew up. The trauma of Pa's letter to him of her murder would be trial enough. "Does Brother Lucas know of this letter and what her journal contained?"

"Of course. I would not keep such a thing from him."

"He read them then." She took another sip of tea.

"Nay. I read certain passages to him." A snigger dribbled from Eliza. "Lucas never learned the gentle art of reading. He never knows if what I read to him is, shall we say, embellished or diminished. He knows what I wish for him to know."

Aveline forced herself to stare at the flame and take another sip. "You embellished her words with 'damnation' and 'wickedness'." This was not a question.

"Of course. In truth, that is what Frances was saying. She just didn't know it."

Fatigue and sadness fell over Aveline. She slumped in the seat. Frances' murder was set in motion by her words that she never wrote.

"I know what you are thinking."

"That you murdered my sister."

A small gasp came from Eliza. Aveline knew she made her point and forced another sip while she waited for a confession.

"How can you think such evil of me?" Eliza whispered.

"It is easy to believe such a thing of you."

"How dare you?"

"I dare. Last we spoke, you said, 'I have sinned'."

"You know not what you speak."

"I know what you spoke, and I know this: you were seen running away from the braid shop the night Frances was killed, with the wetness of blood on your dress." Suddenly, Hulda Cane's words echoed, how the thin cuts may have been made by a woman.

Eliza's rocking became a metronome, *allegro* tempo. "I did not murder your sister."

"Then explain your presence at the braid shop."

"My husband sent me to fetch Frances. I found her in such a condition!"

"Explain the blood on your dress."

The rocking stopped. "I believed blood spilled on her dress and I must have knelt on her dress. I panicked, returned here and told Lucas. He left immediately to the braid shop. When he returned, he said not to speak of this, ever." She whispered "It was not blood. My skirt dried clear, but I burned my dress. I could not abide it in my house."

"Then who did it? Your husband?"

An explosion erupted from Eliza. "Lucas did not do the deed. He is *not* a killer."

"He is a Danite, yes? I have heard whispers of their deeds."

"When he returned to me that night, I asked him if he killed her. He denied the action. Neither of us are responsible for it."

"You hated my sister enough to ensure her fate. You lied to Lucas about her heartfelt words to me, to my parents." Aveline's voice grew to a scream. "You put words such as 'wickedness' and 'damnation' in his head. If you did not do the deed, then you had a hand in it!"

Eliza threw her cup at Aveline's head. Aveline did not flinch. The cup sailed a foot above her and clattered against the log wall. "Get out! No wonder Brother Washington wishes to replace you. Do not ever attempt to return to this house!" She gasped for air as her head fell back against the rocking chair. The effort and the anger sapped her strength. "If you wish to realize who atoned the sins of your wicked sister, ask Thomas Keegan. He was there."

~*~

Aveline trudged down the street with Eliza's screams echoing in her head. Did she believe Eliza that she and Lucas had nothing to do with Frances' murder? She shook her head. They had something to do with her death. Eliza admitted she lied to

Lucas about the words Frances had written in her letter and in her journal. Frances' apostasy and the fabricated words solely to enrage Lucas would be enough for him to kill his own wife.

Keegan was there. Aveline thought back to Keegan's behavior in his store. He appeared to be genuinely sorry about Frances' loss, although he appeared to be angry at being cheated. He blamed Frances, not so much Lucas, but would he kill his son's love simply because he had been cheated at a card game?

How Frances suffered in silence. Sadness and fatigue washed over Aveline. Her feet suddenly felt full of lead. She needed to rest, but there was no place to sit. She plodded past two cabins where the women of the household stood outside. They stopped their discussion to watch her. As she approached, they grabbed their children's arms and yanked them inside. As one door slammed, Aveline heard mumbled bits of a conversation. "That's her … defying … the faith."

Why would they say that about me? I only want to know who committed the murder of a gentle girl. What did Eliza mean about Washington replacing Aveline? She froze. Her breath barely entered her chest. Was he so unhappy with her that he would throw her out, especially now that another wife was on the way? Could he do worse to her than that? A chill raced down her spine. Aveline shook her head. No doubt, Eliza was only disgorging more of her venom, anything to gain a mental and emotional advantage over her adversary. Pity for the suffering Frances rose in her heart.

Plodding down Cahoon Street, Aveline looked further down the street, toward the Council House. The membership of the High Council had concluded their meeting, and members lingered outside. She caught sight of a familiar figure and stopped.

Washington stood beside a young woman, who gazed up at his face. He glanced at the crowd of council members as if to ensure they weren't watching. He smiled down at her and clasped both her hands in his.

Chapter 28

March 18, 1847
Mormon Battalion, Company E
San Diego, California Territory

With a groan, Bedford Bowmore pushed away from the tent pole. He took off his cap and wiped his sweating face with his forearm. He straightened his back, hoping to be rid of the ache that never went away, and put his hands on his hips. His cap dangled from his hand. The wind off the ocean chilled his sweat-soaked scalp. Staring out toward the sliver of Pacific Ocean not hidden by the dunes, he watched distant waves lap the shore, mesmerized by their repetition. He closed his eyes and felt the warm sun on his face. His nostrils flared at the scent of salt.

"Makes you miss the prairies, don't it?"

He looked at the other private, Aron Goodell, and a wide smile spread over his face. Turning back to the ocean, he held out his skinny arms wide, soaking in the breeze as if the moving air could fill his soul. What was it about the zephyr here, a softness that caressed his body like he imagined no woman ever could? The sun's rays weren't harsh, as if their sole purpose was to embrace the world with a soft glow.

"Nope. Don't miss the prairies. I'll never go back if I can help it." Bedford slapped his cap back on his head as if to seal the decision. "The only way I'd go back is if I'm ordered to."

Aron thrust the spade into the earth. He leaned thin arms on the handle and stared out to the ocean. The sixteen-hundred-mile journey from Iowa to California, with little food and the clothing nearly worn off their bodies, had shrunk the once-powerful five-hundred-man Mormon Battalion into emaciated beings. "I know what you mean. I'll never go back either." He shook his head to allow the breeze to flip his long, loose hair over the bulge of his shoulders, forgetting that the month before their commander, Colonel Philip Cooke, had ordered all men to cut their foot-long hair and shave their beards.

He smiled to himself; Aron still wasn't used to his short hair. "Where you from, Aron?"

Aron paused. He yanked up the spade and stabbed the earth. "Nauvoo."

The stories about the looting of Mormons' legal property as they were driven away at musket-point echoed in his mind.

"My people came from Pennsylvania, Chester County. We were lucky, though. There were several neighbors who converted with us. The other neighbors weren't mean to us, just … distant. But we got good money for the farms." Bedford swung the pickax to break up the hard-packed ground for the latest tent he and Aron had been ordered to pitch. He hunched over, panting at the exertion. Their company had left the other four companies in San Luis Rey and arrived in San Diego exhausted and dehydrated the day before. During their duty today, both weary men stopped often to rest and look behind them at the neat rows of white tents, toward an old fort in the near distance.

They watched sea gulls hovering, as if waiting for the men to toss bits of bread at them.

"Not bad duty," Aron said, staring to the distant east horizon. "We're fortunate. No battles, no skirmishes."

He threw his head back and laughed. "If you don't count the Battle of the Bulls. Remember Corporal Luddite, frozen stiff, couldn't move, when the bulls charged us?"

He thought back to when the battalion had marched through Arizona. Wild bovine bulls had charged the convoy. When the dust had cleared, three men were injured, three mules lay dead, and several wagons were knocked over or damaged. Carcasses of nine bulls littered the ground.

Aron laughed. "Yeah, and when he finally thawed out, he almost shot his foot off!" He shook his head. "Good fortune we were there in December, in the cooler part of the year. I can't imagine how it would be in the dead of summer."

A figure approached and shifted his musket to the other shoulder. "Good morrow, gentlemen," Corporal Levi Luddite called out as he stopped to watch their progress. "This is all you've accomplished? Sergeant Smith said the two tents have to be erected today. You only have a few poles dug in!"

"We'll finish today," Aron said. "The good sergeant needn't worry. We may be slow, but it's not like we're frozen in place." A wide grin spread across Goodell's face, clearly enjoying the joke at Luddite's expense.

Luddite's expressionless face stared at Aron's until his smile faded and he picked up his spade to continue his work.

"The luncheon is prepared." Luddite threw a glance at Bedford. "Some wagons came in from Winter Quarters this morning. You got a letter. It's on your bedroll."

"Who's it from," Bedford asked as he threw down the pickax, ready to run to his tent.

A sneer came across Luddite's sallow face. "You want I should tell you what's in it?"

"You probably know," Aron sneered back.

Luddite turned to head back to the tent. "Careful there, Private. Don't make me report you. Just finish those tents today." He scrambled down the short hill toward the cluster of tents and the old fort.

Aron wriggled in an "oh, I'm scared" motion. Bedford broke into a grin as he shouldered his pickax and limped his way down the hill. His boots had worn out on the trek to California. Upon enlistment, many men sent their clothing allowances to their families and most had no change of uniforms. Resupply was almost nonexistent. Most men, like Aron, were barefoot or had wrapped their feet in burlap or animal hides.

"Meet you at the mess," Aron called out to Bedford's back.

Bedford waved his agreement and stabbed his pickax into the ground at the front of the tent. He ducked under the flap and sneezed as the warm, dusty air assaulted his nostrils. The soft snapping of the canvas sides seemed oddly quiet.

He plopped on his bedroll, already laid out flat, and propped his head on his rolled-up jacket that served as his pillow. He spun the letter, seeking the best place to open it.

The address: *Private Bedford Bowmore, Company E, Mormon Volunteers.* He read the return address: *Winter Quarters: Ma, Pa, and Aveline!*

He tensed over the possibility of bad news, noting Frances' name was not included. He sat up, removed his knife from its sheath and carefully slit open the foolscap. Unfolding it, scrolls of his father's tiny copperplate decorated the page.

February 28, 1847
My dearest son,
We hope you are well in California. Brother Younger arrived here from Arizona for supplies for your battalion. He awaits this letter and will return immediately.
I have the worst news a father could convey to his son. Our beloved Frances has gone to her eternal rest. She was found yesterday, her life taken from her in Brother Lucas Bates' braid shop at the hands of one who can only be a devil. Who did the wicked deed is as yet unknown. Frances now rests in the cemetery that overlooks Winter Quarters.
In a past letter, I wrote you she was united in holy marriage to Brother Lucas Bates, Frances being specially chosen to be a plural wife.
Our only comfort is the belief she reigns in heaven as she sits by the right hand of the Lord. We grieve mightily at our loss.
We trust you are in good health. I must close as Brother Younger awaits to speed this communication and supplies to you and your selfless battalion.
Your ever loving father.

Bedford read the letter again, then again, as tears flowed down his cheeks. *This cannot be! This must be a mistake! Frances would hurt no one.* The sobs started deep in his chest and rose to his throat. A wail burst forth as he gripped the letter, crumpled in his fist. Their family was so close. Each cherished the other. The loss of one was unbearable to all—but to lose one to murder!

His howls of grief expanded and contracted with the movement of the canvas walls.

~*~

The sun lowered in the west, and the shadows of nearby tents dimmed the light in the tent. Bedford pushed himself off his bedroll and swayed to catch his balance. His mind refused to think. One foot in front of the other, he stepped down the dirt aisle, and stood at the door flap as if to remind himself to bend.

Outside, he noticed the cooler breeze and the murmurs of approaching soldiers, finished with their day's duties. He turned to walk between tents. The thought of speaking to anyone revolted him.

Trudging, he made his way up the slight knoll where Aron stamped the dirt around the last pole in the second tent. Aron turned and spied Bedford. "Was that a letter from a girlfriend? Did you need some time alone to—" Aron froze at the sight of Bedford.

Bedford held out his clenched fist that contained the crumpled letter. Aron forced Bedford's hand open and smoothed the crumpled paper. His lips moved as he read. Lowering the paper, Aron slid his cap off his head and placed it over his heart. "Brother Bowmore, may your sister rest among the stars in heaven."

Nodding his thanks to Aron's blessing, Bedford gasped in a sob. Helplessness swept over him. There was nothing he could do for his family so far away. Aron moved next to him and patted his back. After a moment Aron said, "Forgive me, Brother, isn't she the one who sent you the letter you got a few days ago?"

Aron's question stopped Bedford's sniffling. He fought to think through the fog of grief. "That's right. She did send me a letter." His voice trailed off.

"Go on." Aron motioned toward the quarters tent. "I'm almost done. I'll finish for today."

Bedford nodded his appreciation and spun on his heels. He ran back to the tent; the light was fading fast. He knelt beside his knapsack and reached in for the last thing he had stored, a letter from Frances he received only two days before. He opened the letter to reread it, desperate to keep from losing his sister.

February 2, 1847
Bedford, Dearest Brother,

I pray you are well as you devote yourself to the defense of our country. Bishop Lang heaps the Lord's praise on you and the other members of your brave battalion.

Ma, Pa, and Aveline are well. Aveline was chosen by divine revelation to marry First Counselor Washington Avery. She excels in this new trial, as she has the strength of the Lord in her.

I beg of you, Brother, to keep this communication silent. I fear for my life here in the Bates household. Brother Bates' wife, Sister Eliza, refuses to abide the revelation of plural marriage. She denies the sanctity of it. Her hatred for the blessing manifests itself in daily curses and bruises. The curses I bear for the promise of eternal salvation, but the bruises are more than I can endure. Brother Bates can be a gentle man, but he is simple and easily influenced by his wife. He is quick to anger and to strike as she directs.

I beg of you, Dear Brother, to forgive me for what I must tell you. I fear and I confess to you I have lost my faith. I am not strong enough to bear this trial. Shame envelops me, when I think of your sacrifice for the Saints and for this country, the country that did not see fit to protect the Saints as they fled before the murderous, thieving fields of Illinois and Missouri. Guilt envelops me when I think of Aveline bearing her trials with Sister Dorris Avery and her husband Brother Washington Avery.

Do not think ill of me, Brother, when I say I have found another, a man who wishes me to be by his side, the only woman by his side. Loyal Keegan is a Gentile.

Please, Bedford, do not think less of me, of us. With Loyal, I am no sinner. I cannot abide such. Loyal is kind, a gentleman who believes in the sanctity of marriage. We have conducted ourselves properly and have committed no sin to violate my marriage vows.

I do fear my presence may anger Loyal's father, Thomas Keegan, owner of Keegan's Mercantile in Kanesville, State of Iowa. Brother Bates boasted how he cheated Mister Keegan out of a great sum of money and the hair comb he presented me as a gift. Brother Bates laughs at how angry Mister Keegan was to lose the treasure, that Mister Keegan promised those involved with the deceit "would pay dearly", and how Brother Lucas made me a part of his unholy scheme. When I meet Loyal next, I shall give him the hair comb to return to his father, with my heartfelt apologies.

When I travel to Kanesville next to trade the braid shop's baskets, I will conceal my trunk and remain in Kanesville. With a heavy heart, I shall soon ask my bishop for a divorce and depart Winter Quarters to join Loyal.

I weep at these words. A letter very similar to this I wrote to Aveline and Ma and Pa. I confess I do not have the strength to face them as the faith is strong in them.

I beg of you to believe I love you, and my heart shall dwell with the Saints.

Your humble and loving sister, Frances.

Bedford read again his sister's cry for deliverance from abuse. Tears welled in his eyes at her suffering. He compared the two letters: one an anguished cry for relief, the other an anguished cry for justice. He stared at the drifting canvas wall as if he could stare through it into heaven. A desperate woman was murdered. All they had to do was let her go.

He flung the letters on his bedroll and stalked outside. Relieving his anger and grief were all he craved.

"Bowmore!"

The shout shocked him from his thoughts. He spun.

Corporal Levi Luddite stood, ramrod straight, before him, his musket slung over his left shoulder. "Malingerer! You left Private Goodell to work alone. He erected both tents by himself. What have you to say for yourself?"

"Corporal, I received most distressing news. I confess my shock took its toll."

"Yes. I heard about your sister, the sinner."

Levi's words boiled over the rage that fell from Bedford's lips. "My sister was no sinner. Who would tell such a lie?"

Levi studied the sling on his musket. "My sister wrote everything that happened. She wrote me a letter I received just today, same as you. Eliza Luddite Bates is my sister—sister-wife to *your* wicked apostate sister."

With a roar, Bedford lunged at the scrawny corporal. "You know nothing. The sin and corruption are in your family!"

Levi stepped back, jerked his musket from his shoulder, and tried to aim the long barrel. The uneven ground kept him off-balance.

Bedford's long legs closed the distance between them. He shoved Levi down the shallow knoll. Both men gripped the weapon, trying to wrest it from the other's hands.

The musket fired.

Chapter 29

March 18, 1847
Winter Quarters, Missouri Territory

Aveline pushed open the door to her cabin and dragged her feet to her stump. No one else was home. Slouching, even staring at the fire took energy she didn't have. Her mind spun from all the words she'd heard and the scenes she'd witnessed. "What a fool," Aveline murmured.

How ignorant she had been to believe Washington preferred her to Dorris, his real wife. Instead, she was a number. Her number was two, the second wife. She was the wife whose gift of marriage allowed the husband and primary wife to ascend to the highest level in heaven. He'd never courted her. He'd never smiled a lover's smile at her. He'd never held her hands until the marriage ceremony and never again since.

She jumped slightly as the door opened. Dorris lugged in the full bucket of water. Aveline shifted her feet to stand and help Dorris, but she had no strength. Numb and aching all over, she could only stare at Dorris while she hoisted the heavy bucket to the table. The cabin was getting hotter, but she had no strength to wave her hands to cool her face. *What is wrong with me?*

"I saw her," Aveline mumbled.

Dorris' back stiffened. She concentrated on ladling water into the teakettle. "Was she pretty?"

"Yes."

"Was she young?"

"Yes."

Dorris sat in her rocker, and Aveline trudged to sit on Washington's chair. She picked up the older woman's hand and held it. "Will you attend the ceremony?" Aveline asked, recalling that Dorris was at her wedding to Washington, but that Eliza had not attended Frances' wedding to Lucas.

"I shall," she said in a small voice. "I cannot deny the wedding, else I will be damned. I must be there for my ritual. I just have to make it through without fainting."

Aveline rubbed Dorris' hand. "I cannot comprehend how you felt as you endured the ritual of placing my hand in his."

Dorris pushed her rocker to set it in motion. "Years ago, Washington had talked about plural marriage. Brother Kimball demanded it for our salvation. With our beautiful marriage, I never expected to give away my husband to another woman. As we walked toward your father's house for your wedding ceremony, I felt so low, so miserable. I prayed the Lord would let me die. The Lord saw fit to make me live and endure it. I forced myself to become numb. My mind was elsewhere except to perform the ritual and run away."

"I remember the look in your eyes," Aveline whispered. "I wish I knew then what I know now." She studied Dorris' aging profile as the woman stared at the flames. "I would have been kinder."

A small smile crossed Dorris' mouth. "You were kind." A small chuckle emerged. "I can almost laugh now recalling how you tried so hard, when you first arrived, in asking me if I wished for some tea when your sister was here that evening." Dorris turned to Aveline. "You know, I could hear you two when you whispered to each other."

Aveline covered her face with embarrassment. Their whispered conversation ran through her mind. "Oh."

"Don't." Dorris reached for Aveline's hand. "Looking back, I know you were being kind. Frances too. I was simply too distressed to receive your kindness."

"Did he ask for your permission for this new wife?" Aveline tensed; the question was not her business.

Dorris shook her head. "Upon his return, he told me Brother Kimball encouraged another union. I know the encouragement from his celestial father, an apostle no less, was the push Washington needed and that he would follow the instruction. Her parents are dead, so he brought the young woman with him."

They sat in silence.

Both women jumped as the door was yanked open. Washington's tall frame blocked the light from outdoors. Aveline pushed herself out of his chair and stood aside. She glanced out the closing door, wondering if the bride-elect was waiting to meet her new sister-wives.

Rising so quickly, the cabin spun. Aveline collapsed on her stump. Sweat beads sprouted on her forehead. She leaned against the wall so she wouldn't fall over. Breathing slowly, she stared into the dark corner until her dizziness faded. Her limbs felt like they weighed a ton.

Washington rubbed his hands more from glee than for warmth and sat on his chair. "What a glorious day! With our tithing paid, Bishop Lang wrote a letter recommending me to be a member of the Pioneer Company, the first group to leave Winter Quarters and the first to arrive in Zion! I will join those chosen to construct our temple." He stood and paced behind his chair in his excitement.

"The leadership understands that I am devoted and want to rise in the priesthood." He stopped and looked heavenward. "I will be a pioneer for the Lord."

"Congratulations, Washington," Dorris said in a quick voice. She hesitated. "You will go alone?"

"The bishop has said I and other men will go. He did not mention anyone else."

"Will ladies go?" Aveline managed to mutter.

"Only men will have the honor of the Pioneer Company." Washington humphed.

"So, my handkerchiefs helped you earn this honor, by paying our tithing?" The words mumbled out of Aveline's numbing lips. She felt foolish and selfish, but she wanted to hear her labors contributed in some way to the family's success.

"I should say my efforts got me this honor."

Aveline's face burned from a hotness that came on suddenly, but not just because of anger.

"Do you feel well, Aveline? You look like your eyes have sunk back into your head." Dorris got up from her chair and walked to Aveline. "I can feel the heat radiating from you out here. You need to get to bed. You've had a stressful time." Dorris held out her arms. Aveline tried to stand from her stump and sank to the floor. The room whirled and she felt nauseous. She heaved.

Dorris spun to grab the washbasin and place it in front of Aveline. She fought the retching urge, and swallowed hard to keep her stomach contents down. Panting, she grabbed Dorris' arm and staggered to her feet.

A strong hand grabbed her right arm. The room spun so fast she couldn't see what she was looking at. Washington scooped her into his arms and carried her to Dorris' bed.

"My bed," she mumbled and lifted her index finger toward the other side of the quilt curtain as if to remind him he was placing her in the wrong spot.

"This is your bed," he said with a sharpness threading his voice. Through the fog clouding her mind, she remembered he would be married again by the day's end.

"Congratulations" tumbled from her lips before she lost consciousness.

Chapter 30

Chickens don't belong in the house. Aveline's dark world whorled like a tornado in her mind. *Whoever brought the chickens in the house should take them away.* The cackling wouldn't let her sleep.

The clucking separated into female voices. Aveline tried to open her eyelids, but they refused to budge. She tried to raise her hand but her arm felt as if a weight was attached.

"She moved!" The voice was followed by other voices calling out "Praise be," and "Thank the Lord."

Rubbing her eyelids, her fingers felt grit. The grit burned her eyeballs.

"Don't rub, honey." Ma's voice trembled as she pressed Aveline's hands to the bed. The warm, wet rag draped over her face felt so good she groaned.

"We're trying to get your eyes open with warmth. It won't take long. Just rest."

Female voices murmured at once. She could make out phrases before the cacophony of voices erupted in a myriad-tone rendition of *Now Let Us Rejoice*. In her confusion, Aveline felt, more than knew, the praises and singing were for her, and she was grateful.

After a few moments, the rag was removed and dabbed to brush away the grit. "Try to see now, honey."

Aveline cracked her eyelids, but her vision was so blurry she didn't know who was before her or where she was. She blinked, but with each blink her eyes threatened to stick closed. "Let's try this once more," Ma's voice said as Aveline heard a splashing, then the warmth of the wet rag on her face.

"Ma," Aveline murmured. She held up her hand, wanting her mother's hand in hers. At her mother's touch, Aveline held up her other hand. "Frances." The background talking stopped as if a conductor had tapped his baton on a podium. She waited for her sister's touch.

A hand clasped hers and pressed it to the bed. "Frances isn't here, Aveline. But I'm here."

"Dorris?"

"Yes. I'm here. And your ma. And several sisters. All here praying for your recovery."

The world stopped spinning in her mind. The rag was removed again. The ladies who hovered over her came into view. "Ma." Ma squeezed her arm. "Dorris." Dorris raised Aveline's hand and kissed it. "Sister Richards, Em, Poppy— bless you all for being here." The words slopped from Aveline's sticky lips.

"Try to sit up, dear. Have some broth." Ma pulled Aveline up, and stuffed another quilt behind her. Aveline groaned as her stiff muscles strained at the simple movement. Poppy handed her a steaming mug.

The hot cup warmed Aveline's cold hands. The heavenly scent brought her to her senses. "What happened?"

Em leaned forward. "Honey, you've been in a faint for three days."

"You had the chills and fever," Poppy added. "We dosed you with quinine, but we feared it seemed to do you no good."

Ma stroked Aveline's hair and cheeks. "I was so afraid I'd lose you." She smiled sadly and cleared her throat. "But you're back with us now."

Sister Mary Richards said, "You don't remember anything of the past days?"

Aveline thought for a moment and shook her head. The slight movement set off the dizziness again. "No." She took a sip of broth. "Oh, this is good," and sipped more. She could feel the drink coursing through her, its strength flowing into her body. Uncomfortable at the five pairs of eyes staring at her, Aveline pretended to rest, handing off the mug to her mother.

"Well, now that I know I can harangue Aveline to work on a quilt soon," Em teased, "I must go. Carissa is slightly ill today. I don't want her to strain herself." She skirted Dorris and bent to kiss Aveline. With a slight stroke of her fingertips across Aveline's cheek, she was gone.

Poppy gripped Aveline's foot and gave it a light shake. "Farewell, my dear. I'll come by tomorrow."

Sister Mary Richards placed her hands on Aveline's head. "You're back among us. I am so pleased our blessing meeting was a success, thanks be to God. Heal quickly. Farewell, Sister. Get strong soon."

The women flung their shawls over their shoulders to leave. "Bless you all," Aveline murmured before they left with a wave. She turned to the two remaining women and caressed their hands. "Bless you both, especially," she whispered. "I'm so sorry for making our lives more difficult."

Ma looked as shocked as did Dorris. "Do not apologize for illness. It is something none of us wish for."

"We are here to care for each other," Dorris said. "You taught me that."

Beyond Dorris' head, Washington's appeared. "She's back among the living. I am pleased, but the quinine took most of our money."

Aveline nodded, silently grateful she hadn't wasted his cash. She couldn't remember why she was in Dorris' bed and not in her own. "Shouldn't I be over there?" Aveline pointed to the curtain.

"No," Washington said. "That is Veil's bed and mine."

Aveline stared into the far corner of the cabin. *I must not have my faculties.* "Why does a veil need a bed?"

Dorris and Ma froze and fixed their gaze on Aveline. They said nothing. Dorris bit her lips to keep from smirking. Washington looked annoyed. He turned slightly. Beyond Dorris, fabric rustled as a figure rose from the rocking chair. He pointed to the young woman whose head Aveline could now see behind Dorris. "This is Sister Veil Thomas. A few days ago, she agreed to grow my kingdom in heaven."

The young woman placed her hands on Dorris' shoulders. Dorris tensed as though forcing herself not to push off the hands. Veil's blonde hair was upswept, her pale blue eyes bored into Aveline's. Her white skin was smooth, a soft blush swept across her cheeks. The lace-edged dress whispered from yards of fine, emerald-green fabric. *Brocade?* Veil said nothing, but only stared at Aveline as if she waited for the sick woman to say something first, a rudeness that irritated Aveline.

Aveline simply nodded her hello. Washington patted Veil's shoulder in a "that will do" gesture. She turned from the small group and sat in Dorris' rocking chair. Aveline glanced at Dorris to see her reaction, but her face remained fixed.

Aveline reached for the mug of broth Ma held. "Thank you," Aveline whispered. To break the staring from the three pairs of eyes, she asked, "I trust everyone is well? Em said Carissa was ill."

Ma nodded her head. "Her condition has made her more sick than she should be. Em made her lie in bed and rest. We can only pray for her and her babe. She is the only one who is ill that I am aware of, thank the Lord."

Aveline tensed, hoping Carissa would be blessed enough to keep this baby. She smiled as she remembered Em's words that she would sit on Carissa to keep her in bed.

"You need to rest and get stronger yourself," her mother said as she brushed Aveline's hair from her forehead.

"Yes, because the weak shall remain behind," Washington said, too loud. "The weak cannot go west to Zion." Aveline, Ma, and Dorris looked up at Washington. "Our leaders have decided that a few women will journey with the Pioneer Company to Zion. Leadership has honored the Avery family."

With a puffed chest, he looked from Dorris to Ma before fixing his gaze at Aveline. He spoke through clenched teeth, "You are one of the women who have been granted the honor to head west with the Pioneer Company."

Chapter 31

With a deep breath of the impending spring air, Aveline sat on the bluff's soft ground west of Winter Quarters. She sneezed again. Something in the air didn't agree with her nose, but she didn't care. She was alive. Her confinement to bed had lasted two more days before Dorris allowed her to get up. On the third day, Dorris gave permission for her to leave the cabin. Walking was still an effort and she tired easily, but she had survived a serious case of chills and fever. Many Saints hadn't been so fortunate and now rested in the cemetery.

In a week, she would leave Winter Quarters for a brighter future in Zion.

The thin cloud shielding the sun withered. The sun's full rays highlighted the cottonwood trees on the north hill. Aveline craned her neck. It couldn't be. Yes! The barest hint of green shrouded the trees like a pea-colored mist. She looked closer at the ground under the trees. A fog of green blanketed it. Scratching at the brittle grass beside her, tiny green shoots pushed their way through last year's dead growth. The grass was growing. Promises of new beginnings were sprouting. The Saints were blessed with the promise of new greenery for the animals to eat, the promise of baby animals and birds to giggle at, the promise of a hard winter gone, and the promise of a new life in Zion.

She watched the settlement awaken and Saints wander to their chores. To her right, a woman replaced a clump on her dugout's roof. A loose cow must have stepped through the roof when it wanted to eat the hay there. The blanket that served as the door swayed gently in the light breeze. Hamish Paddock led a mule to his cabin. Near the town center, a woman climbed down from the wagon where she lived through the winter. Two children lugged a pail to the well. Brother Allred, the carpenter with the sad specialty of making coffins, lugged a small box on his back on his way south; though the number of deaths had dropped, another family had lost a child. Sister Cane herded her brood down Second Street, heading to Brother Cane's police station. Lucas Bates rode a horse up the street, returning home from his mission.

Brother Bates. The person involved in Frances' murder rode back into town. *He looks so relaxed.* She sat straighter. Her eyes narrowed as she tried to think of how she would approach him. Perhaps a talk with Chief Finis Cane was in order first, to let him know Lucas was back in town. Washington was back in town too, and she hadn't heard that the police chief had spoken with him, or at least, neither man bothered to mention it to her. It was time for Aveline to speak with Chief Cane about his findings thus far in Frances' murder case.

Movement at the bottom of the slope diverted Aveline's attention. "Pa!" She waved at her father. He waved back and shifted his direction to meet her.

"Good morning, Pa!" She scrambled to her feet as he reached to embrace her.

"Good morning, Daughter! You are a sight for sore eyes!" Pa sang out. "Shouldn't you be resting at home?" He pushed her back to study her skinny frame.

"I walk up here every morning. I need to exercise my muscles, and the fresh spring air will do me good." She swept her arms to show him the green mist that hung over the trees. "I will go home directly and rest. Oh," she remembered. "Brother Bates is back in town. I saw him ride in. I'm going to talk with Chief Cane first to find out what is happening with the investigation."

At this, Pa shook his head. He sat on the ground and helped his daughter sit down beside him. "I received a letter from Bedford this morning."

Aveline gasped. "How is he?!"

"He is alive and fairly well. When he wrote the letter, the battalion made it to California—threadbare, with no shoes, but they made it."

Pa paused. "There was an accident. A musket discharged. The ball hit his left foot. The doctor almost removed his foot, but decided to wait if it would repair itself."

The thought of her big brother—never serious, always jolly—now perhaps a cripple, cramped Aveline's stomach. She closed her eyes.

"But," Pa said in a loud voice, "he is being treated and is recovering. He hopes to keep the foot." Pa blinked back tears.

"The discharge was an accident. He wrote he bears no ill will for the musket fire. It is an injury for the Saints that he will gladly endure, he says, especially since a corporal—who is now a private like him—keeps him company in the cot next to his. This private is being treated for 'severe bruising'."

Pa stared up at the sky. His faced crinkled in concentration. "I'm not sure how to take such a statement. There's a hint in there somewhere.

"He wrote that the greatest difficulty of his injury will be remembering not to use his crutch to tease the dogs that follow the camp. He says the dogs like to chase a stick, but they occasionally refuse to return it to its owner." Pa chuckled. "Bedford loves California. He confesses to being hypnotized by the ocean. A 'haunting mistress', he calls it. He does not know if or when he will return to us."

Aveline relaxed over her brother's news. Her father stared out over the settlement for a moment. "I can see why you like to sit up here."

She nodded her head. "I know this is idleness to sit up here, but I enjoy it. I feel like I'm a part of the town, yet separate. I can watch what people do. See that brother there?" Aveline pointed at a man who wobbled down the street this side of the settlement. "He often goes home in such condition in the mornings."

Pa watched, incredulous. "Is he drunk?"

"Yes. He is one of the police who confiscated the whiskey from Brother Smith, over there." She pointed to a corner cabin to the north.

Pa shook his head. "Disgraceful." After another look over the town, he turned to Aveline. "I'm told you have a new sister-wife."

"Veil Thomas. I have not yet made up my mind about her. She's an orphan. Her parents died in Iowa on their way to Mount Pisgah. Dorris and I learned to cherish each other. I hope to have the charity to feel the same about Veil."

"I hear she was from a wealthy family."

Aveline barked a laugh. "She has a notion she is to be accorded privileges because of her former family. Dorris told her even if her parents were alive, she doesn't belong to that family anymore. She belongs to the Avery family, a family that must work for its sustenance, and that we have no servants to perform our chores. Veil was not happy about that revelation."

"Have you provided her any instruction, any counsel?"

Aveline laughed. "With my history in the Avery household, I am not the one to instruct her. I try to blend into the walls. It's more difficult for me now because I used to sit on my bed to remove myself from disagreements. Since we all must share a bed, it's not so easy."

At hearing her family's sleeping arrangements, Pa squirmed with embarrassment. The comforting silence between them stretched.

"Why didn't you take a second wife, Pa?" The question was out of the Aveline's mouth before she could stop it. She tensed, not wanting to know the answer, but needing to hear it. "You and Ma never once talked about it."

Seconds passed. Aveline glanced at Pa from the corner of her eyes. His hands clutched his arms and his jaw muscles tightened. He cleared his throat. With a tight voice he replied, "I fear my faith isn't strong enough."

Aveline breathed in silent relief. "So, Ma approves of you not taking another wife." It wasn't a question.

His mouth turned down in a sad grimace. "It is because of your mother I cannot. When we learned of the principle on the trail, seeing the pain in your mother's eyes was more than I can bear."

He shook his head as he stared at the Missouri River in the distance. "I try my best to be a faithful Saint. If I work hard enough, I pray the Lord will allow me to enter the lowest level in heaven."

At that, he turned to Aveline and gave her a sad smile. He picked at the ground and tugged at the grass in hesitation. "About seeing Chief Cane, I would advise against it."

"How can you say that?"

"Your ma and me have reconciled ourselves to Frances' death. I hope you will too."

Aveline shook her head, her mouth tight. "No. I want to know who killed her and see them brought to justice."

"I understand, Aveline. Believe me, I do, but I've heard rumors about Frances." He choked on his words. "That she was an apostate."

Tears formed in Aveline's eyes at the pain in his voice. Through her tears, she whispered, "It's not a rumor. It's true. She removed her sacred undergarment and didn't intend to put it back on."

Pa said nothing, but looked into the distance where the Missouri River flowed. "Perhaps she removed it for an unknown reason."

"No, Pa, she took it off, for good."

"How do you know this?"

She stroked his face to wipe off the wetness from his pouring eyes. "She wrote a letter to you, Ma, and me about it."

At this, Pa turned to look at her full in the face. "Where is this letter?"

"Eliza Bates burned it, along with Frances' journal."

Pa closed his eyes. He sniffled and wiped his nose with his sleeve. "How do you know all this?"

"When I was in Kanesville, I met the man Frances was going to leave Brother Bates and our faith for." She faced her father and stared into his shocked eyes. "He said she didn't have the strength to tell us, so she wrote a letter." She wiped her eyes.

She glanced at her father. "I spoke with Eliza. She admitted to the letter. She read it to Lucas because he cannot read. Eliza admitted she embellished Frances' words to make her seem sinful, wicked." Aveline took a deep breath. "Then she burned the letter and the journal."

Pa sat quietly and watched the ferry cross the river. "I thought she was devout."

"I think, at one time, she was. I think she tried hard to be. Because of the Bateses' and Eleanor's cruelty, she couldn't bear it any more. I think she endured it as long as she could. Then she happened to find another, one who promised to love her and treat her well."

"Do not speak with Chief Cane." Pa's flat tone surprised Aveline. "You must stay out of this."

"Why, Pa? She deserves justice."

"She is an apostate, and one with a lover."

"Pa, they were not lovers. Loyal swears they never did anything inappropriate."

"Loyal Keegan?"

"Yes, Pa, the son of Thomas Keegan."

Pa sighed deeply. "Some say Frances was punished for her sinful deeds, for her wickedness. There are rumors about that nothing shall be done because no sin was committed."

Aveline's eyes widened. "Murder is no sin?"

"There is said to be a band of men, Aveline, sworn to avenge any wrongs against the Saints. Their deeds are whispered. They may be just whispers, but there are many who believe this band exists and that they are powerful."

He looked at Aveline, fierceness glowed from his eyes. "They will not hesitate to fulfill their orders or to protect the Saints from dangers within and without."

Pa watched Hamish Paddock walk his laden animal down Woodruff Street. "Some say that killing an apostate is no sin.

Some say, by the spilling of their blood, the dead may now achieve salvation."

"Blood atonement," Aveline whispered.

"Yes."

"Is that what you think was done to Frances?" She whispered, afraid to speak the words too loudly.

Pa was silent as he scraped the ground and piled the dirt into a little mound.

"Yes."

Chapter 32

"How do I look?" Dorris twirled, wearing her new, green silk blouse. "Sister Paddock got the blouse finished with the cloth you brought me from Kanesville just in time for the dance tonight!" She studied herself in the cracked mirror. "Wait. I need one more thing." She scurried to her trunk and lifted the lid. Peering into the darkness, she pulled out a small, white cloth. At the mirror, she fluffed the white cloth and tucked it into the high-necked bodice. "There! Now what do you think?" She spun for Aveline to examine.

The green silk shimmered in the light from the dying fire and flickered with her movements. The handkerchief Aveline had given her floated at Dorris' throat like a lace ascot.

"You are so beautiful!" Aveline exclaimed. "The green silk sets off your eyes and the handkerchief at your throat sets off your face." She clapped her hands in delight.

Dorris spun again to look at herself and fluffed the handkerchief's lace edging. "Vanity, thou art a sin." She laughed and covered the gums of her toothless mouth with her hand. "Or should be."

Aveline laughed back. "I think vanity shall be set on a shelf at least once in a while for a woman to appreciate her beauty." She smoothed her red dress, her best dress and the same one she wore to the last dance.

A rustling of fabric came from behind the quilt curtain as Veil swept her way into the center of the room. The lighthearted banter between the two women ceased and the tension increased. Veil lifted her skirt's hem to prevent it from scraping the dirt floor and stood at the mirror beside Dorris, who turned to move away.

Veil's red silk sash accented the blue brocade gown. Her décolleté displayed ample cleavage and its brazenness shocked Aveline. In the mirror, she watched Veil push aside the edges of her sacred undergarment and turn down the collar. Veil glanced at the women and stepped behind the curtain. Moments later, Veil emerged. She, too, had tucked a handkerchief in her bodice.

Aveline and Dorris exchanged knowing looks and smiled.

"That's a beautiful gown," Aveline said.

"Yes. My father brought the dress from England for me. He said a countess wore this gown to Queen Victoria's court."

"Ah, he gave you a used gown," Dorris said.

Veil spun to face Dorris, a grimace of anger and embarrassment creased her face. She opened her mouth as if to give a sharp retort when the cabin door opened and a gruff, "Ready, ladies?" stopped her.

The three women twirled to show themselves to their husband. He barely nodded his approval.

"Are you alright?" Dorris asked as she reached for him. "You look exhausted."

"Of course, I am exhausted. These last days, I was ordered to work the fields to prepare for crop planting. Next, I am to build the picket around the town. I do not have the time to work the fields. How am I to prepare to head to Zion if I am to work menial labor? We leave west in a few days. The chosen pioneers should be allowed to prepare for the journey, not work like field hands."

Aveline stopped herself from saying, "Everyone must prepare for those coming after us." She bit her lips to prevent angering Washington more. The evening promised to be a joyous time, and a chastisement from him would spoil it. She rushed to fetch her shawl off the nail in the wall, but decided the evening was too warm.

She and Dorris linked arms, and the two women giggled their way out the door behind an agitated Washington and in front of an even angrier Veil.

"You both are acting like children," he snapped.

Dorris took hold of Washington's arm as Aveline quickly slipped her hand onto his other arm before Veil could move. She wanted Veil to know, as the number three wife, her place was to bring up the rear. "We are blessed by the Lord to feel happy at least once in a while." She smiled up at him, hoping her gaiety would project into him and lighten his mood. She spread her arm wide as if to proclaim to the heavens, "For the evening, we shall throw off our trials and our cares and dance to William Pitt's band." She fought the urge to skip.

Washington looked down at Aveline. He patted her hand. "And you shall step on my feet numerous times."

"Thank you for your permission."

The Council House was lit from within by the glow of candles mounted to the walls. A stream of people stood in line to enter. Laughter met Aveline's ears. Entering behind Washington and Dorris, she gasped at the warmth, grateful she had left her shawl behind. Just inside the door, she hugged Em, Carissa, and Hamish Paddock, dressed in their finest.

"Attention, attention," Patriarch John Smith called out, his arms held wide as silence washed over the crowd. "On our knees, let us give thanks for this evening of relaxation and fellowship. Let us pray."

Almost as one body, the assembly sank. Patriarch Smith intoned his lengthy prayer, and Aveline tried not to squirm. Her knees ached despite the layers of fabric she kneeled upon. At the end of the prayer, the men assisted the women to their feet.

"We shall lift our voices high with the song of *Come Thou Font of Every Blessing*," Patriarch Smith called.

The many-toned voices sang loud. Aveline sang as loud as she could so her happy feeling would reach the heavens.

Sung by flaming tongues above …

Words of unkind gossip about Frances' death came spinning back. She choked on the lyrics.

Prone to leave the God I love …

Aveline blinked back tears. Frances was leaving their faith without the strength to tell her own sister.

Clothed then in blood washed linen …

A gasp for air, then a sob escaped Aveline. She closed her eyes to see Frances lying in the straw pile, dried blood around her throat. Aveline could only listen as others sang the final lines:

Send thine angels now to carry
Me to realms of endless day.

Another sob escaped. She pulled her handkerchief from her bodice and pressed the cloth to her mouth. She squeezed her eyes shut to blot out the feeling that everyone's eyes were upon her. Gulping down the sadness, pushing the grief to her stomach, she took a deep breath and dabbed her eyes. No one watched her, but Dorris stood beside her and patted her shoulder.

At the end of the song, William Pitt's band started the dancing with a tune for a schottische. Aveline took Washington's offered left arm and Dorris took his right. Veil stood, awkward, not knowing what she should do. Aveline turned back, feeling wicked and pleased. Softening, she decided later she would drop off his arm so Veil could take her place as one of Washington's wives.

They marched around the dance floor the second of the three times, crying out "Praise the Lord," before Aveline waved to Veil to take her place beside Washington and parade around the room.

After the final circuit, Washington pushed off Veil's hand so he and Dorris could start a Virginia Reel. Veil stood against the wall, anger flashing across her face. This must be the first time any man rebuffed her for another woman, Aveline thought—for a woman old enough to be her mother.

Clapping her hands in time to the music, Aveline waved at her parents across the room. She squeezed through the crush of people to make her way to them.

Her mother looked radiant in her green gingham dress, and Pa looked very happy. Ma put her mouth next to Aveline's ear. "Brother Younger got a letter from Bedford's commander. In the letter was a message for Brother Younger to pass on to us. Bedford is in better health and hopes to be back to work in his company. That was all that was written."

Aveline closed her eyes in a quick prayer of thanks. When she opened them, her parents looked back with tears welling. "Thank the Lord," Ma murmured and nodded.

"Yes," Aveline said. "I'm grateful to the captain for including the information. If the musket ball had hit higher …" She let her voice trail off. The alternative was unthinkable. She looked up, happy. "But he's fine." Ma hugged her.

A squeal erupted behind her and arms surrounded her. Aveline spun to embrace Poppy Wallace. Husband Anson stood close behind, his hands on Poppy's shoulders. The couple studied Aveline's face with big smiles.

"Oh, Aveline, I am so relieved to see you and looking so well!" Poppy's normally high-pitched voice almost squeaked in her happiness.

Aveline returned the embrace and held out a hand to Anson, who gripped her hand and patted it with his other.

"We are so grateful you've recovered," Anson said.

"I can't thank you enough for your help and support. I'm only here because of such loving care," Aveline said, reaching a hand to her mother, who gripped her daughter's hand.

"I heard you have a sister-wife." Poppy studied Aveline's face for her reaction.

"Ugh, I can't believe it. Her name is Veil Thomas. She's from a rich family and she makes sure everyone know it." Aveline rolled her eyes. "I cannot believe he would take another wife now, making us live and sleep in tight quarters and with food at times hard to get.

Poppy's eyes sparkled. "Want to hear what I heard about why a man takes a third wife?"

Intrigued, Aveline nodded.

"Anson told me a couple men said they have three wives instead of two because it's more peaceful that way."

Crinkling her face in disbelief Aveline cried, "How is that even possible?"

"Because then the women split their jealousy because they don't know who to hate most." Poppy leaned back with a naughty grin.

"Oh, for heaven's sake—

From the center of the room, swaying, glistening dots caught her eye. As she focused on the swinging objects, the room turned dark. The music faded to silence except for the ringing in her ears. The only thing Aveline saw, over a few shorter heads and through the crush of people, cresting an upswept pile of graying hair, was Frances' hair comb. It stood high, its pearls undulating in time with the music.

"Aveline, are you all right? You've turned right white. Aveline? Where are you going?" Her mother's voice sounded a hundred miles away.

She pushed her way through the crowd. She didn't react as she bumped against dancing bodies. Her eyes never wavered from the crown of pearls. The woman turned and caught sight of Aveline staring at the hair comb. "Hello, my dear."

The man beside the woman turned from his dancing and saw Aveline. "Ah. Mary, this is Sister Bowmore. She made the handkerchiefs you adore so. Sister, may I present my wife, Mary Keegan."

Mary's face brightened. "Your work is beautiful, so delicate, my dear. If you can find your way to make more, my husband has already sold out of your work." Mary's face fell as she studied Aveline's shocked expression. "My dear, what is wrong?"

Aveline's anger grew. "Murderer!" exploded from her mouth. She stared at Thomas Keegan, eyes wide. "Murderer! You killed my sister!"

Mary and Thomas Keegan's faces paled from shock then reddened with anger. "Why, she's demented," Mary sniffed. "How dare you?" She whipped open a fan, fanned herself and turned away.

Thomas Keegan turned with his wife, but Aveline grabbed him by the arm and yanked him back around to face her. "Why?" Her voice grew in volume. She didn't care that she was screaming. "Why would you kill a woman? She loved your son!"

Dancers near her stopped to stare. An angry voice pushed through the crowd. "What is happening here?"

Aveline glanced toward the voice and was gratified to see Chief Cane glaring at her. "Brother Cane." She held up her hand to indicate Thomas Keegan. "Here is the murderer of Frances Bowmore, my sister." She stepped aside so Cane could wrestle Keegan to the ground before he dragged the killer away.

Instead, Cane's face turned red. He seized her by the arm, dragged her through the crowd, and out the door. In the darkened street, he pushed her away and yelled, "Woman, what have ye done? Ye accuse a true friend of the Saints of this deed? Are ye mad?"

Mary and Thomas Keegan had followed the struggling pair outside and stood beside Cane. Several others from the dance spilled onto the dirt road to watch.

Chief Cane turned to Keegan. "Mister Keegan, do ye want ta press a charge of slander against this woman?"

Aveline stared with wide eyes at Cane. Her voice was high-pitched as she screamed. "Did you not hear me? He killed my sister. If anyone is to be charged, it is he!"

"Shut up, woman. Yer hurting my ears." Cane shook Aveline's arm to emphasize his words.

Keegan studied Aveline. Calmness washed over his face. He hesitated and held up his hand as if to stop all action. "Chief Cane, I wish to know why she believes I would do such a thing."

"Yer a considerate gentleman, Mister Keegan." Cane turned back to Aveline, but kept his steel grip on her arm.

Keegan shook his head. "I do this out of consideration for Frances Bowmore."

Aveline took a deep breath. His mention of a kindness toward Frances and why he would tolerate Aveline's accusation reeled her back.

"Answer the gentleman." Cane shook her arm.

"Where is Mister Avery's handkerchief?" Aveline stammered, hoping to throw him off guard with a question.

Keegan glanced at Cane, then back to Aveline. "What handkerchief and who is this Mister Avery?" His voice was calm, quiet.

Angrier now, Aveline snapped, "Mister Avery is my husband. He fought you after the last dance, when my sister was killed. He gave you his handkerchief, to sop your blood."

Keegan nodded. "I see. Mister Avery is the brute who chose to fight me. Yes, he did get in a couple licks. He said he was defending his cheating friend's honor, although I don't see how a cheat has honor, Saint or not. To answer your question, he did not give me his handkerchief. If the handkerchief of which you speak is one that you made, he used it to wipe the blood from the bloody nose I gave him. I most certainly would recall it. He gave me nothing, but a black eye and a sore lip."

"What other accusations do ye have against Mister Keegan?" Cane said. This time he dropped his hand.

Aveline tilted her head up, chin out. "You said Frances made Lucas cheat you at cards. You lost a lot of money and a hair comb."

She pointed to his wife's head. "The most condemning piece of evidence of your deed sits on your wife's head: Frances' hair comb, the one she was wearing when she was murdered. The killer must have taken it." *Then the killer took it.* Lucas' voice rumbled in her mind.

Missus Keegan's mouth fell open. She reached up to her hair and fingered the comb as if her touch would confirm the terrible story.

Keegan raised himself up to his full height of five feet, four inches. "I never said Frances ordered her husband to cheat for money and goods. I said his *plural wife* ordered him to cheat. This incident occurred well before your sister married Mister Bates."

Aveline's hands rose to her mouth. It was impossible for Frances to have ordered Lucas to get the comb: Lucas gave the hair comb to Frances when he proposed to her in their parents' cabin. She felt her face grow cold.

"The same woman who ordered her husband to do such a deed must have repented her action because she returned the hair comb to me." Keegan continued. "That is she there."

The body of interested people turned as one in the direction of Keegan's pointed finger.

Eliza Bates ran from the crowd.

~*~

Few of the crowd dispersed at Chief Cane's directive. "Move along now. Go back to the dance." Most ignored the order, too engrossed in the proceedings to obey.

Aveline swayed, horrified. Covering her face with her hands, she wished she could faint to hide from the crowd's disgust and loathing etched on their faces. Shame of slandering a well-thought-of gentleman and his wife, disrupting a crowded dance, and horror at learning who killed her sister washed over her.

Cane moved to stand beside Keegan. They both watched Aveline's reaction.

"Well, Mister Keegan, do ye wish to press a slander charge against the sister?"

Keegan studied Aveline. "I believe the good sister has only the best intentions."

Aveline burst into tears. She leaned toward Keegan for an embrace, but thought better of it. She curtsied instead. "Mister Keegan, Missus Keegan, I, I cannot tell you how sorry I am. I know facts and they led me in your direction. I humbly beg your pardon and your forgiveness." Sobs of shame pulsed from her chest as she again curtsied deeply. "I let anger and despair of Frances' murder take control of my thoughts. I am so sorry."

Grimly, Keegan nodded. He patted her shoulder. "Good sister, let us speak no more of this dreadful business." He turned to look in the direction Eliza had run. "Although I think there is another you may wish to speak with."

"The good sister needs ta stop meddling in this matter." Cane grabbed her arms and shook her. He yelled at her, "But she refuses to listen to authority."

"She will listen to *this* authority." A loud voice startled the gawking group. Washington shoved his way through. Even in the night's dimness, his face was livid-red. His eyes bulged with fury. "Go home, woman. I'll deal with you at home." He glanced at Keegan, then to Cane. "I'll correct her. There will be no more talk of this from her." He fixed his glare on Aveline.

"Now!"

Weeping, Aveline curtsied deeply to the Keegans and ran into the night.

~*~

Slamming the cabin door shut, Aveline threw herself on Dorris' bed. Wailing, she beat her pillow. So many emotions raced through her: anguish at her embarrassing actions, disbelief that the police chief had disregarded her charge of the killer, and terror at her husband's rage. The injustice tormented her. Only Thomas Keegan seemed interested in what was right.

Shouting outside the cabin interrupted her mangled thoughts. The cabin door flung open and banged against the wall. Washington charged in. Dorris was behind him, her hands on his shoulders as she tried to hold him back. "Please, Washington, be kind," she entreated him. Veil followed, curiosity floating in her eyes.

He grabbed Dorris and Veil by their arms and shoved them out the door. "Go elsewhere." He slammed the cabin door closed. His chest heaved.

Aveline sat up. Her trembling hands waved in terror. "Mister Avery, I beg of you—"

"You have disgraced me!" In a flash, he was beside the bed. His fist lashed out and struck Aveline's cheek. She screamed as numbing pain flooded her head. Blinded by the bright lights flashing in her head, she could barely see Washington, his fury unleashed, as he lifted his fist again. She barely felt the blow that struck her temple as her world turned black.

Chapter 33

A drop of water dripped on her forehead. Throbbing enveloped Aveline's head. With a slow turn, she tried to escape, but the pain floated into agony. A soft groan escaped.

"Ssh." Dorris' soft hiss blew into her ear. "Lie still."

Aveline did as Dorris said. Her left eyelid wouldn't open. The right one cracked with only a slit to see through. Dorris was blurry as she glanced over her shoulder, then down to Aveline. She held a finger to her lips.

Aveline tried to nod in understanding, but her neck hurt. She closed her right eyelid and the world returned to black.

~*~

The clattering of a pot awoke Aveline. The sharp sound made her grimace as the pain of it pierced her ears. She opened her right eyelid. Veil dumped water into the coffee pot, then pulled up the bucket, and walked toward the door. She didn't try to keep the pot from clanging or the bucket from banging furniture.

Dorris turned in her rocking chair to Aveline and got up.

"Good morning," she whispered. Her eyes flicked to the quilt curtain. Aveline nodded her understanding that Washington lay on the other side. Veil closed the cabin door behind her with a slam.

Aveline rolled over and forced herself up on an elbow. Her head throbbed and her neck was too weak to hold up her head. Stomach muscles cramped. The side of her left leg hurt.

She pushed herself upright and gritted her teeth, which she had to stop because her jaw hurt. She rested until Veil pulled open the door and staggered in lugging the full water bucket.

At the table, Dorris poured the coffee grounds in the pot, and hung the pot over the flame. Veil tipped the bucket and splashed the water into a washbasin.

Dorris grabbed a rag and carried the basin to Aveline. She dipped the rag into the water, squeezed it out and gently pressed it onto Aveline's cheek.

Aveline winced, but the cold water soothed the pain. "Feelsh goot," she muttered.

Both women jumped as the quilt whipped aside. Washington stood, already dressed. His dark eyes were sunk into his face from fatigue and his lips were tight. "Get dressed and get to work. In three days, the company leaves for Zion. You better be ready."

Aveline nodded. She handed the rag back to Dorris and gave her what she hoped looked like a smile. Dorris took the rag and basin and stepped to the kitchen area.

Washington whipped the curtain back into place. "Dorris, make sure all my shirts are clean and ironed. Pack my clothes and make sure she," his voice indicated Aveline, "has all her clothes, cooking utensils, bedding, and food packed by tomorrow morning. Make sure she uses the Bill of Particulars. That's the list of mandatory items. She's not to leave anything behind. We start packing the wagon tomorrow."

"Yes, Washington. Much of it has already been done. We have not much left to do."

Washington stood at the curtain a moment longer. "There are three other women selected to journey with the Pioneer Company: two Sisters Young and Sister Kimball. None of them cause their husbands any difficulty or shame. They are obedient. I expect you to be as well from here on."

Aveline nodded and looked at the floor through the slits of her eyelids.

"Coffee, Washington?" Veil offered as she lifted the pot from the flame.

Aveline's lip curled. She fought back a sneer at Veil calling her husband by his given name.

"No. I don't want to look at that another moment," he said flicking his head toward Aveline. He grabbed his waistcoat and jacket and slammed the door closed behind him.

In the heavy silence, Dorris sighed, took down two cups from a nail in the wall and filled them with coffee. She brought both cups to the bed, sat down and handed one cup to her battered sister-wife.

"Thank you, Dorris," Aveline mumbled. "I appreciate your kindnesses. This can't be easy for you."

Dorris blew on the coffee to cool it. She stared at the bottom edge of the quilt curtain as she breathed in the scent of the hot liquid. "I fear I have it the easiest." With her finger, she nudged a strand of Aveline's hair behind her ear. "Your sister met a horrible fate, and you have no name to blame for it. Washington is ... difficult now. We have a new wife—another new wife. We're preparing for the journey west. This has been a great trial for him."

Dorris sipped her coffee. "Aveline, hear me. In three days, you leave for a glorious adventure. You are a member of the select few, the Pioneer Company, chosen to enter Zion for the first time. As such, your name will be written in the Saints' history for all eternity."

Dorris took another sip. "You have been granted a great honor. With that honor comes responsibility: the responsibility to be a good Mormon woman and wife. You must demonstrate your worthiness."

Shame swept over Aveline. Washington was brutal in his teaching, but Dorris' gentle instruction eased its way into her soul, its meaning embedded into her spirit. Aveline began to weep. "I want to be worthy. I want so much to do better," she mumbled through her swollen mouth. She tried to stop crying; the pressure felt as if her head would split.

"I know." Dorris put her arm around Aveline. "Don't *want* to be worthy. *Be* worthy. Don't *want* to do better. *Do* better." She gave Aveline a light hug. "Don't cry now; you must save your strength. Soon, you have a great deal of walking to do."

~*~

The next day, Dorris straightened up from leaning over Washington's trunk. She had swept it out with a tiny clutch of willow branches. His shirts she had already ironed so she stacked them inside. His trousers were folded with a spare undergarment underneath. She had darned his socks and brushed his top hat. His trunk was ready. Dorris watched as Aveline folded up the last of her garments.

With a day's recovery and her movements these past several hours, her swollen face had lessened, but the bruising was darker.

"What is left to do?"

Aveline looked around the room. "Finish packing the food. Separate the cooking utensils. I'll fold up the bedding in the morning when I get up."

The two women prepared to separate which utensils would go with Aveline and which would remain with Dorris. Aveline froze. "You will be here alone with Veil." They could talk openly now; Veil had left earlier to visit friends.

Dorris shook her head. "Brother Mattison's family from Ward Six will move in here after you leave. His wife is Prudence. They have two babies. That ward's cabins are overflowing, and the move here will give them more space."

"Children, too? Six people in this cabin? That will be a noisy change for you."

Dorris laughed, "With you and Washington on your way to Zion, I think it shall be a quiet pleasure." Aveline smiled at Dorris' teasing.

"Veil will share my bed." Her tone sounded as if she hated the thought of sleeping with her. "Brother Mattison and his wife will have your old bed, of course. The children will sleep in the loft.

"Besides, we won't have to share the cabin for long," Dorris continued as she inspected a knife. "Washington will return this summer. He'll pack up Veil and me, and we'll make the trek. Until then, our responsibility is to start a garden behind the house. The Saints arriving this fall will find a ripened garden that will sustain them through the coming winter. I admit to looking forward to getting my hands dirty and watching green things grow." She smiled at the thought.

"I should think Veil will relish the experience of tilling the soil and picking weeds," Aveline said, a smile flitted across her swollen lip.

Dorris chuckled at the thought. "I confess, I look forward to that day."

Skirting the boxes and trunks set out for packing, Aveline reached for the Bill of Particulars. Her lips moved as she read the list again to herself, "Five pounds dried peaches, few pounds of bacon, twenty pounds of soap, five pounds of coffee, a pound of tea."

She skipped through the list of other foodstuffs she knew were packed. She ignored the hardware items such as the weapons or the draft animals; those were Washington's responsibility. "A half-pound of mustard! The store ran out when I asked for it last week. Do you think they may have gotten some in?"

"Likely. Those items on that list are mandatory, so I would hope they hurried to fill the store." Dorris stepped over Washington's trunk, lost her balance, and waved her arms to stop herself from falling.

The mustard was necessary not just for cooking, but as a poultice in case of congestion. Aveline considered how frightful her face looked. Perhaps, if she ignored the mustard, she wouldn't need it on the trail. If she needed it, perhaps she could borrow some.

Be worthy. Do better. Dorris' voice rang in her head. The responsibility to fill the list was hers. She would have to tolerate the stares. She reached into the little ceramic pot where Washington kept cash to purchase the remaining items and counted out some coins.

Not knowing how much the mustard would cost, this change had to be enough. If it cost more than this, well, she had a handkerchief she might be able to trade. The bills she had sneaked into her trunk from her earnings at Keegan's

Mercantile flashed in her mind. No, she would use his money for this purchase.

She poured the coins into her reticule, said farewell to Dorris and grabbed her shawl off the nail. The early afternoon sun felt warm against her shoulders, but the shawl would help hide her bruised face.

The Avery wagon was parked in front of the cabin. Stretched taut over the box bows, the pale canvas glistened in the sun. The tongue stretched out in front and almost blocked the cabin door.

Looking up at its rounded height, Aveline's heart rate quickened. She tried to imagine walking to Zion. Her name would be included in an honor for the ages: a member of the Pioneer Company.

Straightening in pride and resolution, she pulled the shawl tighter over her head and crossed one end of it over her face to hide the bruises. She headed north on Second Street.

An excited energy filled the settlement. The first company was preparing to emigrate, and more companies would leave soon after. The Mormon community focused with its characteristic attention not only on surviving winter, but on heading toward a new life over the western horizon.

Wagons had been positioned in front of many cabins in preparation for the journey. Even the dogs seemed caught up in the new spirit of goodwill and didn't fight; they only circled each other stiff-legged. Aveline waited at the intersection of Cahoon and Second Streets while a carriage traveled past. To her right, one pulled up in front of Lucas Bates' cabin. Aveline watched Lucas jump down, unhitch the horses, and drive them off.

Aveline hesitated. Eliza would be home preparing for Lucas' departure with the Pioneer Company. Aveline and three other women had been chosen to head west; Eliza was not one of them.

Thomas Keegan said Eliza returned Frances' hair comb. Since then, Aveline believed Keegan was innocent of Frances' murder. Shame flooded over her as she recalled her demented accusation against him at the dance. The rush of blood to her flushed cheeks pulsed her bruises. Her fingertips brushed the swollen knob on her left cheek.

Staring at Bates' cabin, Aveline took two steps in that direction but stopped.

Be worthy. Do better. Dorris' words echoed in her mind. If Aveline ignored her words now, she was not trying hard enough to be a good Mormon wife. With a gentle toss of her battered head, she turned left and headed into the store.

~*~

The log store was crowded with people trading for goods for the trip west. Conversation snippets sprinkled around her:

"Brother Brigham will lead us ..."

"Brother Cane confiscated two barrels of whiskey ..."

"Yer a tight-fisted man, Brother ..."

No one spoke of fear about the coming journey, only of excitement.

As she glanced around the store, conversations slowed and stopped. A quiet pall settled. She looked up from the shelves of goods to see what caused the silence; all faces stared at her. Ashamed, she pulled her shawl higher around her face, squared her shoulders, and pressed against the quiet.

Brother Younger stood behind the makeshift counter, both hands on the surface. He stared at her a moment longer. "Are ye comin' to claim I killed the sister, too?"

Aveline felt, rather than heard, a collective gasp at the brazen question. A snicker sounded behind her. Only a fool would believe no one knew about her hysterical accusations against Thomas Keegan. Of course, everyone knew. She forced herself to meet his eyes. "No, Brother. I need a half pound of mustard, as required for our journey."

He nodded and headed to the back where the mustard was stored. She watched him through the throng as he scooped out the powder onto a scale. He poured the amount onto a large piece of paper. Aveline ignored the whispering behind her. Brother Younger brought the packet to her. "That's seven cents."

Grateful that she had the needed amount, she counted and placed the coins into his palm. "Thank you, Brother."

No one spoke as they parted to let her pass. She pulled the shawl forward as she fled the store. She brushed past others entering the store and started to run, but the effort hurt her head. She blinked back tears of anger.

Just one more day and everyone might forget what I did. We'll have too many other things on our minds. One more day and I can forget what happened here. Even as she thought the words, in her heart Aveline knew she'd never forget what happened here.

She turned to head south on Second Street. As she glanced down Cahoon, she saw Eliza step down from the wagon parked in front of her cabin and head inside. Aveline froze. She took another step toward home. She hesitated. *Be worthy. Do better.*

Aveline shoved Dorris' words to the back of her mind and turned toward the Bates cabin.

Chapter 34

Aveline's heart pounded louder in her chest than her fist did on Bates' cabin door. She had no idea what to say.

She stepped aside as the door pushed open, and Eliza, the killer of her sister, peered out. Eliza's eyes were swollen, like she had been crying. She had lost so much weight, her clothes hung on her frame. Leaning against the doorjamb, Eliza smirked. "Gonna accuse me, now?"

Anger flooded Aveline. She widened her stance and jammed her fists on her hips, movements to convince Eliza—and herself—of her conviction. "Yes."

Eliza pushed herself off the jamb and reached to close the door. Aveline shoved the door open further and pushed her way in, almost knocking over Eliza. Stink permeated the cabin. Aveline's nose twitched. She flicked her eyes around the interior. It was dark. No fire burned in the fireplace because of the warm afternoon. She pulled the door almost closed; tight enough to keep prying eyes and ears out of their business, but open enough to let in light and fresh air.

"Eliza, why did you do it? How could you?" The questions were flat, monotone.

Eliza snorted. Her hands trembled as she picked up a shirt of Lucas', wadded it into a bundle, and stuffed it into a small wood trunk. She picked up a soiled pair of pants to wad when Aveline took a couple steps and whipped the pants out of Eliza's hands. Aveline threw the pants onto a bed that smelled as if the sheets hadn't been changed since fall.

"Tell me why you committed murder." This time, Aveline let the anger come through her voice as she advanced on the older woman.

Eliza backed up and staggered around her rocking chair, as if the wood piece would protect her. Aveline stood on the other side of the chair and leaned on it, her face close to Eliza's. "Answer me. Why would you kill your sister-wife?"

The question and mention of her sister-wife seemed to jolt Eliza. She tried to appear flippant as she stroked the arm of the rocking chair. "Why do you accuse me of the deed?"

"Confess, you witch. I'm so angry, I could strangle you." She lifted her hands like claws. "As much as justice is carried out in this town, nothing will happen to me for avenging my sister's death."

Aveline stepped around the chair to emphasis her point as she advanced on Eliza.

Eliza said nothing, but she moved to keep the rocking chair between her and Aveline. Finally, buying time, she asked, "*Why* do you think I did it?"

Aveline stopped. "I told you before, Mister Avery said he saw you leave the braid shop about the time Frances was killed. He believes you're the killer too!"

Eliza shrugged. "That means nothing." She stepped aside and behind another trunk set in the middle of the room for packing, and poked at some rumpled clothing.

"The cuts to Frances' throat looked like they had been made by a woman, not deep, but like someone who was afraid of what they were doing."

"I've killed a pig before." The sneer in Eliza's voice was meant for Aveline to interpret her words how she wished. "Slicing up a pig is nothing! Cutting a throat is nothing!"

Knowing her words were affecting Eliza, Aveline pressed on. "You read Frances' journal and letter to Lucas. You deliberately added words to make her appear sinful and worthy of death." She stepped beside the rocking chair and slipped toward the trunk, slowly so as to not scare Eliza to run outdoors.

"He already knew of her sin!" Eliza wailed.

"You murdered a woman who would soon leave you to your husband." Aveline screamed back; her voice rose with each word. "Why didn't you just let her go? You would have had Lucas all to yourself. You were abusive to an innocent woman who only wanted to do right. You are the one who sinned, and you are the one going to hell for it."

"No!" Eliza screamed. Tears poured down her face. "I committed no sin." She convulsed with sobbing. "I cannot abide this anymore. Yes, I found your sister, but she was already dead."

Aveline's eyes narrowed as she pondered whether to believe her. "How did you come to be at the braid shop?"

Eliza sank to the dirt floor. She whimpered, "Lucas sent me to fetch her. She had been gone a long time."

Aveline approached Eliza, stood over her, close, and looked down. "You're saying you only found her. Then how did you get her hair comb? Off her dead body?"

Eliza pulled her knees to her chest. She started to rock back and forth. "I took the comb."

"Why?"

"I knew Lucas cheated the Gentile out of the hair comb. I thought if I gave it back to him, someone might think he did the deed."

"How on earth do you believe you have the right to cast blame on an innocent man —"

"He is not innocent!" Eliza looked up to Aveline. A madwoman's eyes glittered in the dim light. "He is a Gentile! They commit murder, against us, against the Saints. You didn't see what they did in Nauvoo, or Missouri. My little brother — they beat Jack to death."

Eliza rocked faster. Her voice rose. "You didn't have them beating on your door, in the night, throwing you out in the cold, pointing their guns at you like you were criminal. They ruined lives, killed our beasts, ran us from our homes, burned them to the ground. They ran us from our farm — no food, no clothes but what we had on our backs, in the cold."

Eliza flung her arms over her head as if to block the vision of a nightmare. A wailing scream erupted from her. "I looked back. I saw it. My baby brother — tried to stop them from stealing our cow. A horseman hit him with the musket." She rocked faster.

"My sisters—they tormented Eleanor. They hurt her. Esther, Lucas' wife, in the throes of birthing—we ran to the grove while they torched our house." Eliza beat the trunk she leaned against with her fists. "She gave birth, in the cold night. She died there, and her baby boy."

She threw back her head and groaned. "My mother froze that night. They wouldn't let us bury them. We had to leave them. They threw their bodies down a well. Oh, God!"

Aveline's hands flew to her mouth as she envisioned the horror. Eliza's anguish bore into Aveline's soul.

"Keegan killed yer sister as sure as they killed my sister, and brother, and baby nephew, and mother," Eliza screamed as she tore at her clothes. "And nothing happened to them!"

Aveline's legs weakened against the weight of the horror and the torment in the woman before her.

Eliza's breath caught in ragged gasps. "If Gentile Keegan is found guilty of the murder of your sister, then his death will atone for the wickedness of rapists and the killers of boys and mothers!"

Aveline staggered as she absorbed the terror of the scene in her mind. Moments passed before she said in a soft voice, "You cannot send an innocent man to his death. That would make you as cruel and evil as those who committed the atrocities against your family."

"My only sin was taking the comb, but I returned it to its rightful owner," Eliza said, her voice small, shaking. With a vicious swipe of her hands, she brushed off her tears and wiped her nose on her sleeve. "Oh, God," she cried as she looked heavenward, as if beseeching for help in ridding her mind of the horror of that night long past. "I only wanted to protect my husband."

Aveline blinked in the dim light. She whispered, "Why do you think you needed to protect Lucas? From what?"

She could make out Eliza's trembling shoulders. Groans seeped from the bowed head. A lightning bolt of realization struck Aveline. "Why was Frances at the braid shop? It was late. The dance had just finished."

Eliza leaned against the trunk, exhausted and quiet. "Lucas ordered her there."

Aveline's legs gave out. She dropped onto a trunk. She whispered, "You really believe Lucas did this."

In the dim light, she saw Eliza's head nod. "I believe Lucas did the deed." A moan slid from her mouth. Groans escalated to open weeping. "When I found your sister, her face was covered. I moved the cloth." Eliza's hands covered her face as she rocked back and forth. "That is when I realized it was—"

"Your wedding veil," Aveline whispered.

Eliza nodded and swayed faster.

"It was your veil over her face," Aveline felt her face grow cold, not believing her own words, but confirming what Chief Cane had said.

Eliza nodded and began to weep.

"It was my veil. I knew," Eliza gasped for air as she shook her head. "I knew he meant the message for me: Do not betray me or you will suffer the fate of not being resurrected. I was too terrified to take my veil, so I left it covering her face."

Eliza stopped rocking and glared at Aveline with a look as if she were the devil herself. She snarled, "Now, get out."

Chapter 35

Aveline tugged at the door to her cabin. To pull open the heavy wooden door took all the energy she had.

"Did the store have the mustard?" A bright voice asked.

"Yes, I got the mustard," she mumbled.

Dorris hurried to her. She led Aveline to Washington's chair. "Are you all right? You're pure white."

Too exhausted to weep, Aveline took in a deep breath.

"Don't. Don't tell me." Dorris held up her hands. "You talked to the Bateses again."

Aveline nodded. Before she could explain, Washington stepped into the cabin. "There's a meeting at the Council House. They wish to pray for us in the Pioneer Company. We must go." He looked around. "Where is Veil?"

"She has not returned from her visit with her friends," Dorris said.

His lips tight in anger, he shook his head. "Hurry. We must leave." To Aveline, he ordered, "You. Cover your face."

Moments later, Dorris supported Aveline as they walked behind Washington and entered the Council House. The atmosphere of the open room contrasted sharply from the last time she was here for the dance a few days earlier: the lit candles, the gaiety, the music, the expectation of laughter and dance. The mood now was darker, somber, tense about the hardship they knew lay ahead. Several chairs and benches stood in rows, not enough for the crowd that pressed into the building. The sun shone through the windows, a harbinger for a brighter tomorrow.

The two women stood near the back while Washington moved to the front and sat down.

While the gathered waited for the meeting to begin, Dorris leaned over and whispered, "What happened?"

Aveline had hoped Dorris would forget she had disregarded the older woman's advice yet again. "Lucas was not there. I questioned Eliza again, until she threw me out."

Dorris' eyes grew wide. "Oh, Aveline," she sighed.

She cupped her hand around her mouth to Dorris' ear, "But it was worth it. She told me things."

Lucas Bates hurried into the building. Aveline stood straighter and craned her neck as she watched Lucas skirt other men to reach the front and sit beside Washington. A moment later, Chief Cane came in, wove his way to the front and sat behind Washington.

Apostle Heber Kimball stood and led the congregation in a prayer. Aveline paid no attention to his words; she only stared at the back of the heads of her husband and Lucas. Kimball introduced the Saints' leader, Brother Brigham Young.

Brigham Young walked to the front of the room. *How tired he looks*. With a slight shake of her head, she couldn't comprehend his burdens: leading the Saints from Illinois during the worse trials of their history and preparing thousands for the journey west.

As he warmed up to his topic, Young waved his arms. He exhorted the congregants to prepare for the Saints arriving in Winter Quarters behind them, to "cultivate the garden in the Lord's ground like we cultivate our desire to worship Him in the eternal Garden of Eden". Looking down to the group of men seated before him, he thundered on. Aveline thought he looked directly at Lucas while he preached. "The Lamp of God's wisdom will light your journey to Zion. His light shines upon the Lord's commandments, the law that guides us. Thieving, coveting and murder will darken the light of the Lord and will have no sanctuary in the Holy Land."

Aveline's heart raced. Incredulous, she reached for a thread of logic. *The leadership knows he's a murderer. And yet he still sits here.* As the congregation stood to sing *Come, Come ye Saints*, she couldn't mouth the words to the song. Her mind raced. *Why wouldn't they do anything about it? The chief of police is sitting one row behind a murderer. Why doesn't he grab Lucas and haul him away?*

Brigham Young dismissed the congregation with the blessing of the Lord. In the crush of departing worshipers, Aveline lost sight of her husband and Lucas. She and Dorris moved with the crowd outside. They stood aside to wait for Washington to emerge and make their way home.

Aveline was more interested in watching for Lucas. As others appeared from the house, many worshippers noticed Aveline and the bruises on her face. Often, as soon as they saw her, they stopped talking, nudged each other and looked away. Aveline pulled her shawl higher on her head and pulled the edges together over her face. Without a word, Dorris moved around Aveline and stood in front of her, sheltering her from the eyes of passersby.

The congregation dissipated as the Saints scattered to their homes or their duties. There was no sign of Washington. Aveline peeked around Dorris to see Lucas emerge and blink in the bright sunlight. He turned toward the braid shop.

"Dorris," Aveline hissed in a whisper. "I'm going to the braid shop to talk to him."

Dorris grabbed her arm. "You can't! You heard Washington. He'll find out! You know what he will do!"

Aveline gently patted Dorris' hand before she lost sight of Lucas. "I must. He killed my sister." She turned and hurried after Lucas.

Chapter 36

Lucas Bates flung the door closed behind him as he entered the braid shop. The three women hunched over their work looked up. Upon seeing Lucas, they returned to their braiding. Two women braided hats, one a basket. A fourth woman in the rear of the long cabin separated and sorted the straw. The dust tickled his nose. He sneezed so violently the women jumped. "Gesundheit," one woman muttered. Lucas didn't respond, but headed toward the back of the cabin.

He stopped to watch Sister Mattison separate straw, sorting it by size and type. The longer he inspected her work, the more her hands shook.

The shop door opened, and the harsh sunlight silhouetted the small figure that stood in the doorway. He studied the comely shape, but couldn't tell who the woman was. He watched as she stepped into the cabin, into the light cast by the oil lamp and fireplace.

Lucas straightened. His bulk seemed to fill the cabin. "Sisters, stop yer work and leave us."

The four women's hands froze. They looked up in surprise and stared at Aveline as she glared at their employer, her jaw jutting in defiance. As one, they looked back to Lucas, dropped their work and skirted Aveline as they fled the cabin. Sister Ann Cassell, the last to leave, cast a furtive glance toward Aveline and pulled the door closed behind her.

Neither Aveline nor Lucas spoke as their eyes met. Aveline trembled in fear and anger, but she allowed her anger to give her strength. She pushed off her shawl and lifted her head to face him in defiance.

As she opened her mouth to demand why he killed her sister, she decided to try a different tack, an approach that might make him talk. "Where did you get the hair comb you gave Frances?"

Lucas blinked. She had thrown him off guard. "That's what ye came to ask?" He took a step toward her.

Aveline forced herself not to budge and to face him squarely. "That is what I am asking."

Lucas shrugged and brushed a small bundle of straw from a table. "I won it."

"As I heard the story, you cheated for it."

Lucas smirked. "True, at faro, but it ain't really cheatin' if yer quarry is too ignorant to know he's bein' cheated." He took another step toward Aveline. "I took the comb and a lot of money from the simpleton. He deserved it."

"Have you not heard of 'Thou shalt not steal'?"

A snort escaped from Lucas' wide nose. "Oh, lass, it ain't stealin' to take from a Gentile."

Aveline's trembling intensified. "It is stealing, nonetheless. Mister Keegan is a good man, trusted in this community. Think of Colonel Thomas Kane. He is so respected, we Saints chose to call the town across the river after him. For your personal reasons, you have caused grave damage to the Saints' reputation by cheating a man who dealt with you in good faith."

"Don't criticize me, woman!" The bellow of rage exploded from Lucas, the force of which made Aveline step back. "Yer husband said ye have not learned to keep yer tongue in check. Ye believe yer his equal." He took a few more steps toward Aveline.

"Why was Frances in this shop after a dance?" The question was out of her mouth before she knew it.

Lucas' advance stopped. An uneasy silence settled like the dust from the straw pile. "I sent her here." His words were gentle, matter-of-fact.

"Why?"

"The door to the shop had been kicked in. I wanted her to inspect it to see if anything was taken."

Aveline's eyebrows scrunched in comprehension. "You ordered a small woman to check out illegal activity? Suppose whoever broke in was still here? She could have been hurt—"

Her own words caused her to step back in horror. Lucas sent her on that mission on purpose. He knew what would happen. He intended for her to be killed all along. "You killed your own wife," she gasped.

"Shut up, woman." A growl rumbled from the fleshy mouth.

"Why? Why would you kill her? She tried hard to be a good wife to you."

Lucas rushed toward Aveline. She screamed and spun around behind a large worktable. She gathered her skirt in her fists. Lucas went one way as Aveline rushed to the other side. "Why would you treat her so poorly?"

"Yer sister was an adulterous apostate—the lowest of a filthy sinner." Lucas was huge, but his bulk made him slow. He switched directions and closed in on Aveline.

"Only because of you and your wretched wife—"

"Yer sister was an embarrassment." Lucas shouted as he closed the space between them.

She spun and raced toward the back of the cabin. Too late, she realized she had trapped herself. Lucas stood between her and the only door. Aveline tried to think of a bid for time so that someone might enter and save her. "If she was such an embarrassment to you, why didn't you just throw her out of your house and divorce her?"

Lucas slowed his advance. "She and ye other impertinent wives needed to be taught a lesson. She refused to accept her station. I can see from yer face Avery is having the same difficulty."

Aveline remembered the bruises, but didn't try to cover them. She slipped to her left, trying to gain closer access to the front door. Lucas sidestepped to his right, cutting off her escape route. "Even now," he almost purred, "ye keep trying to escape yer destiny." He smiled.

"Why would you cover Frances' face? Why use Eliza's veil?" Aveline glanced at the sunlit strip under the door, hoping to see the shadow of a rescuer. The sunlight was unbroken. If she kept him talking long enough, someone might come in.

Lucas picked up a straw shaft. He poked at his teeth with it while he looked Aveline up and down as if he inspected a cow for purchase. He tilted his head to the side. "Yer sister was not a good wife. She did not deserve resurrection."

Rage erupted in Aveline. She grabbed a half-finished basket and hurled it at Lucas' head, but missed by two feet. "She tried to be a good wife. She deserved resurrection."

"Eliza's veil sent a nice message to her, aye?" The quiet voice from Lucas crashed Aveline's anger into chills of horror.

Her eyes opened wide, her breaths were ragged. "You sent Eliza on purpose. You knew she'd find Frances, and her own veil. You knew Eliza would keep silent from here on out."

Lucas smiled and continued to pick at his teeth.

"Eliza lied to you. You do realize that."

The straw pick froze. "She'd never lie to me."

"She lied to you. She made up what she 'read' from Frances' journal. Frances never committed adultery. She was virtuous. Eliza lied to you about what Frances wrote in her letters. She used words like damnation and sin and blasphemy of the Mormon faith just to anger you. She admitted it this morning. She reads portions to you or makes it up to steer how you act. You murdered an innocent woman because of it," Aveline screamed.

"Ye will regret messin' with my wife." He flung the straw to the ground.

"You are a killer," Aveline whispered.

"There's no proof of such a thing." His silky-soft voice caressed Aveline's ears as he stepped closer.

Aveline glanced at the door, willing it to open. Her heart raced in terror at the fast-approaching Lucas. "How will you explain my death?"

He reached for her. "I won't have to explain anything."

Aveline screamed and ducked as Lucas lunged. His reaching fingers grabbed only her shawl and snatched it off her. She raced for the door, but he was too quick. He seized her arm and whipped her around to him.

The door slammed opened and hit the wall. A shaft of bright light blinded Lucas.

"Halt, Brother!"

The loud voice shocked Lucas. He froze.

With a cry, Aveline yanked her arms from his huge hands. Silhouetted, a man stood in the doorway's glare. From behind him, a woman skirted him and ran to Aveline.

"Dorris!" Aveline burst into tears with relief and gratitude.

The two women fell into each other's arms. Dorris led her away from Lucas. As they neared the door, Washington Avery said, "Go home, Aveline. You're done. It's over."

Chapter 37

Dorris supported Aveline out the braid shop door and leaned the bruised woman against the doorjamb. She hurried toward the back of the cabin, but she didn't look at Lucas or Washington while she snatched Aveline's shawl off the straw-covered floor. As she ran past Lucas, she held it up like a shield. Outside, she draped it over Aveline's head and covered the bruised face with the shawl's edge. The silent crowd outside the shop parted for them. They walked home with their arms around each other.

In sight of the Avery cabin, Aveline started to tremble. The shock was wearing off and the reality sinking in. "How did you know to bring Mister Avery?"

Dorris exhaled a quick laugh that didn't mean humor, but was the release of tension. "You, Lucas Bates," she paused, "your sister's killer—I knew there would be terrible trouble. Him being so quick to anger and you publicly accusing him of killing his wife." She patted Aveline's arm as they walked. "As soon as you went in that direction, I ran in the other to fetch our husband."

"What do you think will happen to Lucas?" Aveline whispered.

They walked on in silence. Dorris shook her head. "This deed is too evil for Bishop's Court. Excommunication? Disfellowship? I don't know. This will be Brother Brigham Young's decision."

As they trudged down the dirt road, Aveline pulled Dorris into a tight hug. "This is the second time you have saved me," she whispered.

Dorris hugged her back. "Ah, the trials of the first wife." She smiled at Aveline.

They pulled open the cabin door. The darkness felt oppressive so they left the door open and sat down, Dorris in her rocker and Aveline in Washington's chair.

Aveline suddenly giggled. She pulled a package from her skirt pocket and held it up, triumphant. "The mustard."

She tossed the package at the trunk that held their foodstuffs where it landed with a satisfying splat. She'd pack it later. Right now, there was left nothing to do except wait for the morning, when the Pioneer Company would head toward the western horizon.

~*~

The shadows grew long when the women stirred from their chairs. Fatigue from the day's tension lingered while Aveline built a fire. "I wonder what is keeping Mister Avery. Do you think he's helping Chief Cane with Bates' arrest?" As soon as the words left her mouth, she held up a hand. "Belay that thought." She remembered not to question her husband's activities. Surprised, she realized she didn't care what was keeping him. She did care that the murderer of an innocent woman no longer haunted Winter Quarters.

Dorris smiled in the dim light. "You're learning."

"When is Veil to return from her friends' home?"

Dorris shook her head.

"How was the ceremony when they married?"

Dorris set the teakettle over the flame and sat down in her rocker. "We met at Brother Kimball's house. Like you, the bride-elect looked beautiful," she said with a touch of envy. "Unlike you, Veil didn't look terrified. She seemed very assured of herself. As soon as the ceremony was over, I returned here."

Aveline poured the boiling water into teacups. She brought one to Dorris and sat down with hers.

"When I got back, your mother was here, tending you. You were raving with the fever. The Paddock women rotated their assistance, as did Sister Richards. Poppy Wallace stopped by too. Later, Washington opened the door and said 'Dorris, make sure the sheets on the bed are fresh', then, 'bring in her trunks'. Your mother and I just stood there as if we had taken root in the dirt floor.

"There you were, deathly ill, and he was worried about the sheets." Aveline was surprised at the mockery in Dorris' voice. "He said, 'Sister Veil has enlarged my kingdom in heaven'. He stood aside. Veil walked in as if she owned the cabin. I guess you can say, at that point, she did."

The cabin door opened. Washington swept into the room with Veil close behind. Their giggling annoyed Aveline. Her jealousy spiked—an emotion she wasn't used to, but he had saved her life so she set aside the bad feeling.

Washington placed his arm around Veil, an act that made Dorris look away and watch the fire. "Aveline, get Veil some tea. Dorris, allow Veil to sit. She needs her rest. She is with child."

Chapter 38

For an instant, both women froze. Dorris' face went blank, her wide eyes unseeing from shock, but her movements to obey her husband's command were automatic. Aveline reached out to touch the older woman, but Dorris held up her hands to stop her. She stepped to her bed behind the curtain. Aveline took a cup from the nail on the wall, and poured in tea flakes and boiling water. Veil sat like a queen on Dorris' throne and accepted the cup without a word.

She returned the kettle to its place near the fire, and glanced at Dorris, who sat on her bed staring at the curtain's bottom edge. Deciding the water bucket needed filling, Aveline headed for the well to escape.

At the well, her mind raced. Would she have to stay behind at Winter Quarters so Wife Number Three could have the honor of heading west? If Veil were with child, the safest time for her to travel was now, not when she was several months along and might have to deliver on the trail.

Dorris' reaction upon learning that Wife Number Three was with child reminded Aveline that Washington hadn't asked for Dorris' permission to marry, as required. As she wrenched on the windlass to pull up the bucket, fury overcame her. She balanced the full bucket on the well's edge and stood with her arms resting on it. Why was she angry? Jealousy that Washington's affection was elsewhere? He was considerate of Dorris and very affectionate with Veil, but never bestowed affection on her, although he could be gentle when he wanted to be, when it served his purpose. She wasn't fond of him, but she could gaze upon his handsome face and softly curling hair all day.

So why be angry that Wife Number Three would bear his first child? *Dorris.* Aveline's heart bled for Dorris and her heartache. Aveline clearly would not, could not, feel the same emotions as Dorris. When Dorris and Washington first married, she expected to live her life with and through her husband as the sole wife. She had vowed to spend her days with that man, only to see his devotion to her deteriorate while another young bride took his attention and affection. With every new wife, another chance to bear his child was lost. Dorris was his stepping stone into heaven as she watched her husband of nineteen years bring young woman after young woman into her home.

Thinking back to the first day she entered the Avery cabin, Aveline recalled her own confusion why Dorris would hate her so, why Dorris was so angry when all she wanted to do was follow the Lord's command.

How painful those next months had been. How wonderful the two women's lives were now. They depended upon each other like caring sisters.

Veil also had sacrificed to follow the Lord's command. Aveline resolved to be kind to Veil and kinder to Dorris. The three women deserved a life where they all got along.

She unhooked the bucket from the windlass, hefted the bucket to head back, but halted.

Veil stood on the path to the cabin. Her wool shawl was wrapped around her shoulders. With a toss of her head she said, "I know the old Dorris is upset, but I cannot read how you feel about my news—the first in the Avery household to produce an heir."

Heaving the bucket back onto the well's edge, Aveline leaned an arm on its rim. "Do not—ever—call Mother Dorris 'old'. She deserves your respect, your reverence, and compassion." Aveline hoped the angry shaking in her voice was not interpreted as nervousness in the presence of this overindulged simp. "Let me tell you, Veil, from experience, from Wife Number Two: you will have a happier life if you could find it in your heart to accept Dorris as a cherished sister. She will support you and care for you, if you let her." Aveline doubted Veil would heed her advice.

"I am with child. That makes me superior."

"You are not superior. You are Wife Number Three. You're just another woman in this household. Furthermore, you would be wise to understand that Washington will marry another wife, and another, after we reach Zion."

"He would never replace me!" Veil let her anger show. "He loves me."

"Perhaps, but he loves more to reach higher into the heavens." Aveline nodded. "You are but another rung in his ladder. He *will* add another wife."

The two women stood and judged each other as the sinking sun's shadow crept higher on the cabins. Veil broke eye contact by looking down at her stomach and stroking her flat abdomen.

Aveline used the movement to launch into her next point. "Keep in mind, Sister Veil, that you have yet to produce an heir. Many women in this settlement have lost the babe before its birth. Dorris did. Many more lost their babe after its birth."

"I will not lose this child."

"Every woman with child believes that. That is their hope. That is not necessarily their reality." She pointed to the cemetery up the hill that held Frances' remains. "There are many babes in that bluff, and many new mothers, and many more women. Even Brother Brigham has two wives resting there."

Thoughts continued to flow from her mouth. "But there's something else on my mind. I am uncertain how I feel about your glorious news. You have been married only a few weeks. To be honest, I am undecided whether you are actually pregnant."

Veil gasped. "You doubt my word?"

Aveline sensed an advantage. She tsked. "Veil, you have been here three weeks. Do you expect me to believe you know you are with child? You might fool Mister Avery, especially since he is distracted with the preparations to head west. I'll venture a guess if I were to point this out to Mister Avery and Dorris—if she hasn't realized it already—this news is uncertain indeed."

Veil wavered in her response. Her mouth worked, as if choosing to spew a curse or give an explanation. She moved closer to Aveline as if to share a secret.

"Since you and I are not the primary wife, I can tell you this." She looked behind her to make sure they were alone. She whispered, "We have been together longer than three weeks." She stepped back as if that were all the explanation she needed.

In shock, Aveline stood back. Her eyes wide, her hands went to her mouth.

"Yes," Veil whispered, "but I am ashamed of it."

"Infidelity is a sin of the highest order, punishable by death," Aveline loudly whispered. "What was he thinking? What were you thinking?"

"He said he was a rising star in the Church. He was First Counselor, and such sin was forbidden to others lower than he. He said if we laid together, he would have the strength to rise higher." She twisted back and forth like a child singing a song. "The First Counselor is the church leader's right-hand man, the second highest man in the faith. I intend to be a part of his becoming the leader, the seer of our faith."

Aveline squinted. Her mind couldn't understand. It still reeled from the admission of a great sin. "The President's right-hand man is his first counselor, yes; but Mister Avery is First Counselor … to our ward's bishop."

Veil's sashaying stopped. Her mouth dropped open. "He said he was First Counselor."

The realization of Veil's misunderstanding came to light. "He is."

"So, … he is not first counselor to Brother Brigham?" Veil whispered.

Aveline shook her head. Wickedness flowed through her as she realized she was enjoying this moment as conceited Veil was receiving an awakening into reality.

Veil sank to the ground, but her carriage was erect, a product of her upper-class breeding.

"Did he tell you he was first counselor to Brother Brigham?" Aveline asked.

A moment passed as Veil's memory worked. She shook her head. "He talked so much of Brother Brigham to me. He said they were intimate, close. He spoke how he advised him in matters of our faith. He is so handsome, so regal. When he told me in Mount Pisgah, I just assumed ..." She turned her head to watch the shadow climb up the side of a distant cabin. Veil wiped her face with her hands.

"He is still handsome," Aveline offered. "Your family's wealth and generous tithing might have assured he will rise in the church. With his desire and his work to elevate his standing in the church, you — we — may actually achieve that goal."

Veil's head snapped up. She fought an internal battle. "We *were* wealthy. We lost everything in Illinois." She swallowed hard. "I lost my parents on the trail."

Sympathy for Veil filled Aveline. The great loss of her parents and wealth forced her to seize the first favorable opportunity to regain protection and station.

"Come." Aveline reached down to help Veil. "Your life in the Avery household can be happy and fruitful, regardless of Mister Avery's station, if you allow it."

With a toss of her head, Veil rose, grabbed her skirt in her fists, and hurried up the path to the cabin.

Aveline turned to the heavy bucket and muttered to herself, "Why, thank you, Veil, I would appreciate assistance lugging this bucket." She grunted at the dead weight. "You are most kind to help me."

As Aveline rounded the cabin corner, Washington and Veil stood beside the wagon. Neither one offered to help her. Veil's hand lingered on Washington's arm as she forced a smile at him.

Her peals of laughter at his funny story made Aveline angry. Envy bubbled in her stomach; Mister Avery had never told her a funny story.

She started the fire and ladled the water into the kettle for more tea. Dorris hadn't moved from her bed. Aveline sat on her stump as she stared into the flames for a moment.

The light outside dimmed as the sun finally sank under the western horizon. Aveline heard Washington and Veil move around the wagon as he explained all that was packed, and what was left to place for the morning's start. Now, Aveline was not sure if she would head west tomorrow.

Darkness fell over the settlement before Washington and Veil entered. Even with the knowledge that he was lower in rank than she had realized, she still carried herself as if she were queen of this log palace.

Washington again offered Dorris' rocking chair to Veil.

Aveline's eyes grew wide with shock. Why didn't he offer Veil *his* seat? His eyes met Aveline's. "Are you ready for tomorrow morning?"

Pride swelled within Aveline. She would be the one to leave in the morning, the chosen one to head west. She nodded, unable to speak.

"Then go to bed. We shall have an early rise." Since his wedding to Veil, he had stopped his weekly change of wives. He slept only with her.

Aveline stood to head toward Dorris' bed, but her eyes lingered on Veil.

She looked up. Their eyes met. Aveline glared as if to say: *You're a sinner; you're poor; and you ignored Mister Avery's true station. You have no reason for arrogance.*

After a long look, Aveline stepped behind the curtain and sat next to Dorris, who still sat hunched on the bed. She leaned close, careful not to touch her. Aveline whispered, "Dorris, I am so sorry."

Dorris nodded. Tears spilled over her cheeks; dark spots sprouted on the front of her dress. Aveline didn't know how to comfort her. She couldn't leave the older woman in peace as she had no place to go. Her trunks stood on the other side of the cabin, ready for packing into the wagon. She wanted to get into bed, but she had no nightgown. She stepped aside, removed her dress, and tugged off her boots. Wearing only her undergarment, Aveline pulled the quilt down and slipped under the sheet. Facing the wall, she stared into the dark corner. After several moments, her sister-wife slipped under the covers still wearing her dress.

Aveline wondered if Dorris had bothered to remove her boots. She rolled to lie on her back. In the flickering light and out of the corner of her eye, she watched Dorris stare at the ceiling. Veil rose from the rocking chair and walked to her bed. She bumped the curtain as she removed her dress. After a few moments, Washington walked over to the bed. He bumped the curtain with his elbows as he took off his shirt, then with his backside as he stripped off his boots and pants.

Aveline tried to ignore the rustling of fabric as they struggled to remove sections of their undergarments. In the dark, Aveline covered her head with her pillow, hoping to block out the soft grunting.

Chapter 39

The quilt was yanked off. Aveline gasped as the icy blast powered her into full wakefulness.

"Get up."

Aveline clambered over Dorris, who didn't rise, but curled up in a ball to stave off the frigid air. The fireplace flickered a sleepy flame, like it too was shocked by the cold. The oil lamp's weak flame barely pierced the dark. Shivering, she pulled on her dress and searched with her hands to find her boots for her frozen feet. She pulled back the bed's quilt and draped it over Dorris.

Washington was already dressed, and he dragged his trunk outside. Through the open door, Aveline heard the yoked oxen snuff and wondered how long he had been up. She peeked through the door. It was still dark outside with no hint of light in the eastern sky.

She poked the fire, added another branch and filled the pot with water and coffee. Using Dorris' knife, she sliced off some bacon and tossed the slabs into the skillet and placed the skillet on the spider over the coals. Washington had packed the remaining items: rifle, box of nails, tent, and the bedding.

Aveline poured a cup of coffee that she took to Washington, which he accepted without a word. She filled another cup for Dorris and sat on the edge of the bed and waved her hand to waft the heady scent towards Dorris' nose. "Wake up, sleepyhead," she whispered and hoped the older woman could hear the smile she forced onto her lips.

Awkwardly, Dorris pushed herself to a sitting position and took the cup. Aveline took a deep breath and tried to relax. This moment would be her last to enjoy the comforts of home for several months. Physical struggles, deprivation, disease, and accidents lay ahead. She would face them essentially alone. Aveline didn't know the other three women selected to travel.

Their status in the church was higher than hers, and she only knew them by sight. She was not privy to their blessing meetings where they spoke in tongues and translated the meanings. Perhaps she would get to know them better on the trail.

Tears formed in her eyes as she studied the older woman.

"I will miss you," Aveline whispered. "Please, please, take care of yourself," she begged. "When you arrive in Zion this fall, I shall have the finest house waiting for you." Aveline hesitated. "Of course, the largest bedroom shall be yours." She forced the smile and nudged Dorris with her shoulder.

Dorris gave a light exhalation that told Aveline she tried to see the humor in her teasing. Brimming eyes flickered in the firelight. "I shall miss you terribly. Please take care yourself." The older woman forced a smile as tears broke loose from the pools in her eyes. "I shall look forward to that bedroom."

Neither one spoke as they sipped their coffee, each woman's warmth comforted the other. The sizzling bacon brought Aveline back to the reality at hand. Reluctantly, not wanting to leave Dorris' side, she shifted her feet to stand and remove the bacon before it burned.

From the other side of the curtain, Veil emerged fully dressed. Aveline hadn't heard fabric rustling or saw the bumps on the curtain to know she was getting dressed. She and Dorris watched, amazed, as Veil grabbed the rag draped on the table to lift the piping-hot skillet, take a fork and move the bacon to two plates.

She took one plate outside to Washington. Within seconds, she returned and picked up the second plate. Veil took a deep breath, exhaled, and spun on her heels. She approached Dorris' bed and offered the plate with both hands to Dorris and Aveline.

"Good morning, Sisters," Veil whispered.

In stunned silence, Dorris and Aveline slipped a piece of bacon from the plate. Veil turned, placed the plate on the makeshift table, and brought the coffee pot to refill their cups.

Dorris found her voice first. "Thank you. Most kind. Veil."

"Thank you, and good morning, Veil," Aveline said.

Veil looked deeply into Aveline's eyes. Last night's message had affected her. She turned to hang the pot in its place by the fire.

Aveline took a deep breath. Dorris' eyes lost their dead look at the change in Veil's attitude and they appeared brighter. Relief flooded Aveline. Dorris would be fine, Veil too. She would never divulge Veil and Washington's terrible secret. The deed was done, and its disclosure would devastate Dorris. Aveline gave Dorris a quick hug.

Outside, the chilly air went through her thin dress. She wrapped her hands around the coffee mug. Dread and excitement coursed through her.

"Check the cabin. Make sure we have everything."

"We're leaving now? But my parents, the Paddocks, and Poppy aren't here yet — "

"I am not delaying this most holy journey for lie-a-beds. We have a destiny in Zion." The set of Washington's jaw and his tight lips meant there would be no discussion.

Gasping, in a panic, she turned to Dorris.

Dorris threw off the quilt and stood, barefoot, in her wrinkled dress. She whispered loudly, "I will tell them farewell for you. I will tell them." She peeked around the quilt in Washington's direction. Aveline understood. Dorris would tell her parents and her dear friends that Washington gave her no opportunity to say farewell.

Aveline spun on her heels. She stood in the center of the cabin and looked around, blinking back tears. How she wished she could tell those she loved most what possibly could be her final farewell.

The trunks were in the wagon. Foodstuffs had been loaded the day before, as had the kitchen utensils. Washington's chair would make the next trip in the late summer when he returned for Dorris and Veil. They were ready. There was nothing left to do except say goodbye.

Dorris pulled on her boots behind the curtain. Veil sat on Washington's chair looking like she didn't know what to do next. *Veil made a good start this morning. She'll be fine.* Aveline sat beside Veil and held out her hands.

She took the hands and squeezed them. "I will remember what you said." Veil lowered her head. "I confess, I feel better."

With a quick breath and a tightening throat, Aveline gave her small home a last look.

Washington entered the cabin and pulled the door closed. "We are ready." Taking in the tense silence, he said, "Let us pray for a safe journey and good health until we shall see each other next."

The poignancy of his words caused Aveline's eyes to tear. She blinked hard while the four held hands. Washington gave a prayer of thanks for their good health and begged the Lord bless the trail and the favored pioneers who would travel its length. "May the three women of this king's castle obey and strive to provide for a happy household, and would the Lord smite any woman who lags in her wifely duties."

A jolt raced through Aveline. The message was a clear sign. Anger sliced through her. She had forgotten during the morning's excitement, and with thoughts and fears of the journey, that she had solved her sister's murder. Her sister-wife and husband saved her from the brutal Lucas. Squirming in discomfort, Aveline fought her anger at Washington's wish to smite a woman. *This? From a man who committed infidelity? And in a prayer to the Lord!*

"Amen."

"Amen," the three women echoed.

The hard knocks on the door made all four jump. Aveline rushed to it, thrilled her parents had come in time before her departure. Two men whom she'd never seen before stood outside, their hands clasped in front of them. Their dour expression made Aveline wonder if they would give the news that Washington and she had been dropped from the Pioneer Company roll.

"Brothers," Washington said. An angry cloud passed over his face as he pushed Aveline aside. The three men walked to the wagon. Aveline peeked out, and the door almost pinched her nose when Dorris pulled it closed.

"Those brothers are actually inspecting the provisions," Dorris whispered, her eyes wide with indignation.

"Inspecting?" Aveline asked, shocked.

"Washington told me yesterday they would come. Their mission is to ensure you have all the provisions required to make the trip, so you won't burden the company with a spare amount. He was not pleased to submit to inspection," Dorris said, low.

A wave of relief swept over Aveline. Thank goodness she chose to face the people at the store to purchase mustard. "Do you think I can run home to say farewell to Ma and Pa?" Aveline pleaded.

"Don't risk it. I cannot believe the inspection would take long. If you're not back in time …" Dorris held out both hands, unable to finish her thought.

Light raps on the door sounded, and Dorris opened it to Ma, Pa, and the Paddocks. Hamish, Em, and Carissa each held the hand of a sleepy child.

Aveline rushed to them and pulled them inside. "Oh! I am so happy you made it in time!" She held her mother and kissed her cheek, then Pa.

Hamish gave her a quick hug, then stepped back, looking uncomfortable with tears in his eyes. Em and Carissa held her and pressed a "Godspeed," and a "Farewell" into her hair. She patted each boy lightly on the back.

Ma handed Aveline a packet of biscuits baked fresh that morning, and Em and Carissa gave her a package of a pocket pie. "To make your journey easier today so you don't have to worry about cooking," Ma said. Ma wiped her tear-drenched face as Pa put his arms around his wife in comfort.

The cabin door opened. Washington, already angry at submitting to an inspection, took in the small crowd in his house. "We may proceed." He let the sneer in his voice carry outside to the two men who still stood beside the wagon.

Washington reached for Dorris and held her in a lingering embrace. He reached for Veil. She dropped her arms after quick pats on his back and stepped beside Dorris.

Aveline hugged Veil and whispered, "Take care of Dorris. She's a wonderful woman." Veil nodded solemnly. Aveline embraced Dorris while she stroked the older woman's face to wipe off the tears. "I love you," Aveline whispered.

Dorris could only nod, too overcome to speak.

As one, Washington and Aveline turned. She took her place beside the wagon. She would walk to Zion as Washington took his place to the left of the lead ox. He lightly tapped the beast with his walking stick. The oxen leaned into their yokes. The wagon lurched forward.

Aveline giggled like a little girl. She waved at her family and friends as they watched outside the cabin in the growing light. "See you in Zion!"

Chapter 40

The wagon rolled south on Second Street. In the brightening morning, more wagons than usual stood outside cabins. Men hitched horses and oxen while women watched their men prepare to head west. The work was quiet. Instructions from one person to another were softly spoken. The loading of belongings were muffled by sacks of foodstuffs. The oxen snuffed in exertion. Even the dogs didn't bark.

Aveline walked ramrod straight and pulled her shawl tighter around her. She hadn't warmed up yet, and the cold air burned her lungs. She glanced at Washington. He walked erect, and gave a quick nod to those who wished him farewell and Godspeed.

The small noises of the Camp of Israel faded. Creaking wheels, oxen snuffing, and the plodding of their hooves were the only sounds. The two pioneers walked past the collection of cabins. The straight rows of sturdy, temporary homes passed from view. Washington and Aveline stared at a few wagons with tattered coverings that served as homes for some Saints. A feeble cough leaked from one. Aveline pulled her shawl closer, tighter, and she wondered how the occupants survived the winter. A quick prayer of gratitude for her comforts over the winter floated in her mind.

They continued west up the bluff. Rows of dugout cabins squeezed the road between the hills. Dug into the hillsides, their fronts and the bulk of the sides were log. Few had doors; the others had only a blanket or a cloth doorway. Most flapped in the morning's gentle draft. Fireplace smoke dribbled from chimneys. An infant's thin wail stopped, cut off. Another dugout was creased with the collapsed, burnt remnants of a roof. This was the place where a boy had played tag with his toddler sister and knocked over the oil lamp onto the woodpile by the door. The flames had reached the bone-dry shake roof in seconds. The family escaped before the fire consumed the dugout's contents, but not before the oil that splashed onto the little girl's dress ignited. The two-year-old girl died two days later.

Aveline glanced at Washington. She couldn't decipher the angry look on his face as he stared at the dugout's remains. He was probably angry at the thought of a boy who played, she thought, before ashamedly recalling his traumatic boyhood.

The outskirts of Winter Quarters fell behind them as the trails unified ahead. The area of dead grass, crushed by wagon wheels during the past several days, narrowed into two tracks carved into the prairie.

Their wagon creaked as the two pioneers stepped beyond the bluffs. The oxen maintained their steady crawl even as the terrain leveled. The standing dead grass tugged at Aveline's skirt. She lifted the edges in her fists and wondered if she would have to hold her skirt the entire way to Zion. At the peak, the trail turned to the northwest. Aveline spun and walked backward for her last look at Winter Quarters.

The rising sun's rays fanned upwards to the heavens. Bright pink and dusty blues saluted farewell.

Below her, the Camp of Israel was still waking. Lagging members of the Pioneer Company hitched horses or oxen to their wagons. Herders walked south to care for their charges in the stockyard. Ma and Pa would be roasting their coffee.

Beyond the settlement to the east, the Missouri River moseyed to its destination down south. The ferry pulled away from the Missouri Territory on its way to Iowa. A small ship floated south, making use of the great Missouri's power.

The bluffs glowed from the first light of the rising sun. Frances would remain forever in this wild country. Tears formed in Aveline's eyes. She felt comforted that her sister rested in holy ground glowing with the power of the universe.

"Move on. We'll noon about six miles out."

Startled from her reverie, Aveline blinked back her tears. Turning back toward the wagon, she was surprised how far it had rolled ahead. The breeze swallowed the creaking sounds. Lifting her skirt, she hurried to catch up.

~*~

The sun beat down, centered between the horizons, yet low in the early spring sky. The wind blew harder, chilling Aveline's sweating skin. She sat on the blanket she had spread on the sea of dead grass while she and Washington ate their lunch of biscuits smeared with peach preserves and chunks of the last bit of cheese.

She rose to her knees to get a better look at the western horizon. "How long before we see the mountains?"

"Weeks."

Aveline thought about weeks of trials that lay ahead. The enormity of their task sank in. She felt small, as if the universe had suddenly expanded to prove her insignificance.

"Will we see Indians?"

"Yes."

Picking up a crumb off her skirt to pop it into her mouth, thoughts of an attack on their company frightened—and excited—her. "Will they attack us?"

"Don't know."

"Where is the rest of the company? I cannot believe we're going by ourselves."

"There's a small camp by the Elkhorn River. They're waiting for Brother Brigham whilst he travels back and forth to Winter Quarters doing church business. We'll remain there while the group organizes. There's another group that's gone ahead to the Platte River."

"Why don't we go on ahead to the Platte?"

"Brother Brigham will use the Elkhorn camp as his base until we're ready to proceed. I will not go beyond where our leader's light shines." His tone cut off any potential for debate.

Images of Indian attacks and accidents swirled in her mind as she chewed the last bite of biscuit. "We'll face many dangers on this journey."

"And we will face those dangers. The lamp of God's embrace will light our journey. He will hold us in grace and protect us from harm."

Aveline watched Washington and envied his highest level of religious fervor and confidence. The defiant set of his jaw dared the scythe of Death to cut his life short.

"What does Zion look like?"

He stopped his chewing and studied Aveline. "Since when do you ask me so many questions?" He ripped off another chunk of biscuit and stuffed it into his mouth.

"I never had you to myself before." The words were out of her mouth before she even considered what they meant.

The words surprised her as much as they appeared to surprise Washington, who stopped chewing to scrutinize his young wife.

She realized they'd never been alone together. Dorris or Veil had always been near: on the other side of the quilt curtain, in a chair, beside her as they walked.

Uneasiness grew as she wondered how she should act, a wife of six months alone with her husband for the first time.

~*~

Whipping the blanket to flick off dead grass, Aveline watched the gold straw blow in the breeze to land some distance away. While she cleaned up from lunch, Washington checked the oxen and ran his hands between their thick necks and the yokes.

He stepped up on the wagon to peer inside to check the interior. As he stepped down, he stopped short as he caught sight of something approaching from the southeast.

Aveline followed his gaze. Another Saint headed west.

Washington inspected the area to ensure nothing was left behind. He took his place to the left of the lead ox. "Hey, yup." He tapped the ox with his walking stick.

Aveline's legs had stiffened during the lunch stop. On her right heel, a burning sensation meant she'd have a blister soon. In addition to the concern for her feet, worry that her illness the week before had sapped too much strength and jeopardized her walking to Zion weighed heavily on her mind.

The plains of the Missouri Territory stretched before them. The land rolled on in a gold sea of dead grass, punctuated with islands of cottonwoods draped in the misty green of budding leaves. At her feet, delicate shoots of new grass pushed through.

A robin, in a barely perceptible squat, deposited yesterday's worms on a gnarled tree stump. The wind carried the pollen of new growth. Aveline sneezed. Her nose and eyes felt pressure, a pushing from within—the downside to the spring's new beginnings.

On the trail ahead, a caravan of three wagons dipped in and out of Aveline's view in time with the rises and depressions of the plains. Washington tapped the lead ox, ordering it to quicken its pace in an attempt to catch up. The road dipped into a hollow.

Trail ruts scarred the soft mud. Scattered boot marks punctured deep holes in the muck. Two thin tracks evaded the muck to the north. Washington tapped the lead ox to shift its course and walk the thin, hard tracks.

Beyond the three wagons, a line of cottonwoods sheltered the Pioneer Company's camp. This was the smaller, second camp. In this spot, members of the company gathered to organize for the coming journey. The larger main camp was further west, near the Platte River.

Smoke from the campfires drifted in the stiff breeze. Seeing other hand-selected pioneers drove home the honor bestowed upon Aveline. Any concerns for the dangers ahead vanished in her joy and pride.

The three wagons ahead reached the encampment. They circled behind the group and slowed to a stop.

"Hello!" Washington called to a man removing the yoke from his oxen beside the encampment. He waved at the man, who motioned for their wagon to follow and stop beside the three-wagon caravan.

"An adventure in praising the Lord!" Washington said aloud, more to himself than Aveline. She smiled at her husband's zeal.

The newly trod and uneven ground caused her to lose her balance. She lifted her skirt. At the camp, wagons stood in a circle, tongues pointed out in a radiating star. The campfires' smoke roiled in the growing wind. One man, enveloped in the smoke, rose from the log stump, pushed against the gale, walked to another man and stood over him, upwind, to continue gesturing in their lively conversation.

"Ho, ho," Washington said low, as he tapped the lead ox on the chest, a signal to stop. Several yards more and the wagon groaned to a halt. Aveline stopped her march and dropped her skirt. The wind rumbled in her ears, and she heard only the oxen's snuffing.

A tall man strode toward Washington. Fatigue etched the man's leathered face. "Brother Avery."

"Bishop Rolfe." The men shook hands as Aveline stood behind her husband. Bishop Rolfe ignored Aveline as he pointed west. "For water, over that knoll is the Elkhorn." He shifted his arm to point east. "You can clog your beasts downstream."

He looked at Aveline, his first acknowledgement of her, and tossed his head toward the grove. "Lots of cottonwood branches for fuel." Rolfe said, "We'll camp here until Brother Brigham returns."

A glum expression passed over Washington's face. "He's not here? I wished to speak with him."

"He and other brothers had business requiring their attention back in Winter Quarters. He's returning this afternoon. After that, he figures we'll be here at least a few more days." Bishop Rolfe nodded his head at Washington, turned and strode toward the three wagons. She felt a flash of relief; she would have a few days' rest before pushing west. Washington walked away from the wagon toward the encampment without a word to Aveline.

"Bishop Rolfe!" One of the men by the lead wagon sang out.

"Brother Younger!" Both men smiled as they greeted the other. Each gripped the other's shoulder in a near-embrace.

Aveline watched as Bishop Rolfe waved the same instructions to Brother Younger, but with more animation. She wondered who would receive the directive for the female to collect wood for the fires.

Brother Younger acknowledged the information with a nod. Bishop Rolfe strode back to the center of the wagons' circle. Brother Younger turned and hollered toward the back wagon. "Luke! I got instructions for ya!"

She turned to watch another pioneer jump from the back of the last wagon, a large man. He sauntered to Younger and listened while Younger relayed the instructions.

Younger noticed Aveline watching him and stared back. The big man noticed Younger's attention was elsewhere, so he turned.

She focused from Younger to the big man.

Lucas Bates stared back.

Chapter 41

The world spun as Aveline's senses shut down. She couldn't breathe. The sun's glare darkened to a tunnel where only the smirking face of Lucas shone.

Lucas turned back to Brother Younger, said something, and both men laughed. He spun toward Aveline. Hands crammed into his dirty pants' pockets, he picked his way across the prairie grasses. Occasionally, he stopped to make sure Aveline still watched him, his smirk ever widening.

As he neared Aveline, Lucas stopped, removed his hat and, in a grand gesture, gave her a deep bow. "Good afternoon, Sister Bowmore."

He spread his arms wide. "Here we are in the Lord's country." He slapped the drooping hat on his head and tucked his thumbs behind his suspender straps.

No words came from Aveline's mouth although it furiously worked. The sounds of the world and the light of the sun returned, but Aveline remained frozen.

He took another step closer. The smirk faded and his brow furrowed. His lips tightened. "Not so full of accusations now, are ye?" A sneer crossed his mouth. He turned back toward his wagons.

"You were hidden to escape your arrest in Winter Quarters. I'll tell Brother Brigham." The choked words stumbled from her mouth.

"Ye'll keep yer damn mouth shut if ye want to live longer," he called over his shoulder.

Lucas' threat snapped Aveline from her shock. "Get away from me, you murderer!" She pointed at Lucas and screamed, "Killer of women!"

Lucas halted, his face had gone pale. In a flash, he stood chest to breast with Aveline. "Ye should stop with the screamin', lass, or you'll be in dire trouble yesself." His voice was silk-soft, low, and stank of whiskey.

He glanced toward the encampment. Men stood by the campfires and watched. Lucas looked back to Aveline. "Now, don't go getting them people in our business."

Aveline took a step back, but Lucas stepped forward. She leaned back to put some distance between them. "Why aren't you in jail?"

"Ye can't throw an innocent in jail."

"You're lying. You're not innocent. You admitted—"

"I admitted nothing, woman." Lucas flinched, showing his growing anger. "Ye just made yesself believe it. Ye wanted to believe it." He looked down his nose at Aveline. "Now, no more about it, hmm?"

"You killed her. How else did Eliza's veil drape across Frances' face? Eliza was terrified of it; she wouldn't have done such a thing."

The smirk crossed Lucas' face. He leaned in. "Maybe, when Eliza was out, say, someone took the veil from Wife's trunk and gave it to the one who did the deed. Wife would see the veil draped over the sinner's face. She would understand the message."

Confusion washed over Aveline. "Why would anyone not close to Eliza or Frances do such a thing? That could only have been you—" Aveline choked on the words.

Movement to her left pulled her attention from him. Desperate for help, she was grateful to see Washington rushing to her aid. "Mister Avery, Lucas escaped—"

Her words were cut short by Washington's steel grip on her arms. His face was red. His eyes squinted. "Silence, woman!" His voice screamed in her ears. "I ordered you to stop your meddling!" He released his grip on her arm to slap Aveline's face.

The slap wasn't harsh, but the pain caused by the bruising from the earlier beating sent her reeling.

"Mister Avery!" She gathered all the energy she had and pushed him away. Washington only staggered back a few feet, but he stayed away. "I don't understand," she cried, eyes wide in pain, fear and confusion. "Why is he not in jail?"

"The Saints do not jail innocents."

"He's a murderer!"

"Stop this accusation. He is my friend, my blood brother. I will vindicate him and defend my faith from all outsiders—"

"He is not your friend!" Aveline screamed. "He was abusive to my sister. Even you said Frances told you how poorly he and Eliza treated her. She told you the night of the Council House dance. You told me how upset she was."

Tears streamed down her face. Aveline pointed to Lucas. "At the dance, he asked me to seal to him, that your children and I would be his for eternity. He said not to tell you!" She swiped at the tears with her hands. "*That* is your friend."

Washington's mouth twisted. "You fool. Frances never told me the Bateses were abusive. I told you such to get you to stop asking questions. I asked her to seal to me, and for her not to tell Lucas." He paused. "It was a test of your faithfulness to us."

Aveline staggered from the two men. Her legs gave out and she sank to the ground as she now understood. Her shock gave way to disgust. She pushed herself off the ground and faced them, her legs apart, arms out to her side. "Did we pass?" Her words were spit from her mouth; she was beyond caring.

Both men nodded. "The test was to see if you would betray your husbands with another and keep silent about it," Washington said. "Very good."

The flippancy of his words removed all traces of fear. "You seem to know all. Tell me, Husband," the word oozed from her mouth. "How did your handkerchief, my gift to you, end up around Frances' throat?" His past words seeped into her mind how he had dropped the cloth near Thomas Keegan during their fight. She shoved the words away.

Washington stared at Aveline. "Just as Eliza's veil was a warning to her, the handkerchief was a warning to you and for all you arrogant women. You failed to heed the warning."

Her face felt cold. The blood drained from her head. Her vision narrowed and her words softened.

"You knew what was to happen. You meant to send such a message." She gagged. Barely able to look at Lucas, she croaked, "You were home the whole time she was being killed. You knew she was being killed."

"Aye. Now yer understandin' I am innocent. I won't have a wife's blood on my hands, no matter how sinful she is." Lucas said, pleased as if hearing his child comprehend a spelling lesson.

"Blood ... brothers," she whispered. "You would vindicate him ..." Eyes wide in understanding, she looked into Washington's.

All three knew the truth. She staggered away from her husband. "You murdered Frances."

"She was a sinner," Washington snarled. "An adulterous apostate. The lowest sinner condemned to the hottest level of hell."

For the first time, she saw her husband as he truly was: a religious madman. Her stomach retched.

To Lucas, she said, "You sent my sister to check on the braid shop. You knew she would be alone. You delivered Eliza's veil."

With movements jerky from shock, she faced Washington. "You said you had church business to attend to. *You* received the veil from Lucas. *You* knew Frances would be alone, you murdered her, and you draped Eliza's veil over Frances' face. Both of you knew Eliza would find her veil and that message would come back to me." Her voice got louder with each word.

Washington hissed, "The only reason you were granted permission to be a member of this glorious journey was so you would be silent."

They glanced over at the encampment. Several men walked in their direction. "Lower your voice, damn you."

Aveline's head flinched as if he had slapped her again. "To be silent over blood atonement," she whispered. "She had only apostatized." Her voice rose again. "She was leaving the Camp of Israel. Why couldn't you just let her leave? *Why did you have to kill her?*"

Washington leaned close and whispered, "I bestowed forgiveness and eternal salvation to an apostate, my greatest proof of devotion to the Saints and to Brigham Young."

Chapter 42

Gasping for air, Aveline gagged. Falling to her knees, bent over, nothing came out of her convulsing stomach. She heard Lucas' voice. "Ta ta, lass. See ye down the trail." The booted feet stomped away.

"Get up," Washington hissed. "Here approaches Brother Brigham." When Aveline didn't rise, he yanked her to her feet. In her mindlessness, she clawed at the air as if she could gain a grip from the nothingness.

Washington stood at attention. "Greetings, Brother Brigham! Welcome to the Avery home." He clenched Aveline's arm to keep her upright.

Afraid her legs would give out on her, she refused to curtsy and said nothing. Brigham Young stood before them, his long hair drifting in the wind. He looked from Washington to Aveline. "I heard shouting. I trust all is well here in the Avery home."

Washington squeezed Aveline's arm in warning. "All is well here, Brother. A family squabble; we have settled our differences."

Brigham Young stood for a moment longer as he watched them. He noted Aveline's bruised face. "We have a long and dangerous journey ahead. The Lord will assure our safety to Zion, but we must assure each other of our safety from each other."

The Lord would ensure their safe passage, but only if the Saints didn't kill each other first, Aveline thought.

Young nodded. "All is well in the home of the Averys, as it should be." He turned to leave.

"No!" The scream was out of Aveline's mouth before she knew it. She groaned and winced at Washington's crushing pressure on her arm.

Young turned back, his eyes wide in surprise.

Aveline yanked her arm from Washington's grip. She stepped aside, away from the swing of his fist. She held out her arm and pointed at Washington. "All is not well. He admitted to murder! Brother Young, I beg of you, arrest this man. He killed my sister, Sister Frances Bowmore."

Young's eyes grew wider as he stared at Aveline. She thought he looked through her.

Washington knelt in front of Young, both hands together in prayer. "Brother, I confess to the killing of a sinner, the lowest of the low, a traitor who confessed to her sin of apostasy and infidelity. I granted her eternal salvation through the spilling of her blood."

"She was leaving the Camp of Israel! There was no need to kill her," Aveline screamed.

"Brother Young, Frances Bowmore faced damnation to writhe in hell's fire for eternity. Thus by God's words, revealed by you, blood atonement was her only promise of salvation. I beg for forgiveness and mercy for my deed," Washington pronounced.

"Brother Young, I beg of you, bring justice to my sister, a righteous woman who only tried to be a Saintly wife for the Lord." Aveline placed her hands together in supplication. Her eyes pleaded with Young.

Young stood tall, and brought his hands to clasp the front edges of his jacket. He faced Washington. "I am well versed in the circumstances of Frances Bowmore. Rise, Brother Avery."

Aveline noted Young did not address Frances as "Sister".

Washington stood, his hands clasped in prayer before him.

"You desire forgiveness for your deed," Young stated with a stern voice as he lifted his head to look down his nose.

"Yes, Brother, I beg forgiveness," Washington said.

"Denied."

Aveline closed her eyes. Justice would finally be served for Frances. The leader of the Latter-day Saints would ensure it.

Washington stood, mouth agape.

"Brother Avery," Young intoned. "I know of this woman's immoral and grave sins. You have committed no sin for which to be forgiven. Granting a sinner eternal salvation is no transgression, an act requiring no mercy from judge or jury. You saved the damned so she may enter heaven."

Aveline sank to the ground, numb.

Washington placed his left hand over his heart and reached to shake Young's hand. "Brother Young, I pledge my blood, my loyalty, and my salvation to you."

With a grimace, Young yanked his hand from Washington's. He looked down at the woman at his feet. "Know this, Sister, such sin cannot be forgiven, but redemption may still be granted for those who sin. If you love your sister, if you wish for her to reign in heaven, then rejoice in her salvation."

Aveline shook her head. "But she was righteous."

"You reject my declaration?" A bellow erupted from Young.

Again, Aveline shook her head. Washington yanked Aveline to her feet and the pain made her cry out. "Stand in the presence of our leader," he hissed.

"I am well versed in your disobedient activities. Perhaps you wish to choose the path your sister chose: apostasy." Young's voice was stern.

A chill raced through Aveline. Would they kill her as Washington did her sister and in plain view of the camp's witnesses? "No, Brother," Aveline whispered.

Young nodded. He looked at Washington. "Counsel your wife on devotion, Brother." He headed back toward the camp.

"Wait!" Aveline screamed. Her heart raced in fear. "Brother, I beg of you two things."

Young turned back again, his lips tight as his patience wore thin. "Your lack of womanly obedience is deeply disturbing, Sister."

Aveline bowed her head. "I beg for your forgiveness. I so wish to be a good wife and a good sister to the Saints."

Young seemed interested. He nodded in a slow fashion. "Continue."

She looked directly into Young's eyes. "I beg to be released from the privilege of being a member of the Pioneer Company, that you allow me to return to Winter Quarters."

An angry murmur rose from the bystanders. Young's face contorted. "Do you realize you cast aside the Lord's honor?"

"Yes, Brother, I do. I fear I am not worthy of such privilege." Other reasons weighed on Aveline's mind.

Washington seized both her arms in painful grips. "Has the devil entered you? You are to be exalted in the Saints' heaven as a pioneer. By going back, you deny me the honor of the Avery family entering Zion."

Aveline wrested herself from his hands and pushed him away. "I do not wish to accompany you."

"Evil resides in you!" Washington screamed. "You deny your faith! You deny me—"

"How can I could abide someone who murders a virtuous woman? Someone who commits adultery, a sin worthy of your death penalty? How does a man commit adultery, yet becomes revered, while an abused woman is falsely accused of adultery and is murdered? If this is your faith, I want no part of it." Aveline screamed back.

Washington reached for Aveline but Young held out a hand to stop him. Young's face was purple with rage. "You reject our faith."

She braced for a blow.

Washington paled. He turned to Brigham Young, whose brow furrowed as he studied Aveline. "What is it you *truly* desire?" Disgust dripped from each word.

She squared her shoulders and looked into Young's eyes. "Truly, I desire a divorce, Brother. I cannot live in this man's house." She gulped and paused. "I decline the great honor of being in your Pioneer Company and ask to return to Winter Quarters."

Young turned to Washington. "You were not married in the temple so you did not receive the ordinance of marriage. Thusly, I grant you a divorce. You are free of this woman."

He turned to Aveline. "You are no longer married. For your headstrong refusal of faith, you forfeit the honor of membership in the Pioneer Company."

Aveline closed her eyes in relief. She was free from Washington. She was safe to return to her parents ... alive.

Young spun on his heels and raised his hands high. The spirit of rage appeared to take over his body. "Hear me."

A hush fell.

"Aveline Bowmore is no longer a member of our blessed Pioneer Company ..."

The crowd whispered in shock.

"For she is no longer a member of the Church of Jesus Christ of Latter-day Saints."

Aveline barely heard the collective gasp of the crowd. Her bones felt as if they had disappeared from her body and she collapsed to the ground. Tears poured from her eyes. All feeling in her mind and heart vanished.

Young pointed to Bishop Lang. "Strike her name from your bishopric rolls."

Raising both arms, Young shouted. "Every member shall erase 'Aveline Bowmore' from the list of the Pioneer Company.

"All will strike her existence from every company roll, journal, and letter. Speak no more of this woman.

"I damn her to writhe in agony in hell."

He turned back to Aveline, kneeling on the ground. A mixture of disgust and pity splayed across his face.

"And the Gentile Frances Bowmore shall be removed from the holy ground in the Winter Quarters cemetery.

"Leave us."

Aveline bowed her head.

Epilogue

Too numb to feel shame for herself or anything at all for Washington Avery, Lucas Bates, or Brigham Young, Aveline watched a man throw her two trunks from Washington's wagon. All other items of hers, bedding, kitchen utensils and foodstuffs, Washington refused to allow her to take.

No one spoke as the man pitched the trunks onto a trader's wagon. A Gentile from Kanesville was set to return after he had dropped off last-minute supplies to the pioneers. He agreed to take Aveline and her trunks to Winter Quarters.

The wind moaned in her ears as he helped her climb up to the seat. The intense glares from the Pioneer Company members conveyed their disgust of her. Aveline stared straight ahead even when the trader glanced over to her. He picked up the reins and flicked them.

With a jerk, the wagon lurched and headed east—

"What are you staring at, darling?" Loyal Keegan's chipper voice sang out behind Aveline.

May 1, 1848
Kanesville, Iowa

Startled, her remembrances vanished. The staring pioneers, the wagon, the Elkhorn River, and the hatred and shame were a long time and distance away.

Standing near the window in the back room of Keegan's Mercantile, she turned and gave him a sad smile.

His arms encircled her in a quiet embrace. He held her for a moment then murmured, "Still thinking of them?"

Her throat was tight, and she blinked back tears. She couldn't speak so she nodded. Loyal pulled her back to him. He rubbed her back.

"I'm sorry," she whispered as she embraced him. "I should not look to the past when I have such joy now and in the future."

Loyal sighed and nudged a wisp of hair behind her ear. "Our past doesn't just vanish, no matter how hard we may wish it. We must deal with it as best we can."

The little bell over the front door tinkled. They both looked through the back room's curtain to see the front door open and hear female voices exclaim.

Two women entered and looked around, tentative in their amazement at the colorful displays.

Aveline started in their direction, but paused. She brushed a quick kiss on Loyal's cheek. "Thank you for being so kind."

He blushed and glanced at the customers to make sure no one had seen her affection. "Why, Missus Keegan, that's my job." He smiled at her as she walked toward the women. "I'll be heading to the livery to check on that horse for you," he called out as he waved his farewell.

"Good afternoon, ladies. How may I help you?" Aveline stood with her hands folded. She fought the urge to curtsy. The Keegans had taught her that such a move was passé in the modern society of Kanesville.

"Good afternoon, miss," the older woman answered. "I have some baskets I'd like to trade for goods."

Aveline's eyes fluttered as she fought to keep the remembrance of Em at bay. She turned slightly, saw Loyal leaving and, at his backward glance, waved.

"Mister Keegan will assist you with the trade. One moment, please." She headed to the storeroom. "Mister Keegan, two women are here about a trade of baskets."

Thomas Keegan stood as he tossed his round-rimmed glasses on the desk. As he passed Aveline, he paused. "Some day you will address me as Thomas."

A smile flitted across his mouth as he pushed aside the curtain. "Good afternoon, Sisters!"

In the storeroom, Thomas could tell which customers were Gentiles and which were Mormon. He liked to address them accordingly. To learn more, she watched how he interacted with the women. She stared toward the windows, then pulled her handkerchief from her bodice.

Without meaning to, she pushed her fingers down her chest to ensure her sacred undergarment didn't peek above the lace that lined her vest. Feeling only skin, she closed her eyes and smiled, promising herself she'd remember not to do that anymore.

Aveline sat on Thomas' chair and swiveled to inspect the storeroom. She thought back to the months before when she had approached Mister Keegan, desperate for a job. She felt sick as she approached the door of the man whom she had publicly accused of cold-blooded murder.

The sounds of those dreadful moments vibrated in her mind as if they had occurred underwater. She remembered the store's door bell tinkling as she pushed it open.

Her boot heels thumped on the wood floor as she stepped toward Loyal and his father. She barely recalled her words as she begged Thomas Keegan for forgiveness. Her heart pounded in her ears as they stared. Keegan dragged a wood chair closer. "Sit down, child."

Then she heard his clear, blessed words: "I understand. I forgive you."

Keegan had walked her into the storeroom and sat her by his desk. He told Loyal to take care of customers. She and Thomas talked until the sun sank below the western horizon, and he lit the wood stove to stave off the chill that crept into the room. At one point he hesitated. "Are you staying at Winter Quarters?"

Aveline nodded; the tears welled again. "My parents are hiding me in their cabin. Word has spread about my former husband's deed. They know of my excommunication." Aveline choked on the word. "My parents leave in a few days to head west. The bishop said once they leave for the trail, I must leave Winter Quarters and never return." She twisted her handkerchief. "I must find a new home and a job."

Thomas nodded. He rubbed his jaw as he spoke, as if he were thinking out loud. "I could use some help in the front room, taking care of customers, helping stock and sort. Arithmetic is not my strong suit nor is it my son's. Figuring is a skill we don't find pleasant." He pointed to a dark corner. "In that corner is a small bed. It's not much, but Loyal can hang a curtain for your privacy. On top of that—if you're of a mind to—you're welcome to take your meals with us. I can pay you twenty cents a day in wages."

Her eyes grew wide at his generosity: a job, room and board, and wages—at a queenly sum! She clasped her hands. "Mister Keegan, I am obliged to you!"

With a wave of his hand, he dismissed her words. "I need help. You need a home and employment. Move forward, we shall both succeed."

Within weeks of moving into the Keegan's storeroom, Aveline had learned the retail business well. She had finally made sense of the jumbled mass of ledgers and papers, and had established some sort of order. A week later, Thomas had exclaimed how he could enjoy the luxury of a day off for fishing.

Soon after, Loyal kissed her on the cheek. Two weeks after that, Aveline and Loyal married and moved into the third-floor attic above the mercantile.

How wonderfully her life turned out, Aveline thought as she stared out the window. She reminded herself of her good fortune whenever the horror at Winter Quarters and on the trail flooded back. A light smile flitted as she smoothed her ballooning abdomen.

On Thomas's desk lay an open letter. Ragged creases from being folded and unfolded untold times threatened to split the letter into several pieces. She picked up the paper and reread the letter she could recite.

January 15, 1848

Dearest Daughter,

We pray you are well. Brother Hamish Paddock brought us your last letter and we are grateful for his bearing your communication. We are thankful for your wonderful news. We wish you all happiness with Loyal Keegan and in your chosen life.

There is much to tell you of our journey to the Promised Land. Your father and I navigated the difficult trail, and, thanks be to the Lord, the company suffered few losses. In the mountains, your father suffered from the mountain sickness. With prayers and the laying on of hands, he recovered. With other brothers, your father is now in California to fetch seeds and plant cuttings. Brother Paddock's wives, Em and Carissa, walked to Zion. You will be pleased to know Carissa added to the family and her son, Brigham, is one of the first boys born in the new country. The Paddocks' four boys are all healthy, praise the Lord.

We have worked hard and Zion is rising in its glory.

Your brother Bedford has won his release from the Mormon Battalion after he had reenlisted for six months. His injury healed and he remains in San Diego, California. He and your father are together now while your father collects plants and seeds.

I hesitate, but I feel I would be negligent if I did not notify you about your former husband and his cohort Lucas Bates. On the trail west to Zion during our journey, their second journey in late summer, both men were ordered to divert from the train to perform a mission in San Diego, California, near Bedford's fort. Word has it that they were not happy in this directive and had words with the President, Brigham Young. The ugliness of the disagreement was legendary, this from a witness. The president said with the blasphemy Brothers Avery and Bates spewed, if they did not repent and report to California, they would be disfellowshipped. They obeyed.

In your father's letter to me a few weeks ago, he wrote both men are dead, found with their throats cut. Their blood had spilled on the ground. He and Bedford say the assailant, or assailants, is unknown.

May God forgive me, but I cannot in my mother's heart feel sorrow for the dead men. I can only wonder if they, too, have now attained eternal salvation.

Your loving mother.

Aveline dropped the letter on the desk and strolled to the windows. Through the panes, she watched a short line of covered wagons stop along the dirt road. The bearded drivers jumped down and walked toward the lead wagon. They huddled together, arms pointing in various directions.

Two women, one younger than other, sat on the bench seat of the second wagon. Their difference in appearances indicated to Aveline they were not related. The younger clambered down and helped the older woman to the ground. They stood, side by side, and looked at the town. The older woman pointed at a distant building.

Aveline leaned close to the window. Her breath threatened to fog the glass. She placed her hand on the cold pane and watched the women stroll, arm in arm, up the street.

The End

Afterword

Winter Quarters was a real place in the Missouri Territory. Its formal name was the Camp of Israel. The Latter-day Saints established Winter Quarters in 1846, and in 1848 the Saints abandoned it. The site later became the town of Florence, now present-day Nebraska.

When tensions between Mormons and non-Mormons escalated in the Midwest, Gentile mobs eventually forced the Mormons out of Missouri and Illinois. The Mormons made their way west — via Winter Quarters and other settlements in the region — to their final destination in Zion, now present-day Utah.

While most characters in this novel are fictitious, the lives of actual people are interwoven in the story. They are:
- Captain Daniel C. Davis, commander of Company E, Mormon Battalion, commander to the fictional Private Bedford Bowmore
- Colonel Thomas Kane, a trusted non-Mormon for whom Kanesville was named
- Apostle Heber C. Kimball
- Bishop Thomas Lang [possibly spelled Laing], Ward Nine, the ward of the fictional Bowmore and Avery families
- Wealthy Richards and Phineas [also spelled Phinehas] Richards, Mary's parents-in-law
- Mary Haskin Parker Richards
- Apostle Willard Richards, Phineas' brother
- Bishop Levi E. Riter, Ward Three, ward of the fictional Abernethy family
- Bishop Samuel Rolfe, Ward Thirteen, ward of the fictional Bates family
- Patriarch John Smith
- Brigham Young, the leader of the Latter-day Saints.

For the purposes of the story, I chose to fictionalize the Winter Quarters' chief of police, Finis Cane. The actual chief of police was Hosea Stout.

While the atrocities against Eliza Bates' mother, brother Jack, sister Esther and her newborn son, and sister Eleanor in the novel are fiction, in real life such brutality did occur.

The most heinous action during the period known as the Mormon Missouri War took place at Haun's Mill in Caldwell County, on October 30, 1838. During an armed conflict between Mormons and members of the Missouri militia, unarmed women and children were shot at or assaulted as they fled. When the battle was over, seventeen Mormons lay dead, including a ten-year-old boy who had his head blown off at point-blank range. Their bodies were thrown in a well. No one was tried for the crimes.

Most Latter-day Saints were in Missouri when a group of Mormon men swore to avenge every wrong against them by those within and outside the church. This group came to be known as Danites or the Avenging Angels. In 1838 more than 80 men signed a letter eventually named the Danite Manifesto, a written threat to antagonists to leave the Missouri region or face death. The Danites carried out this threat and drove many non-Mormons from the region.

Whether the Danites continued their vigilante activities, with or without church leadership approval, is debatable. Excommunicated Saints, such as "Wild Bill" Hickman and John Doyle Lee, wrote in their memoirs that they had murdered certain individuals at the request of church leaders, though these missions were carried out as independent men and not as Danites. Their well-publicized stories contributed to the perception that the Danites still existed and continued their vigilantism. Secrecy, lies, myth, and lore cloud the facts.

Suggested Readings

The reader may find these sources and selected writings useful in learning more about the faith, the times, the overland trails, the actual people included in the novel, and modern views on Mormon history.

- Bailey, Paul. *Polygamy was Better than Monotony*. Los Angeles: Westernlore Press, 1972.
- Beecher, Maureen Ursenbach, ed. *The Personal Writings of Eliza Roxcy Snow*. Logan: Utah State University Press, 2000.
- Beecher, Maureen Ursenbach, and Lavina Fielding Anderson, eds. *Sisters in Spirit: Mormon Women in Historical and Cultural Perspective*. Urbana: University of Illinois Press, circa 1987.
- Campbell, Eugene E. *Establishing Zion, The Mormon Church in the American West, 1847-1869*. Salt Lake City: Signature Books, 1998.
- Cannon, Frank, J., and Harvey J. O'Higgins. *Under the Prophet in Utah*. Boston: C. M. Clark Publishing Company, 1911.
- Cross, Mary Bywater. *Quilts and Women of the Mormon Migrations, Treasures of Transitions*. Nashville, Tenn.: Rutledge Hill Press, 1996.
- Darter, Francis Michael. *Celestial Marriage*. Salt Lake City, circa 1937.
- Denton, Sally. *Faith and Betrayal: A Pioneer Woman's Passage in the American West*. New York: Knopf, 2005.
- Hafen, Leroy R. and Ann W. Hafen. *Handcarts to Zion; The Story of a Unique Western Migration, 1856-1860*. Lincoln: University of Nebraska Press, 1992.
- Hatch, Charles M., and Todd M. Compton, eds. and trans. *A Widow's Tale: The 1884-1896 Diary of Helen Mar Kimball Whitney*. Logan: Utah State University Press, 2003.
- Kimball, Edward L., and Kenneth W. Godfrey. "Law and Order in Winter Quarters." *Journal of Mormon History* 32, no. 1, (Spring 2006): 172-218.
- Lee, John Doyle. *Journals of John D. Lee: 1846-47 and 1859*. Charles Kelley, ed. Salt Lake City: private printing for R. B. Watt by Western Printing Company, 1938.

- Mormon Battalion Association. https://www.mormonbattalion.com, 2009.
- Mulder, William, and A. Russell Mortensen, eds. *Among the Mormons; Historic Accounts by Contemporary Observers*. NY: Albert A. Knopf, 1958.
- Peavy, Linda, and Ursula Smith. *Pioneer Women, The Lives of Women on the Frontier*. NY: Smithmark Publishers, 1996.
- Rea, Tom. *Devil's Gate: Owning the Land, Owning the Story*. Norman: University of Oklahoma Press, 2006.
- Ricketts, Norma Baldwin. *Mormon Battalion, U.S. Army of the West*. Logan, UT: Utah State University Press, 1996
- Stegner, Wallace. *The Gathering at Zion; The Story of the Mormon Trail*. Lincoln: University of Nebraska Press, 1992.
- Stenhouse, Fanny. *Englishwoman in Utah: The Story of a Life's Experience in Mormonism*. London: Sampson Low, Martson, Searle, and Rivington, 1880.
- Stout, Hosea. *On the Mormon Frontier: the Diary of Hosea Stout, 1844-1861*. Salt Lake City: University of Utah Press, 1964.
- Tobles, Douglas F., and Nelson B. Wadsworth. *The History of the Mormons, In Photographs and Text: 1830 to the Present*. NY: St. Martin's Press, 1987.
- Van Wagoner, Richard S. *Mormon Polygamy, A History*. 2nd ed. Salt Lake City: Signature Books, 1989.
- Ward, Maurine Carr, ed. *Winter Quarters: The 1846-1848 Life Writings of Mary Haskin Parker Richards*. Logan: Utah State University Press, 1996.
- Williams, Jacqueline. *Wagon Wheel Kitchens: Food on the Oregon Trail*. Lawrence: University Press of Kansas, 1993.
- Winter Quarters Project. 2007. http://winterquarters.byu.edu/

About the Author

Barbara Townsend's writing journey began at the University of Wyoming. During her first fiction writing class she felt compelled to write a mystery. The thought of twists, turns, red herrings, clues and making them all fit into one story fascinated her. That first short story, *Murder at Wainwright,* she later wrote into *Clear and Convincing Evidence*.

An internship in the Toppan Rare Books Library led her in another direction. With books dating from the 1800s, she wrote a thesis that examined women in nineteenth-century Mormon polygyny. That paper won a student competition at the university's American Heritage Center. Her accumulated research led to *Blood Atonement*.

Her writing credits include the university's newspaper and Air Force newspapers. She was first a student and then a faculty member of the Wyoming Writing Project. She graduated *summa cum laude* with a Bachelor of Arts degree.

Before becoming hooked on writing, Barbara had entered the U.S. Air Force at 17 and retired 24 years later.

She lives in Wyoming's Wind River Mountains.

Books by Barbara Townsend

Clear and Convincing Evidence
Blood Atonement
Tarnished Gold